*To Ena and Roy
with very best wishes
Keith Michel
December 2010*

CORSAIR

A novel by

Keith Michel

Published by

MELROSE BOOKS

An Imprint of Melrose Press Limited
St Thomas Place, Ely
Cambridgeshire
CB7 4GG, UK
www.melrosebooks.com

FIRST EDITION

Copyright © Keith Michel 2009

The Author asserts his moral right to
be identified as the author of this work

Cover designed by Jeremy Kay

ISBN 978-1-906561-88-8

All rights reserved. No part of this publication may be reproduced, stored in a retrieval system, or transmitted, in any form or by any means electronic, mechanical, photocopying, recording or otherwise, without the prior permission of the publishers.

This book is sold subject to the condition that it shall not, by way of trade or otherwise, be lent, re-sold, hired out or otherwise circulated without the publisher's prior consent in any form of binding or cover other than that in which it is published and without a similar condition including this condition being imposed on the subsequent purchaser.

Printed and bound in Great Britain by:
The Good News Press. Ongar, Essex.

Mixed Sources
Product group from well-managed
forests and other controlled sources
www.fsc.org Cert no. SGS-COC-2315
© 1996 Forest Stewardship Council

All characters and events in this book are fictional and any resemblance to actual places, events or persons, living or dead, is unintended and purely coincidental.
The events depicted take place in the present day.

★ ★ ★ ★ ★ ★ ★ ★ ★ ★

Also by Keith Michel

Contraband (1988)
Countdown (1991)
Caracara (1995)
Karakan (2000)
War, Terror and Carriage by Sea (2004)

★ ★ ★ ★ ★ ★ ★ ★ ★ ★

For Rosie, Vera and Edward

★ ★ ★ ★ ★ ★ ★ ★ ★ ★

Prologue

Sandakan, Sabah, East Malaysia

Jean-Yves Bertrand stretched awkwardly. The scar on his left shoulder started to chafe against the steel frame of the worn seat in which he was slouched. The ageing twin-engine aircraft lurched into an air pocket.

"Sorry, mate. Hate these flights early in the morning. We should right ourselves in a moment. At least I hope so."

"I thought you Aussie bush pilots knew something about flying by the seat of your pants."

"We do, mate. Believe me. But this crate's buggered and should have been scrapped."

"Some comfort. Is it always like this?"

The Frenchman's question was lost as the cockpit radio crackled into life. It did nothing to improve his humour.

"That was Sandakan control. They say it's all clear once we've passed the Kinabalu range."

Bertrand peered down at the hazy cloud clutching at South East Asia's tallest peak.

"Ever climbed it?"

At least the pilot was back with him again.

"Once, it was a piece of cake. I did it with a couple of guys, before we got shipped up to Diego Garcia."

"Air force?"

"Yeah. We did the reconnaissance for the poor sods on the ground in Afghanistan. My grandpa was at Gallipoli. Have you ever done time in the military?"

Bertrand nodded.

The plane ploughed on. Despite the early hour, there was as yet little daylight. The two men fell silent.

The Frenchman's eyes narrowed. His face was lined and he felt tired. Things didn't change. The landscape and the language might be different but he was still pushing uphill. He always had and he guessed that he always would. His head fell forward and he tried to sleep.

"Hell mate, you look horrible. Are you OK?"

Bertrand had no wish to cross the youthful aviator. He had seen men like him smile and die a hundred times. All they sought was the sight of their mother's eyes. Few had succeeded.

"Thanks. I'm OK."

The Frenchman forced a thin but genuine smile. The boy was lonely despite the bluster.

"You had me worried for a minute there. Didn't they feed you in Labuan last night?"

Bertrand smiled again and shook his head. What passed for a guest house in the only town on the tiny island, off the north west coast of Borneo, was hardly worth its name. He had hoped to learn something, but the hours spent in the only bars open had yielded nothing that he did not already know.

As if intruding on his thoughts the pilot lent over, removing his earphones for a moment.

"You work for the Government don't you?"

"Not exactly." Bertrand's answer was non-committal.

He had seen and heard enough of the ways and means of governments in a dozen or more countries. Corruption, self interest and a reluctance to advance the causes of the needy seemed to prevail. It was always easier to hold out a palm to a willing contributor. Favours would always be called in at a price. The rulers of the former protectorate of North Borneo were no different.

"Sit tight. We're cleared for landing."

Bertrand arched his stocky frame.

The pilot began to throttle back.

"Shit."

Suddenly the plane was swallowed in a column of oily smoke, thick and seemingly endless. The engine coughed. The young Australian struggled to retain height. He looked anxiously at the swarthy figure slumped in the co-pilot's seat. The Frenchman put his hand on his shoulder.

"Calm, my friend, we'll be OK."

Seconds later they were through. Below lay the jungle clearing and the red earth airstrip of the sanctuary; ahead the azure blue of the Celebes Sea, crystal clear as the sun rose far to the east. To their right, rafts of timber and logs floated within the confines of the harbour of Sandakan, awaiting shipment.

The plane came to an uneasy halt.

"Well done."

Bertrand's compliment was genuine. The pilot shook his head and spoke slowly.

"The log fires are getting worse. They're burning the forest like there's no tomorrow."

The Frenchman nodded.

"It's everywhere. The whole of the Kalimantan region down south looks like a desert, brown, dry and dirty. You've got to strain your eyes to see anything of the rainforest that's left."

Bertrand stepped down from the aircraft. It was not yet eight in the morning but the heat was already intense. He walked slowly towards a one-storey timbered building, ducking under the aircraft's port wing.

The pilot's voice was hoarse.

"Did you see the logs in the harbour?"

Bertrand nodded as they walked, and replied, "It's been the same for months. Now there's something else."

Bertrand continued as the pilot cast him a sideward glance. "If you look upriver the water's yellow. There's acid residues from the new mine and it's deadly. The whole area is polluted and no one cares."

"Is that why you're here?"

Bertrand seemed almost surprised at the question. His reply was swift.

"I'm here because I've got a contract. But I care. Like hell I care."

The two men stepped up on to the veranda. The slow draught from the overhead fans gave some relief as they walked inside. Bertrand pushed open the rear shutters of an untidy office. Behind lay a small compound and the kampong, which housed the mainly volunteer staff of the Kepilok orang-utan sanctuary. Despite international acclaim for its conservation efforts to save the threatened primate, the sanctuary had existed for a decade on a meagre charitable budget and the unselfish efforts of its supporters.

Then the provincial council of elders had decided that the sanctuary would have to pay a local community levy, from which it had previously been exempt. Days later the perimeter fence, enclosing the tiny enclave of virgin forest, was breached.

The pilot peered at the faded map pinned to the wall and looked across at the Frenchman. Before he could speak the calm of the morning was shattered by the roar of an engine and the shriek of brakes.

The two men dashed outside in time to see a battered pick-up truck grind to a halt in a cloud of red and brown dust. A middle-aged local man and a young English girl, her blonde hair swept back by a tiny scarf and her t-shirt stained with blood, leapt out.

Bertrand jumped on to the rear fender. His face paled, he bit his lip and his eyes welled with tears at what he saw.

Sprawled across the running boards were the bodies of the sanctuary's oldest and most revered residents. Their docile gentle faces still carried the mask of love, in death, as the old man of the forest lay slumped beside his mate of three decades. Their long tactile fingers almost touched, but they were motionless.

The girl sobbed uncontrollably as the driver put his arm across her shoulders, as much to shield his own grief as to comfort her. Bertrand closed his eyes. They had been his family. People had trusted him to protect them. He had failed, just as he had failed in Rwanda.

As the commander of a Foreign Legion paratroop company, deployed as peacekeepers, he had been forced to watch the tribal bloodletting unfold. Yellow-livered bureaucrats in the Quai d'Orsay and at the United Nations had decreed that his unit would breach its terms of engagement if it took offensive action. As a result, a bunch of drug-crazed thugs continued unchecked with their rampage of pillage, rape and murder.

How the creatures slumped at his feet, their fine chests torn by bullets, reminded him of those disembowelled children and their parents. As it was then, it was nothing but pitiless, bloody slaughter.

The girl hesitatingly opened the passenger door of the pick-up. She grabbed a battered-looking cap and handed it to Bertrand. He glanced at it and slowly turned the peak round. The pilot read the logo deliberately.

"Globex International Mining."

The Australian looked at the cold contempt in the Frenchman's face. Bertrand's voice was hushed. "Rahman Mansur."

The pilot gave a sympathetic half-smile. "I know, mate. I'm sorry. Believe me."

He turned to leave and then stopped. He paused for a moment before speaking again. Perhaps Jean-Yves Bertrand was the kind of man they were looking for. He held out his hand and his eyes met Bertrand's. It was worth a try.

"Call me at Brooke's bar in the old Sabah hotel. Maybe there's a way to put this to rights."

The two men looked at each other and shook hands. Bertrand nodded his agreement.

"I'll see you there."

* * * * * * * * *

Les Deux Croix, Vaud, Switzerland

The early afternoon sun glistened on the late spring snow of the distant Alpine peaks. The mountains began to reveal the craggy slopes and high pastures that had been hidden during the winter months. Occasionally a gleam of light sparkled like crystal, and then, as quickly, it was gone.

Hugo Jackson peered down into the steep valley below, picking out the familiar landmarks that he had known since he was a boy. He turned to look up towards the towering slopes behind, but before he could do so he felt a hand on his shoulder.

"I'm sorry about your father. You've lost someone very dear to you."

The words of his late mother's brother seemed empty. He suddenly felt much older than his twenty-four years. His heart was heavy. It had been just two years since his mother had died of cancer. Her death had left an unbridgeable gap in his life.

It had also forced the closure of the children's hospice that she had established and where she had worked selflessly until her last days.

"Thank you." Jackson's words sounded hollow.

"It's time we went in."

The older man spoke softly. His words were almost lost in the peal of the church bells.

The two men heard the clock tower strike three and began to walk towards the porch entrance. Jackson noticed the first signs of spring flowers peeking through the remaining pockets of snow. The names on the gravestones testified to the years that the English church of St Martin and St Paul had provided a last resting place for early Victorian mountaineers and others who had come from afar. The tiny village of Les Deux Croix in the Swiss canton of Vaud, where the church overlooked the old town square, had changed little.

The congregation filed quietly into the body of the church and took their pews. The organ played the haunting strains of Land of our Fathers.

After a seemingly unending pause the young priest climbed awkwardly into the pulpit. His words came slowly. His face and eyes belied his years. He had the air of a broken spirit, one who had witnessed much and somehow found it difficult to adjust to the daily round.

The funeral service sheet recorded his Distinguished Conduct Medal. It had been awarded to the youngest member of the British Army Chaplain's department, for bravery under fire and saving a wounded man in the battle for Iraq.

Jackson looked up, as if seeking courage himself to face the truth of what was to come.

His uncle, Michael Crosfield, looked down and shifted uneasily. The cut of his dark overcoat emphasised his heavy build. He was in good shape for a man in his mid-fifties, despite a life spent in the long hours of a City of London law office, or travelling the world as his firm's senior partner and legal ambassador.

"Ladies and gentlemen, may I welcome you all."

The soft words of the priest seemed to bring the congregation to order.

"We are gathered here in the sight of God to remember and give thanks for the life of Richard Jackson and to ask His blessing and sympathy for his family, and in particular for his son, Hugo."

There was an uncomfortable shuffling of feet and the clearing of throats as the young priest hesitated. It was as if he was suddenly mindful of other supplications given in less tranquil surrounds.

Jackson gazed out of the stained glass window beside him depicting St Martin's famous act of slicing through his Roman centurion's cloak before forsaking the military for a life of piety. It all seemed strangely ironic.

The priest recovered his composure.

"This church, for a century or more, has welcomed the souls of those whom the mountains have taken. Men, women and children have all been innocent victims as they sought adventure amongst the peaks that surround us. Richard Jackson is now tragically among them."

The priest motioned his head towards the polished oak coffin, standing proud of the front pews, before the altar rail in the tiny church.

Jackson remembered only too clearly how they had broken the news. He could not understand how the accident could have happened. Then the details came through.

The newspapers had made much of the fact that Richard Jackson was an experienced skier. Despite enquiries by an investigating magistrate and the cantonal police, no explanation had been given as to why his father had ventured alone to an area notorious for its precipitous rocks and glacial movement.

Jackson scarcely noticed that the priest's address had ended. The choir of three local schoolchildren sang the haunting tones of the Nunc Dimittis. As the service ended his thoughts turned to the future. He knew that there would be further interest from the media. His father, after all, had been one of the club.

After obtaining a first at Oxford, Richard Jackson taught English literature at Harvard and the Sorbonne. He was then recruited by the *World Economic Monitor* and was based at the journal's headquarters in Geneva. He rapidly gained a reputation as a fair and fearless journalist and broadcaster, frequently emphasising the need for economic globalisation to respect and protect the traditions and ways of life of tribal societies worldwide. His love of the mountains had led him to write two bestsellers highlighting the threats that the peaks of the world faced as a consequence of mass tourism.

The service was over. The burial party gently hoisted the coffin on to their shoulders and began to process out of the church. Crosfield stepped aside and allowed his nephew to lead the mourners. As he did so he glanced at his watch. There was much to be done.

The sun was lower now, and the shadows of the mountains longer, as the group walked slowly towards the graveside. Jackson placed a wreath of alpine flowers on the coffin as it was lowered. He bowed his head. He promised himself that he would always remember that simple wreath. It would be his final memory of a mother, lost through illness, and of his father, taken by an accident. An onlooker from the village cast a handful of snow over the newly dug earth.

The priest's farewell was lost in the swirling roar of a helicopter's twin rotors, as the aircraft manoeuvred overhead and headed for the open terrain of a nearby sports field. The down-draught threw up a cloud of powdered snow.

Crosfield looked towards the opening door of the helicopter. He spoke without emotion, almost carelessly, now that the funeral was over.

"Sorry, Hugo. I have to leave. They'll look after you at my apartment. It's all been arranged."

"Thanks." The younger man's voice was non-committal. He was still unable to understand why his father had been so keen for him to join Crosfield's firm after he had completed his Master of Laws at Kings College London, and qualified as a solicitor. It troubled him at the time and still did. Only now, there was no one with whom he could share his concerns.

It was true that Layton and Springer, with its head office in the City and a dozen offices worldwide, was a leading corporate and business law practice. But the firm's allegiance to the moguls of the energy, mining and shipping industries scarcely seemed to fit the profile of his father's journalistic crusade. Nonetheless he joined the firm, as his father had wished. Perhaps he needed to put the uncertainty of his student days and the loss of his mother behind him. He was far from certain, however, that he had done so.

The helicopter's two passengers walked slowly towards the church gate. Several journalists covering the event hastened towards the new arrivals. There was no logo on the side of the aircraft to identify its ownership but there was no mistaking its occupants.

A tall man of heavy build, with dark hair, a swarthy complexion and a moustache flicked with grey strode up to Crosfield.

"I hope that we have not disturbed the occasion."

The accent was almost unnoticeable, the tone soft and the smile genuine. If there was a hint of condescension in his voice, Crosfield did not notice it.

"Of course not, I'm delighted you're here."

The two men were obviously well acquainted. Crosfield called to Jackson, who was beginning to walk away.

"Hugo, let me introduce you to one of the firm's most valued and respected clients."

There was a pause.

"May I present Mr Rahman Mansur. As you know, he owns Globex International Mining."

"I'm pleased to meet you, Sir."

Crosfield stepped back to make way for Mansur's fellow passenger.

"And this is Hedizah Mansur. You'll have read of the wedding in the office newsletter."

Jackson looked at the young girl in front of him. He thought that she could be no more than twenty. Hedizah Mansur wore a fur scarf, a long ankle-length coat and dark boots. As she removed her sunglasses and tossed back her black hair, Jackson thought that he had never seen anyone quite so beautiful. Her dark brown eyes, high cheekbones and her soft delicate skin captivated him instantly.

If Rahman Mansur had noticed the shy, almost vulnerable, glance with which his young bride returned Jackson's smile, he chose to ignore it. He spoke quietly and extended his hand.

"Mr Jackson, I'm delighted to meet you. Please accept my condolences for the loss of your father."

Almost at the same moment, Mansur glanced at his watch.

"Please excuse us. We have to leave."

As he ushered Hedizah back to the aircraft, he already appeared deep in conversation with Crosfield. The helicopter shaped up to take off. As it did so, Jackson felt a surge of nervous apprehension, for reasons that he did not understand.

Chapter One

Two months later

Kimberley, Western Australia

THE START TO THE DAY HAD NOT been promising. Jean-Yves Bertrand looked at his watch and patiently awaited the arrival of the yute that the caller said would meet the arrival of his flight from Darwin. The flat one-storey terminal building at Kununurra's municipal airport in the Kimberley district of North Western Australia was almost deserted. Bertrand's fellow passengers had already left to seek shelter from the torrid early morning sun and to find some breakfast at the nearby country club. The welcome sign that the region represented the country's last frontier seemed apposite.

The landscape that he had flown over was arid and dry, broken only by escarpments and ravines left behind by time, and the curious beehive contours of the Bungle Bungle range.

Not for the first time, Bertrand wondered why he had agreed to come. In truth however, he knew that he had had little choice.

Within days of the killings at the sanctuary two armed policemen had informed him that his work permit had expired. They had only allowed him time to pack his gear. He had then been escorted to Kota Kinabalu and placed uncompromisingly on a plane to Singapore.

But they had been too late to prevent his meeting at the old Sabah hotel. The Australian had told him that there might be a chance of further employment. It might suit a man of Bertrand's experience. With no job and less prospects, he had nothing to lose.

Then, there had been a hint that he might not have been the only one to witness the hand of Rahman Mansur in the pursuit of mineral riches on a global scale. He had read of the aboriginal protests at the reopening of the open cast mine in Kakadu in the Northern Territory way to the east. Maybe someone had a conscience after all.

The battered yute screeched to a halt.

"Are you Bertrand? Sorry for the delay, mate. We've had bloody poachers at the homestead, just before dawn."

"Sorry to hear it."

"Don't be, mate. It's what keeps us going. Jump in. Be careful."

Bertrand dumped his bags in the open trunk and gently picked up an ageing Lee Enfield rifle, with a well worn stock and trigger guard. Just as gently he checked the safety catch.

"Over fifty years old and still packs a punch. The old .303, I like it."

Bertrand smiled wryly as the driver coaxed the engine into life and headed out from the airfield's perimeter. The Frenchman pulled down his bush hat. The red dust began to dry his throat.

"Where are we headed, if you don't mind my asking?"

"Sorry again, mate. We've been all over the place, what with the mine at Goran Creek being sold and a whole lot of guys we've never seen coming up from the south looking for work. They say the wages are like the gold rush. If you understand what I mean."

"I'm sure I do. But tell me, how far are we going?"

"No worries, mate. Two hours and we'll be at Shark Bay."

The outer suburbs of the small town were soon left behind, as the yute made rapid, if uncomfortable, progress. Rough scrub country with nabob trees and giant red termite mounds gradually gave way to fringes of palm and rocky outcrops, as they neared the coast. The Timor Sea glistened blue in the mid-morning sun, as the vehicle drew to a halt outside the reception office of the Shark Bay Eco Resort.

The driver motioned Bertrand towards a dry timbered building with open shutters and a veranda overlooking a narrow jetty. Bertrand watched as several slothful salt water crocodiles settled on a nearby sand bank, and a school of bronze whaler sharks sliced through the clear inshore waters. He motioned Bertrand towards an open door.

"Wait in there. It'll only be a few minutes." As an afterthought, he added, "Help yourself. It's an open bar."

Bertrand slumped into a wicker chair, adjusted the floral cushion, and began to drink a cool beer.

The door was closed behind him and a muffled voice came over the room's intercom.

"Mr Bertrand. You are free to go at any time but I am interested in what you may have to offer us. Shall I continue?"

Bertrand put down the beer, stood up and looked around.

"Please nod if you are staying."

The Frenchman did so and sat down.

"First, I need to ask you a few personal details, if you don't mind."

Bertrand shrugged his shoulders.

"Date of birth?"

"Seventeenth of July, 1961."

"Place of birth?"

"Marseilles."

"Nationality?"

"French."

"Did your parents live in Marseilles?"

"My mother lived there for a short time after I was born. We moved to Bordeaux when I was about five or six."

"Your father?"

"I never knew him. My parents were farmers in Algeria. They were Pieds-Noirs and lived in the hills behind Philippeville. That's the name I remember. It's changed now of course."

"What happened to your father?"

There was a pause. Bertrand looked out as a small boat began to disembark a party of tourists, returning from a bird watching trip.

"He was killed by the rebels, the FNLA. As best I know, my mother returned to the farm one morning to find my father's body slumped against the front door of their house."

There was a further pause.

"She hardly ever spoke of it. He had been garrotted and mutilated. The police said that my mother had been lucky. In the village it had been worse. Young mothers and their children …"

His voice tailed away.

"And then?"

"Like thousands of others, my mother fled by ship to Marseilles. She carried me, one suitcase and a few hundred worthless francs. She found work where she could. The OAS was starting its campaign on the mainland. My father had been in the army in Indo China. Some of his old friends helped out. But when the army revolt collapsed in Algiers, it must have got too dangerous to stay in Marseilles."

"How did you survive in Bordeaux?"

"My mother did what she could. She kept me at school as long as possible. But we were outsiders. No one wanted to know. I quit school as soon as I could, and did pretty much anything to earn some money. I worked on oyster boats in the Bassin d'Arcachon and up in vineyards in the Medoc."

"And your mother?"

Only now did it strike Bertrand that the interview was taking place in bizarre circumstances. He could hear but he could not see his inquisitor. But then, for reasons that he did not understand, Bertrand almost welcomed the chance to talk. It was a distant past that he recalled with affection, despite its penury.

"I was just eighteen. My mother was working in a shop near the docks. One evening the owner attacked her. She was in a really bad way when they found her. She never recovered from the shock."

"And you?"

"When I saw her, I went straight to the man's home."

"Go on."

"He confessed to what he had done."

Bertrand paused. He continued slowly. "I made sure that he suffered just as my mother had done when he attacked her."

He looked down. "Then he fell on the ground, bleating for forgiveness. I cut his throat and left."

There was a further short silence.

"The next morning, I signed on for the Foreign Legion at their base in Pau. I assume you know the rest. Twenty years of work carrying out government policy in Africa and the Middle East. War, peacekeeping, death, we saw it all."

"And then?"

"I took work where I could find it."

The voice was silent for a moment, before continuing slowly.

"Is that what brought you to the East?"

"Yes, and also perhaps some kind of desire to help."

The voice continued. "Go on, Mr Bertrand."

The Frenchman's reply came quietly. "What happened at the reserve? Perhaps there's a chance to put it to rights. It's part of something much bigger."

Bertrand looked out of the window. The crocs had shifted their position. The tourist boat was moored up to the jetty. Several light clouds were blowing in from the north east. The tide was turning.

Bertrand spoke slowly. His tone was sardonic. "If there's a job, I'm interested. As you are no doubt aware, I have no other offers."

The Frenchman smiled to himself. It might be the start of another mission. He needed something to retain his self respect or to assuage the constant feeling of guilt. The helpless bodies of the children in Rwanda continued to haunt him. The quiet sadness in the faces of the dead animals had moved him in a way that he had not expected. Bertrand needed to make sense of where he was, or might be, going.

"Do I take it that we can count on you?"
"You can. For sure, you can."
The voice died away.

Bertrand walked from the building. Once again, it would be a new beginning.

* * * * * * * * * *

The City of London, England

Hugo Jackson hastened his step. The rain was falling heavily as he passed the Temple Bar and approached the main entrance of the Royal Courts of Justice in London.

He edged his way through groups of bewigged, confident-looking barristers and solicitors as they waited impatiently to pass through the Court's security check.

Crosfield had asked him to meet him in the centre of the cavernous galleried hallway, beside the glass panelled stands, that displayed the day's lists of cases.

One of those cases, which had been set for judgment in the Commercial Court in the early afternoon, was listed under the title 'Globex Transport Inc. versus Johnson (Underwriting Syndicates) Limited'.

Jackson had worked on the periphery of the case shortly after joining the firm. Soon after his father's death, Crosfield, without explanation, had moved him on to a research project, which involved a historical paper trail enquiry into the legal title to an obscure islet in the Arabian Gulf. It was a case of little or no public concern, unlike the matter that had that day been brought to a judicial conclusion.

But as Jackson had discovered, within a few days of joining Layton and Springer, the affairs of Rahman Mansur often attracted unwelcome press attention.

Already reporters and cameramen were taking up positions at the foot of a stone twisting staircase that descended to the paved floor of the Court hallway. It was unusual for the trial of an action, relating to the unexplained sinking of a cargo vessel, to have attracted such public interest.

The doors of the Court opened. Lawyers representing the contesting parties filed out, each in muted conversations with their clients, expert witnesses and industry observers. An obedient coterie of barristers' clerks struggled to cope with volumes of files and bundles of documents, as they made their way back to the Inner Temple across Fleet Street.

Crosfield nodded to Jackson and the two other young lawyers from the firm. Papers were shuffled. Within minutes, microphones and cameras were pointed towards Crosfield.

He motioned for quiet. There was, for an instant, only the sound of the passing traffic to be heard before Crosfield began.

"Members of the press, we have called this short conference following the conclusion today of a case that has attracted unwarranted media intrusion, in order to allay once and for all the unjustified allegations that my client has faced over the last months."

A voice called out. "It's true then, that you are still acting for Rahman Mansur, despite all this."

"We are. As the content of the judgment handed down by the Court shows, my client's conduct has been vindicated. There has been no finding that either he, as the principal of the Globex group, or anyone in his employment, had any direct or indirect responsibility for the total loss of the *Globex Mariner*, her cargo and crew last year."

"Does that mean that the insurers have lost the case?"

The legal editor of *Insurance Weekly* seemed more concerned with the formal outcome of the action. Others from the popular press impatiently sought to address their enquiries for the benefit of a hungrier public.

"Yes. The judge held that the loss of the vessel occurred in circumstances that raised no undue suspicion. It was an unexplained loss at sea. The risk was properly and fully covered by the terms of the Lloyds of London policy of insurance."

Jackson shifted his position. His eyes met the stare of another young member of the firm and as quickly looked away.

The team of lawyers representing the losing insurance interests had reached the main exit. Their leading barrister, a Queen's Counsel of many years' experience in the commercial field, looked back at the impromptu press conference and shook his head slowly, as if in disbelief.

"For the record, Mr Crosfield, are you willing to confirm at least some of the details of the vessel's loss?"

The representative from *Insurance Weekly* was keen to keep the debate focused on the key issues.

"Yes I am, so far as the judgment permits me."

Crosfield cleared his throat and started to read from a prepared note.

"The *Globex Mariner*, a cargo vessel of some 5,000 tons, was built in Gdynia, Poland, five years ago to the highest modern specification. She had traded successfully and safely for my client's organization until the time of her loss."

The tone was slow, slightly defensive. Those present sensed it.

"Didn't she fly a flag of convenience?"

Crosfield had been expecting the question.

"Yes, she flew the Liberian flag. But, as the Court found, there were no defects in the vessel's safety and inspection records. Anyway, as I'm sure you know, the Liberian Registry is managed from New York and has an excellent reputation."

"What voyage was she on when the vessel disappeared?"

The group seemed to accept that the *Insurance Weekly* representative had become their spokesman.

Crosfield continued in the same matter of fact tone.

"The *Globex Mariner* loaded consignments of agricultural machinery at Karachi for discharge at the port of Yanbu in the Kingdom of Saudi Arabia. The equipment was destined for an up-country irrigation scheme designed to support new crop research in desert areas. The project is one of many sponsored by the United Nations Research Agency into global warming."

The questioning continued.

"How many crew were on board?"

Crosfield leant towards an older man beside him with a weathered face.

"Captain Johnson will answer that question. He is a senior marine superintendent with my client's organization."

Having checked the notebook that he was holding, the old seafarer spoke softly. "There were twenty officers and seamen in total."

The response came quickly.

"What was their nationality?"

Crosfield motioned to the older man, who spoke in the same measured tone.

"They were all Filipinos. Their families and next of kin have been compensated in accordance with their articles of service."

Crosfield nodded, as if relieved that he had been spared a display of ignorance as to the number of men who had lost their lives.

The journalist from *Insurance Weekly* showed no sign of letting up.

"What was the Court's explanation of the casualty? From what we know, there were no reports of bad weather at the time and no distress calls were received."

Crosfield looked again for assistance. "I'll ask Captain Johnson to answer that question also."

The old seafarer spoke slowly. "As far as can be presumed, the vessel was lost through contact with a floating mine. Her last reported position was some fifty nautical miles west of the port of Hodeidah in Yemen. The last vessel to observe the *Globex Mariner* reported nothing untoward as she entered the Red Sea, having passed Aden in passage from Karachi."

The assembled gathering seemed to appreciate the weary authority of the elderly sea captain as he continued to recount such further details of the vessel's last hours as could be ascertained or assumed.

He continued, glancing again at his notes. "There's been damage reported by other vessels striking mines in the same area. They are thought to have been laid by rebel groups, several years ago, along the coast, to try to hit Saudi-bound vessels. NATO naval forces in the area have investigated but there have been no definite sightings."

"Is that the conclusion that the Court reached?"

"It was."

Crosfield's intervention was noticeably swift. The atmosphere seemed to lighten. Perhaps, after all, the press campaign had been mistaken. Perhaps the loss of the *Globex Mariner* would not be the catalyst that would force Rahman Mansur to shed the obsessive secrecy and obscurity that shrouded his business empire.

There was perhaps even an acceptance that, with the Court's ruling that the insurance claim for the loss of the vessel had been upheld, nothing more need be said.

Crosfield looked around and decided to bring the press conference to an end. Before he could do so, however, a young female voice spoke quietly from the back of the group.

"This is Ann Sutherland from the *World Economic Monitor*."

Jackson looked up instantly. It had not occurred to him that the result of the case would have been of interest to the journal to which his late father had contributed for so long.

"Mr Crosfield, will the Court's finding today be sufficient to put an end to speculation that the loss of the *Globex Mariner* might be attributed to the fact that she was carrying an undeclared cargo of explosives, which detonated accidentally and caused the ship to sink?"

There was a pause as Crosfield looked across at the barrister retained for the case on behalf of Rahman Mansur. He shrugged his shoulders disdainfully.

Crosfield's reply betrayed a hint of anger.

"Miss Sutherland. That baseless accusation has been levelled at my client throughout this case. It was the central theme of the insurers' defence that somehow there was conspiracy, involving unlawful activity that directly caused this tragic loss."

He paused for a moment before continuing with an air of derision.

"The judge has stated categorically that there was no evidence whatsoever on which this allegation could be supported. That is the end of the matter. Thank you. I will not be taking further questions."

Crosfield ended the conference and gradually the group began to disperse. He called across to Jackson and the other lawyers.

"Take the judgment papers back to the office and post them on the office information website. I've some calls to make and I'll see you in the eighth floor conference room for a debriefing in an hour."

Jackson and the two other lawyers hailed a taxi for the short ride to the City office of Layton and Springer, a new twelve-storey building overlooking London Bridge.

The rain had eased a little as Jackson looked through the taxi windows at the lengthening queues of tourists snaking into St Paul's Cathedral.

Admittedly, he was new to the world of international litigation. His legal training, however, had taught him the essential rubric of the laws of evidence, causation and probability. He had also read only a small clutch of the mountains of documents that had been assembled for the trial. Nonetheless he felt uncertain over what he had seen and heard only minutes before.

"Good result, Hugo."

The chirpy tone of one of the associates on the case caused him to start.

"Is there something wrong?"

"No, I was just thinking about the judgment, that's all."

"It's over now. A good result in Court means it's good for my CV and even better for my bonus."

The third passenger in the taxi nodded in agreement.

"Maybe you're right. What's done is done." Jackson's reply sounded distant.

"Quite so; you worry too much, Hugo."

"Perhaps I do."

The result of the case, however, was not the only thing on Jackson's mind. There was no explanation to the origin of the Paris newspaper photograph of Hedizah Mansur that had been left anonymously on his desk earlier in the day.

As the taxi slowly edged its way towards the City, Crosfield turned out of the High Court building in the opposite direction. He took shelter under the arches leading to the Judges' entrance and accessed his mobile phone.

"This is the private office of Rahman Mansur. Who is speaking please?"

"It's Michael Crosfield. I've some good news for him if you could put me through."

The response was polite but unexpected.

"I'm sorry, Mr Crosfield, but he's in conference at present and not taking calls."

Crosfield's fingers tightened on the phone and his knuckles showed white. It was the second time in as many days that Mansur had avoided him. He turned away, pulled his collar up against the damp of the afternoon and walked towards his apartment.

Ann Sutherland watched him go and then made her way down towards the river. Finding a quiet corner in Temple Gardens she too accessed her mobile. Within seconds she heard an automatic recording. She had needed to leave a message by 1530 hours London time. She had now done so.

* * * * * * * * * *

Villefranche, France

The midday sun glistened on the still waters of the Mediterranean, lapping the rocky foreshore of Cap Ferret, on the south coast of France. There was a strong scent of frangipani as Hedizah Mansur gripped the wooden railing of the veranda of the secluded villa set above the harbour of Villefranche.

She looked down to the private beach and mooring below. The slope was fringed with tropical ferns and palms, and radiant with bougainvillea.

Hedizah heard the soft whirring of a marine diesel engine as the bow of the motor yacht edged alongside the jetty. Within minutes, Rahman Mansur appeared at the top of the winding stone staircase that led down to the water.

He was fit and in good shape for a man in his late fifties. Tall, dark skinned with a greying moustache and swept-back wavy hair, it was hardly surprising that his handsome looks attracted attention, whether on the alpine slopes of Gstaad or the casino in Monte Carlo. But he frightened Hedizah, and had done so ever since he had first set eyes on her.

"So, my dear, have you had another pleasant day?"

Hedizah smiled thinly. Her reply was formal.

"Thank you. It's beautiful here. I've everything anyone could need."

"You're not lonely?"

"No. I have Sophie if I need to talk."

Hedizah had been unable to speak a word of French when she arrived less than six months before. Now she could converse quite freely with the housemaid, who had become her friend. She was indeed the only person whom Hedizah was permitted to meet, when Mansur was away on business.

She returned his kiss as he expected. In the same way, she had had no choice but to become accustomed to a way of life that she had not wanted and one from which she could presently not escape.

Mansur seemed noticeably distracted as he spoke.

"I have some people to meet in an hour in the office."

Hedizah forced another smile and turned towards the open veranda windows. She felt his hands under her blouse, as he began to draw himself towards her.

Once upstairs she undressed and waited as she always did. She knew what he expected. Minutes passed. The door to her room remained closed. Through the open shutter she could hear the telephone ring, and the sound of angry voices. There was a knock on the door. It was Sophie.

Sophie had the eyes of a middle-aged, unmarried woman, who had lived and worked amongst the rich oligarchy that, for decades, had colonised the Cote d'Azur. She had seen film moguls, ship owners and oil barons of a dozen nationalities come and go. She had witnessed the tortured souls that they had left in their wake, as new opportunities, younger women, drugs and unfailing egotism had driven them forward.

She spoke softly, holding her hand out to Hedizah. "He sent me to say that he's not coming up."

Hedizah smiled and went across to her maid, gently touching her on the side of her arm.

Sophie was afraid for this beautiful young girl in her early twenties, who stood before her. She had a soft sallow skin, deep brown, trusting eyes and flowing dark hair. Tall, slim and with a fine figure, Hedizah would have attracted many admirers had she been allowed to stay in the small village in northern India, where she was born and raised in her early years.

Hedizah quickly pulled on a loose fitting robe and went outside. There were more clouds but the air was still balmy and dry. She closed her eyes and felt the warmth on her cheeks. She had willed herself to think about what had been her home, on other occasions, when Mansur had used her and left. She could imagine it all in her mind's eye but could never recapture the familiar, comforting noise and smell of India.

Hedizah fingered a treasured photograph of her parents taken outside their tiny one-storeyed house. It sat on the edge of the field that, somehow, had sustained their livestock, as well as her parents and five brothers and sisters.

She remembered the occasion well. It was a traditional Hindu festival of thanksgiving. The children were all in their finest and brightest clothes. Parents and elderly relatives patiently attended to the performance of time-honoured rituals.

Then the drought had come, quickly followed by famine and an outbreak of cholera. Within weeks she had lost almost all of her nearest family.

At the age of six, she found herself as an unwanted additional mouth to feed in a distant uncle's home. The family lived in an untidy industrial town, further north in the Punjab, between Simla in the east and the border with Pakistan in the west.

She had worked hard in the house and at school, but was always a stranger within her own kind. Her good looks had attracted jealousy and suspicion in equal measure. The area remained confused and uncertain of its norms and beliefs, despite the passing of the decades since the bloody days of partition had divided one man from his neighbour.

The kind attentions of an elderly nun had helped Hedizah to pass through secondary school to begin training as a teacher. Then, again, outside events were to determine her fate.

A serious accident at the steel mill where her uncle worked had resulted in its closure. Food and resources in the family became scarce. Hedizah sought guidance from her mentor, but her elderly friend had become too sick to assist.

Then, it seemed, a saviour for the town's ill fortunes had arrived. A wealthy entrepreneur from Lahore, reputedly Kurdish by birth, but then based in Pakistan, was prepared to rebuild the mill, in order to provide cheap steel to support his growing industrial empire overseas.

But there was a price to be paid. Hedizah's uncle, a spokesman for the town's union of workers, had been only too willing to listen to whispers that surrounded the takeover.

Rahman Mansur was known to let nothing stand in his way. A devout Muslim he may once have been, but the trappings of wealth and public acclaim had led him to abandon, without demur, the strict adherence to faith that his elders had once demanded.

Mansur had seen Hedizah but once. However, within a week, she found herself without a home and an outcast from the surrogate family where she had, reluctantly, once been welcomed.

Her uncle had been only too willing to secure his appointment as the foreman of the new plant by informing Mansur that he had no objection should Mansur wish to take his distant niece. She no longer had any place amongst his kin.

Hedizah had been forced to become Mansur's mistress. Despite her Hindu origin, he made plain to her that she could either choose to live with him as his wife or he would offer her to his associates to make what they could of her.

The wedding in Paris had attracted wide attention. The good-looking middle-aged entrepreneur, with international fame and charisma, had chosen to marry a lovely young woman, of another faith, from a poor background, in a neighbouring, sometimes hostile, state. It was a story that the media readily absorbed. The origins of their meeting were not divulged.

Now, only months later, Hedizah had become merely a trophy. She felt herself no more than a detached and lonely adjunct to Mansur's impatience for further and wider business success. She dressed quickly and made her way downstairs.

Hedizah could hear Mansur's raised voice coming from the private office wing of the house. She listened cautiously and recognized the voice of Mansur's Chief Executive, Max Herlov, an expatriate Lebanese of mid-European extraction.

"I believe that we should wait. It was a close thing."

Mansur looked at the other man across an ornate Louis XV desk and smiled.

"We didn't achieve all this by hesitating, my friend, as you well know."

Mansur stared at Herlov. They had been together since the early days in Southern Turkey.

It had all started with cross-border smuggling from Northern Iraq. It had been easy, before politics and religion – on both sides of the border – had made life dangerous for those outside the ruling cliques.

Herlov smiled and nodded. His eyes played over the priceless Byzantine artefacts and ornaments that adorned the desk, and the gold embossed shelves of the study. Impressionist masterpieces hung on heavily embroidered wallpaper.

He walked towards the window and turned to Mansur, speaking almost distantly.

"It's true. But this time we needed our lawyers. That's never happened before."

Mansur's response was swift. "Everyone needs lawyers. You can't survive without them, at least to ensure that the regulators and tax people are kept at bay."

Herlov wondered whether Mansur was starting to feel infallible. He had seen it before in Beirut and Grozny. He walked towards Mansur and this time spoke more slowly. He needed to make his point.

"But the *Globex Mariner* was different."

Mansur said nothing.

Herlov persisted. "This time, we had to go to Court. It was a risk but we had no choice. You know that."

Mansur's response was swift. "I know why we did it. There were too many voices to silence, if we didn't clear our name."

Herlov was undeterred. "But can we afford to take the same risks again so soon?"

He continued hurriedly. "Crosfield left several messages. He wants to speak with you. He says that there are things that you should know."

Mansur was becoming irritated. "The judge found for us. That's all there is to it."

Herlov looked up at the taller man. "I don't think so. Crosfield's heard what was said in the corridors outside the Court. We should postpone for a while, until things settle down."

Mansur was unmoved. "You know that's not possible."

He stood up, walked round to the front of the desk and spoke slowly. "Max. I love you like a brother, as you know. I've trusted you as I would my son."

Then his face hardened. His eyes looked coldly at the other man.

"Should I be worried about you, Max? Is there something that we should share?"

Herlov had known his master long enough. There was a pause and a moment of mutual understanding.

"There's nothing for you to be concerned about."

Mansur spoke slowly. "I accept what you say, my friend. But I can't agree with you."

There was a moment's silence. Mansur seemed to reflect. "Perhaps you're right, Max. Call Crosfield, tell him that we need to meet."

"So you'll go ahead?"

"Of course I will."

Herlov reached out with his hand. Mansur took it. The two men embraced. The meeting was over.

Hedizah made her way quietly towards the lobby of the glass-walled spa that adjoined the house. The young, square-shouldered personal trainer welcomed her. She disliked the way that he watched her swim and his unwillingness to allow her to be alone.

"I'm taking a sauna this morning."

"Not using the pool, Madam?"

Hedizah watched as he prepared the sauna. She then walked into the adjoining dressing room. Closing the door behind her and keeping her back to the entrance, she carefully extracted the mobile phone that Sophie had handed to her earlier.

She spoke quickly, clipped the receiver closed and left it beneath her clothes.

* * * * * * * * *

Piraeus, Greece

Stelios Kyriakos smiled to himself. It was an unusual assignment but, after a lifetime spent in the Greek shipping industry, nothing surprised him any more.

The morning traffic running down the main thoroughfare from Athens city centre to the port of Piraeus was lighter than usual. He had received a call in his apartment in Faliron on the other side of town late the previous evening.

Kyriakos had moved his office, from the old yacht harbour, back to his home. Business had been slow for months now. There seemed little market for a recently-retired ship's master, offering his services to survey second-hand cargo vessels for prospective buyers.

The maritime world was no different to the rest of modern business. There was too much technology, too much money and too many slick deals. The old days of tramp steamers, family companies and loyalty to the owner had gone forever.

He had been told to take a taxi to a shipyard on the outer side of the harbour. The caller had merely said that a foreign principal was looking for a suitable vessel for a specific assignment. He had located a twenty-year-old vessel, called the *Aegean Dolphin*, that was available for purchase.

The vessel had apparently been impounded for a breach of European Union customs arrangements. The former owners had been unable to pay the fine that had been levied, and the vessel was being sold by the local court bailiff.

The taxi made its way past the Piraeus passenger terminal and headed out towards the industrial area beyond. Run-down low-rise apartment blocks and closed warehouses slipped by as the vehicle approached the entrance to a privately-owned ship repair berth.

Kyriakos paid the fare and walked towards the locked gate. He was a tall man with slightly stooped shoulders. He bent his head towards the intercom at the dock gate.

It opened quickly and he was met by a stocky man, in his mid-thirties, who introduced himself as the dockyard superintendent.

The other man eyed Kyriakos suspiciously.

It was Kyriakos who spoke first. "Have you worked here long? It's some years since I've been to this yard."

"Long enough."

The man's accent was guttural and slow. Bulgarian or Romanian, Kyriakos guessed.

"Do you have some ID?"

Kyriakos produced his Greek identity card and seaman's ticket. The other man nodded.

"They said that you're authorised to sign certificates for the flag state and the classification society."

Kyriakos paused for a moment. The other man continued.

"There's been a change of flag, from Greek to Liberian Register. The new classification society is the East Asiatic. Do you have any problem with that?"

Shaking his head, Kyriakos walked along the pier towards the gangway. As he did so, he stopped as he passed several shrink-wrapped crates and equipment, awaiting shipment on board.

Kyriakos looked at the other man whose response was quick, perhaps too quick.

"Engine room gear ordered by the new owners, I believe."

Nearing the gangway leading from the pier to the main deck, Kyriakos paused again.

"Mind if I check the bow and stern areas before I board?"

"Go ahead."

The surveyor walked along the pier and looked up at the side plating of the port bow. Picking his way over a tangle of mooring ropes, he made his way to the stern. He took out his notebook but said nothing.

Perhaps there was nothing wrong, but it had been well done. Only the closest inspection would reveal that the former name and place of registration of the vessel had been skilfully erased. She had not been the *Aegean Dolphin* for long.

Kyriakos walked back towards the gangway.

"Thanks. Let's go up. I'll do the bridge inspection first, then I'll go down to the engine room."

The main deck showed signs of significant activity. Steel girders and frames were being fixed into position. The hatches were open, and Kyriakos could hear the sound of welding torches below decks.

He opened the main door into the accommodation block and climbed the internal stairwell, through three decks, to the bridge. What he saw surprised him.

"I didn't expect to see that kind of gadgetry on an old vessel like this."

He passed his hand over the new radar receivers, navigational equipment and digital weather recording systems. The other man began to look at him uneasily.

"As I said, the new owners seem to have plenty of money to burn."

"But why on this vessel I wonder? She's seen the best of her trading days."

He spoke almost with affection. His whole life had been spent on vessels like the *Aegean Dolphin*, plying the world's oceans. They had been his home.

"No idea."

Kyriakos looked out across the bridge wing. A tear came to his eye and he bit his lip. He had longed for the day when they would no longer have to spend months apart. Then, within months of his retirement from the sea, his wife of forty years had died. There had been no warning, no time to make up for the long years of loneliness and no children or family to share the grief.

"You OK?"

Kyriakos nodded and turned away from the wheelhouse. He looked at the bronze plate screwed to the bulkhead, which showed the vessel's building and registration details. Kyriakos had seen it done before. The telltale cracks in the interior paintwork showed that the plate had been replaced recently, and with care.

"I'll get on with the survey then."

He expected to be left alone to inspect the vessel in his own time but it became immediately clear that this would not be permitted.

"I'll come with you."

The two men traversed the vessel. Kyriakos recorded his findings, as they progressed. Steel strengthened tweendecks, new gantry hoists, engine room power packs and powerful thrusters awaiting installation. It was far from what he had expected and it made him uneasy.

What he had witnessed bore no resemblance at all to a semi-salvaged vessel, awaiting a judicial sale after confiscation for carrying contraband. What he had inspected was an old frame with a new mission. Someone had gone to a good deal of trouble and expense, and had done their best to provide the ship with a new identity.

But despite all that had been done, the vessel could not sail without current valid papers.

Kyriakos felt an involuntary shiver down his spine as he followed the man who purported to be the dockyard superintendent into the captain's office on the bridge deck. A set of papers were laid out neatly on the table.

"Sit down. Take your time. Can we offer you coffee?"

Kyriakos shook his head as the mess steward closed the companionway door behind him.

He started to examine the documents that the other man motioned that he should sign. The flag state and classification certificates had been prepared with several copies. They had all been carefully printed and bore the correct security sequence numbers. There was, however, no doubt in Kyriakos' mind, that the papers were forgeries, skilfully done, but forgeries.

It was all too obvious now. He had been asked to sign off on documents that, somehow, were to validate whatever makeover the vessel was undergoing, and for a purpose which he could only speculate.

The superintendent sensed his hesitation. "Sign, old man. You've seen everything."

Kyriakos looked up. "What's going on?"

"You don't need to know. You've done your inspection. Sign the papers now and we can finish."

As he spoke the man produced a clutch of tightly bound United States hundred dollar bills.

"Here's your fee, Captain. Sorry you've got no one to share it with."

"What are you up to?"

Kyriakos' voice sounded old and hoarse. He felt a sense of cold fear. The door behind him opened. The man who entered levelled an automatic pistol at Kyriakos' head.

"Just sign, Captain. That's all we need you to do."

Kyriakos' head slumped forward. He pushed aside the wad of notes and despairingly signed as he had been asked.

The superintendent nodded to his companion, motioning him to open the door. Kyriakos walked slowly down the passageway towards the main deck and the gangway. He almost felt a surge of relief as the warm afternoon breeze from the bay fanned his cheeks. What he had done was clearly wrong. Already his mind was made up to alert the port authority.

As he approached the top of the gangway, Kyriakos turned to see one of the deckhands raise a heavy wrench above his head. It was over in seconds.

Kyriakos' body slumped on to the deck and slipped down towards the pier. His shattered and bloodied head struck one of the steel stanchions of the gangway as it fell.

The superintendent watched from above. The noise of the yard equipment fell silent. As it did so, Pytr Majec withdrew his mobile phone and sent two texts in quick succession. The first was routed to a computer, in a one-man yacht agency, on the island of Saint Croix in the Caribbean. The second was to a waiting answerphone, in a private room on the tenth floor of the offices of Layton and Springer in London.

Chapter Two

Geneva, Switzerland

MICHAEL CROSFIELD CLOSED THE TAXI DOOR, PAID the fare and looked up at the imposing portico of the Hotel Belle Montagne. He walked quickly into a tall galleried hallway, with faded Victorian décor.

An attractive uniformed receptionist welcomed him graciously to the hotel.

"Monsieur Mansur asked that you meet him in the bar."

Crosfield stepped into a panelled lounge, adorned with hunting trophies and sepia photographs, and entered the Salon des Anglais. Fine leather chesterfield sofas and a range of English Eighteenth Century furniture exuded a warm sense of comfort and security. Little had changed since his first visit some ten years before.

He checked the discreet bar at the end of the room. Mansur had yet to arrive. Crosfield let himself out on to the stone flagged terrace. There was time to take in the view over the still, opaque waters of Lac Leman below and the jagged peaks of the French Alps on the opposite side.

He could not be certain of the outcome of the forthcoming meeting. Crosfield had managed to ensure that Mansur's Globex group of companies had remained his own favoured client for the last decade. He had guarded his position jealously. No one else had access to any information or details that would prejudice his position of client exclusivity, should professional regulators or his firm's compliance department enquire too closely.

Crosfield adjusted his sunglasses as the lake shimmered in the glare of a sudden burst of sunshine and the sweep of a cloud of mist. He smiled to himself. It had worked well enough. No one at Layton and Springer had seen fit to check the manner in which his own profits had increased so spectacularly ahead of his contemporaries', in the firm's annual review.

The figures and the international profile that Mansur attracted had ensured Crosfield's unopposed election to the position of senior partner. It seemed like another life. Crosfield smiled to himself as he recalled his final report at the middle ranking private school to which his ageing parents had scrimped and saved to send him.

The headmaster, a saintly cleric, with a lifetime's experience of his pupils, had written that Michael Crosfield had an unpleasant personality. He was, sad to relate, a sycophant and a bully. As such, he would likely do well in the world of business.

The words had been prophetic. After engineering a place at university through a combination of lies and cheap blackmail, after learning of the admissions tutor's secret trysts with a first year male undergraduate, he had never looked back, until now.

"Reflecting on your success, Michael?"

Rahman Mansur's meticulously polite enquiry almost startled him.

He turned quickly around. Mansur and Max Herlov were standing next to him, each with their hands on the balustrade.

"Always a fine view, I feel."

Crosfield was uncertain at Mansur's tone. Something was different. He had sensed it when he had spoken with him the previous morning. He needed time to think. That's why he had travelled by train from London, under an assumed name. The call from Piraeus had confirmed his fears. Mansur, without doubt, had another agenda.

For the last decade, Mansur had instructed Crosfield to navigate his way through the jungle of myriad money laundering and anti-corruption legislation that the world's trading nations had put in place.

But Crosfield needed certainty. He still needed Mansur, in order to stay one step ahead of his partners.

Now Crosfield could not be so sure. He sensed that there might be outsiders taking too close an interest. Brief unattributed comments or soundbites in the legal press caused him to wonder. They were of no consequence individually but over time the uncertainty grew. Then came the death of Richard Jackson. It was unexpected, somehow unsettling.

"Shall we go in?"

Mansur's voice remained deceptively benign.

The warm glow of the sun had gone and the mist began sweeping up over the terrace.

The three men sat down at a table by a long window that overlooked the hotel garden, as it gently sloped down towards the lake shore.

"As I said, Michael, you and your people did well but you had us worried at the start though."

Crosfield needed no reminding of the day when a courier package, containing confidential documents about the *Globex Mariner* case, had been delayed somewhere in the Layton and Springer office building, before being belatedly delivered to Crosfield's private suite.

"You needn't have worried." His reply sounded hollow.

Mansur seemed unconcerned. He looked at Herlov, seated opposite him. A waiter approached.

"May we have coffee for three, please?"

There was a moment's silence until the waiter withdrew.

Crosfield cleared his throat. "The newspaper response to the judgment has been quite muted. There were some awkward moments at the press conference outside the Court but there's not much more that can be said."

Mansur nodded. "I read your report and agree with your advice to keep a low profile for the moment."

He continued, as if with an afterthought, "And you're sure that there's no chance of an appeal?"

Crosfield surprised himself with the confidence of his reply. "It's all evidential surmise. The insurers have accepted that they've no alternative. They're now legally obliged to pay."

"But will they?"

Mansur's tone was almost deliberately disinterested, but Crosfield continued in the same confident vein.

"I'm sure that they will. They've had their day in Court and lost."

Mansur looked at Crosfield and then out towards the lakeside gardens. The mist was thicker now. He turned to Herlov.

"Are we sure about the documents, Max?"

Mansur's associate glanced quickly at Crosfield, who replied on his behalf.

"They're secure."

But Herlov was persistent. "What about the first coastguard report? It was very specific as to the outbreak of fire."

Both men were looking closely at Crosfield, who was determined to stand his ground.

"We never disclosed it to anyone. The original data has been destroyed."

Herlov glanced at Mansur, who urged him to continue. He spoke quickly.

"We went down there immediately we heard of the casualty. No one will talk. We can be sure of that."

There was a further uneasy pause, before Mansur broke the silence.

"Michael, we have been thinking. You and your people have helped us.

We've all been grateful for what you've enabled us to achieve."

Mansur's tone gave every indication of what was to follow. Crosfield almost expected it. Whatever decision was made, he knew only too well that his window of opportunity was short.

"You must let us have your account for the *Globex Mariner* case. Max will settle it by return."

Crosfield nodded in appreciation. The fees would secure his position in the firm, but for how long he could not be sure. His obsession with personal wealth had already led him covertly to use the Mansur account with Layton and Springer as a vehicle for business schemes of his own. He had gambled, and gambled rashly, on the market movements in precious metals.

He had been closed out of several favourable mid-term options on the London International Metals Exchange and his collateral security was exhausted. He knew that there were people who would soon be beating a path to his door.

Six months before, he had taken short positions on industrial diamonds. He desperately needed a sizeable facility to cover his exposure when he discovered that a cash deposit had been credited to his account by a corporation in Nassau. Someone had bailed him out.

Days later, there had been an announcement of a major find by Globex Mining at their new mine in Kimberley.

He had survived, but not without substantial outside support. He could not be sure, but he suspected that the hand of Rahman Mansur had somehow been involved. Crosfield needed to know. He needed to know where Mansur was leading him.

He also wondered if Mansur and Herlov were reading his thoughts.

Mansur again adopted the benign tone with which he had started the meeting.

"We do feel, Michael, that we should take stock and consolidate for a month or two. We want to let any waning press interest die down. We should concentrate on our core business, perhaps pause for a while, before our next move. As you said yourself, a period of low profile might be best for us all. That doesn't mean that we're going to lose touch. But we'll just put some business distance between us for a while."

Crosfield's reply was sharp and to the point.

"I understand, but don't forget, my good friend, that Layton and Springer helped put you where you are today. I need hardly remind you that, without us, you and Globex would on more than one occasion have been in seriously deep trouble. That's even before the *Globex Mariner* episode."

Mansur gave no indication of concern at his lawyer's rebuke.

"Don't think, Michael, that we haven't appreciated what you have done for us. But times are changing. You've often said so yourself."

Both men looked at each other. The message was clear after all.

"Let's not part on bad terms, Michael. We've been through a good deal together. I don't regret that."

Crosfield was not to be deterred. "You're the client. Your decisions are your own. I've often said that too."

Suddenly there was quiet in the room, broken only by the soft strings of a harpist, playing in the hotel lobby.

Mansur broke the silence. He spoke slowly, thoughtfully. "Perhaps now is a good time to end our meeting."

Mansur stood up. "Goodbye for the moment, Michael."

The two men shook hands, and looked into each other's eyes.

Without saying more, Mansur motioned to Herlov to follow him, and the two men headed towards the hotel reception. Crosfield watched them go. He had been right to act as he had done. He needed information and insurance. Pytr Majec would provide both.

Majec had been difficult to locate. However, once Crosfield made him aware that the prosecuting authority at the International War Crimes Tribunal in the Hague was showing an interest in his activities in Kosovo, he had been more amenable to negotiation.

He finished his coffee and took out the magazine that he had carefully folded in his briefcase. The current edition of *Celebrity International* had run a feature on the lifestyle of Rahman Mansur and his new consort.

Crosfield knew only too well that the contents bore scant resemblance to the true state of Hedizah's marriage. He checked again. She would be in London within a week, at a charity event, in support of the world's poorest nations. That would be his opportunity.

He felt a surge of his old anticipation, as he left the hotel and climbed into a taxi.

"Take me to the airport please."

* * * * * * * * *

Taipei, Taiwan, Republic of China

The job of cargo dispatcher for China Interfreight had been an undemanding one, for the two years that Lee Chin had held the position. It had paid reasonably well. The job had also provided some security for his growing family, after the accident on board a Taiwanese frigate during national service days that had left him lame in his right leg.

Chin had made good progress from the suburb where he and his family shared a home with his elderly parents. The rush hour traffic on the main freeway between downtown Taipei and Chiang Kai Shek International Airport had eased.

He approached the perimeter gate at the cargo terminal some minutes before his shift was due to begin. The clouds lay low over the mountains behind him and it was beginning to get dark.

The security guard at the gatehouse, who had joined the company at the same time, waved him through. Chin looked across the airfield tarmac as he turned into the car park in front of the one-storey offices of the air cargo terminal. Immediately in front of him stretched a long line of warehouses. It was twenty-four hour work, and the area was busy with trucks and trailers being manoeuvred into position to await incoming aircraft.

Chin walked through the reception to an open plan office. In front of him were several neat rows of computer terminals and an array of maps and files to support a global air freight organization.

"Tea, Mr Chin?"

The staff had been kind to him since the day of his arrival. He could hardly walk unaided, and had felt sick with worry as to how he would cope with his first employment after the accident.

He smiled at the beaming young face beside him. "Of course, and thank you."

An older man at the next desk stood up, stretched stiffly and reached for his jacket.

"I'll leave matters in your capable hands. Time I went. There's Japanese baseball on the TV tonight."

Chin smiled and responded affably. "Good luck. The Tigers have been out of form. Perhaps things will get better this time."

"Maybe." The other man sounded unconvinced.

"Anything special I should know about?"

"Not really. It's been pretty routine."

Chin's colleague made to leave and then paused, as if he had forgotten to say something.

"We got that shipment out to Hong Kong at midday."

Chin looked up. "I didn't know that there'd been a problem."

"It wasn't too bad, only an hour or two's delay."

"Why?"

Chin's colleague glanced out into the dark of the early evening. The sky was starting to look stormy. He looked behind him. Several other members of the office were also starting to leave as their shift ended.

"Nothing really."

There was a moment's hesitation, before he continued. "It was something to do with air traffic wanting to bring in a Starlifter from Guam. It seemed a bit strange, but you'll see the details on the screen."

He paused as if wanting to say more. Instead he nodded to Chin and joined the lengthy queue of staff waiting to clock out.

Chin knew that he would be alone for the first part of the evening shift. He had not minded it at the start, but for reasons that he could not understand, he had begun to count the days until he would return to the morning roster.

He turned on his personal computer and accessed the day's cargo movements. Chin was a careful man. His line manager had complimented him on more than one occasion on the way in which he had kept his freight movement files.

Chin checked the departure and arrival shipments against the air cargo documents, with which he had become familiar. Handling airway bills, cargo manifests, certificates of origin, invoices and insurance covers had become routine.

Chin sipped his tea. As he did so, his attention was drawn to the dimming of the arc-lights that, moments before, had silhouetted the huge airframe of the Starlifter. It was the aircraft that Chin's colleague had said had arrived that afternoon. However, as Chin realized only too well, the arrival of the Starlifter was certainly not routine.

China Interfreight had not, to his knowledge, accepted goods inward or despatched goods outward to Guam. He also knew, from his days in the military, that United States supply aircraft from Guam would never use the civilian side of Chiang Kai Shek airfield.

Covert arms supplies, to support Taiwan's continued standoff with mainland China, needed to be delivered well out of sight of the prying eyes of undercover agents who were known to frequent the island.

As he continued to watch the aircraft, he saw the approach of several powerful tractor vehicles, towing what seemed to be a series of long crates on low-loader trailers. The leading vehicle slowed as it approached the rear cargo ramp that the ground crew had just lowered. An arc-lamp from an adjacent cargo bay suddenly illuminated the scene. Other operational equipment began to arrive, fuel and air tankers and, in their wake, what Chin could make out as a dark coloured Hummer truck. Its doors opened. Four men alighted and took up surveillance positions at the four points of the aircraft.

The logo on the upper fuselage was visible to Chin, as he moved to the side of his desk, and extinguished the light above his head. The reflection from his computer screen created a shadow on the wall behind him. Chin ducked down and keyed in a search.

He had not previously encountered any movements by China Interfreight that had involved flights by what he assumed was a chartered aircraft. Chin entered his employer's password. Within seconds he had opened the confidential register that listed the world's international airline operators.

His eyes had become accustomed to the darkened interior of the office. Outside he could see that the Starlifter was being readied for loading. A lightweight hoist had been positioned to steady the crates as they were shifted from the low loaders on to the ramp.

Chin entered the name of Globair Express. He had been right. It was a chartered aircraft. He had no means of verifying the register and survey record of the Starlifter itself, without details of its licence and manufacturer, but the name was listed.

It appeared that Globair Express SA had been incorporated three years before in Saint Croix, in the United States Virgin Islands. Its principal office was registered at what appeared to be the address of a local yacht agency and broking business. Chin tried to access the details of the directors and shareholders. The directors' register was unavailable, owing to it being updated. The shareholding was stated to comprise one hundred bearer shares, held by a bank in Miami, as trustees.

Chin closed the screen and sat back. The office began to feel cold. He was suddenly aware that he was alone. Wiping the cold dampness from his hands, he stood up, carefully moving across to the window.

His nerves began to feel taut. The nagging pain in his leg caused him to stiffen momentarily. Involuntarily he started, as the clatter of his desk phone shattered the eerie silence that had settled on the office. Outside, loading was underway. He could hear the muted sounds of electrical equipment and the odd shout from the ground gang.

Chin snatched the receiver.

It was the superintendent of the weighbridge over which all outward booked cargo had to pass. It was routine for him to call before sending through the weight checks that Chin would need to complete the export cargo documentation.

"You'll have the details in two minutes."

Chin navigated his way through the darkened office to a small private room where the documents would be printed out. He closed the door and switched on the light.

There was quite clearly something wrong.

The figures showed that five trailers had passed over the weighbridge, carrying almost fully loaded crates and containers. What Chin had seen on the tarmac, however, was the type of equipment and labour that would be needed for a much lighter load. He read off the cargo description, which was stated to comprise piping and irrigation materials destined for Jeddah in the Kingdom of Saudi Arabia.

Chin left the room and returned to his desk. He accessed his screen again. A familiar set of documents came up almost immediately. They were no different to the dozens of movements that he had handled in the last month. None of these, however, had involved any chartered flights to the Middle East.

Chin suddenly began to perspire. He felt empty and sensed the first pangs of panic in his stomach. Then he froze in disbelief. On the screen in front of him, the image was only too clear. Lined up against the rear wall of their tiny house were the figures of his parents, his wife and their children. Masked men were holding weapons to the heads of the two youngest. The other members of his family were facing the wall with their hands upwards and outstretched.

Suddenly, the light above his head came on. In the same instant, a desk light was swung into his eyes. He felt his neck being pulled back and the tip of a blade at his throat. The man behind him tightened his grip.

A second figure appeared. Reaching into his pocket, he threw down a ring on to the desk. Chin recognized it immediately. It was his wife's wedding ring. The same man then opened an attaché case and thrust a set of documents at Chin's face.

"These need to be filled in, as we tell you."

Chin froze, unable to speak or move.

"We'll give you five minutes."

He must have looked defiant.

"Do it, Mr Chin, or you'll see your family die in front of your very eyes."

The man holding Chin nodded. The other man unclipped his mobile phone video screen to reveal an image of terror on his mother's face.

Chin nodded frantically.

"That's better, better for all of us." The man released his grip. "Get to work."

Chin could see from the package of documents that a flight plan had already been filed. It showed that the Starlifter with her cargo was bound for Tripoli, Libya, via Tehran.

* * * * * * * * *

Keith Michel

Kensington, West London, England

The Eastbound District Line train juddered to a halt. The lights flickered and passengers stumbled into each other. Travellers had packed into the carriage as West London's rush hour service began to recover, after an earlier security alert had delayed services at Hammersmith.

Jackson glanced at his watch. He had time enough. On other days, he would have been late to arrive at Layton and Springer's City office, but today he had another assignment.

Suddenly, the main lights in the carriage went out. Seconds later, the pale glow of the emergency system silhouetted the passengers as they struggled to regain their balance.

Jackson shifted his weight from one foot to the other. The atmosphere was becoming thick and unpleasant.

His mind wandered to the date when, a few months before, he had joined the firm. Then his eyes clouded at the memory of his mother's death, two years before, and his father's all too recent funeral.

Jackson lived alone in a small apartment in West London. Its solitude had given him time to think. It had not been easy to decide on the direction that his life was to follow. He was still unsure how he had been persuaded that a career as a young City lawyer was one to which he should aspire. But his father had been keen that he should do so, when Jackson's instincts told him otherwise.

It was strange. Perhaps explained by uncertainty or a lack of security after his mother's death, but he wasn't sure. After all, it was his father who had initially encouraged him to read social anthropology when he had won a scholarship to St John's College, Oxford.

Tribal systems, their social structure, the mysteries of religion, magic and taboo had fascinated him. Field studies in New Guinea and among the Bushmen had persuaded him that modern man had much to learn from first nations or indigenous peoples. It was a theme that his father had eagerly espoused in his articles for his journal.

The train jolted and slowly ground forward. The lights came on. Jackson was still lost in thought. He started upright to find a tall black girl standing beside him, slim, smartly dressed and with quizzical eyes looking into his own.

"You look a million miles away."

"I'm afraid I was." Jackson offered a half smile, not being quite sure how to respond.

"It's OK, you know, to think aloud." The tone was friendly and vaguely inquisitive.

"Was it obvious? I'm sorry if I troubled you."

"Don't worry. You didn't."

The girl sensed a note of embarrassment, and gave him a wide grin. She seemed somehow sympathetic, as if looking for understanding and yet, at the same time, not a little seductive.

The girl glanced out of the window. "This is my stop I'm afraid."

The train edged its way into the platform at Gloucester Road. She moved closer as other passengers started to make for the opening doors.

"I'm getting off at the next one." Jackson's reply was hesitant.

Within a moment the girl was beginning to thread her way towards the door. She turned and looked at Jackson. "Take care, my friend. Perhaps I'll see you again sometime."

Her look had changed. Without another word, she thrust a folded newspaper towards Jackson and was gone, lost in the throng winding its way towards the platform exit.

Jackson took it and looked down at the open centre page of the morning edition of *London Free*.

The advertisement immediately caught his eye. In bold copy it announced that Layton and Springer, international lawyers, were proud to host the opening of an exhibition of ethnic art works from sub-Saharan Africa at London's Natural History Museum. The exhibition, it stated, had been sponsored by the Globex Charitable Foundation.

The train began to pull out towards South Kensington where he would alight. He looked almost urgently for the girl, as if seeking an explanation. She was gone.

Jackson was due at the opening. Crosfield had asked him to attend. He had been given no explanation, other than he wanted someone reliable to report back on who was attending.

That had been strange in itself. There had been rumours around the office that all might not be well with the relationship between the firm and Rahman Mansur's Globex group of companies.

Jackson had been out of the main building for some days, continuing his research in the archives department of the former Indian Government offices in London. Title enquiries into the origin of the disputed Arabian Gulf oil concessions had continued to prove elusive, when he had received Crosfield's call.

There had been nothing to suggest that anything was amiss. Crosfield's private office had, however, remained closed to members of the firm.

As a consequence, Jackson had to await the departure of a group of visitors from the adjacent conference suite, where Crosfield eventually saw him. They had apparently arrived at the main ground floor reception unannounced an hour beforehand.

Crosfield explained that he would not be present at the opening. This had been agreed with Mansur's charitable foundation to avoid, it was said, any inappropriate enquiries about the *Globex Mariner* affair.

All that was needed was a discreet observer, who was unconnected with the conclusion of the case. Hugo Jackson was such a person.

Jackson left the train at South Kensington, and walked briskly through the tiled Victorian tunnel towards the Gothic entrance of the museum. A crowd had gathered and coffee and cold drinks were already being served.

The exhibition had been mounted in one of the upper floor galleries. Jackson made his way through the exotic displays of fauna and flora dating from the present to the depths of prehistory.

As he did so, he thought back to the chance encounter with the girl on the train. It was the second coincidence in less than a week. Both had involved Rahman Mansur. Jackson could only speculate, but he could not rid his mind of the image of Hedizah, caught for those few fleeting moments after the funeral, nor did he wish to do so.

A podium had been erected and several museum staff were looking towards a side entrance. A group of invited members of the press were taking up positions, opposite the door through which Mansur would shortly enter, to open the exhibition. Tall and impressive in his demeanour, Mansur stood aside as the Museum Director called the gathering to order.

The doors behind the gallery closed. Jackson noticed that several uniformed security staff had formed a line across the entrance.

"Ladies and gentlemen, it is my privilege and pleasure to welcome you all this morning to the private opening of a remarkable collection of exhibits, which the Museum is proud to display. Without the generosity of the Globex Charitable Foundation and its founder, the renowned businessman and philanthropist, Rahman Mansur, this exhibition could never have taken place."

The tone of the museum's Director was professional and urbane. It was the voice of a man accustomed to standing alongside the rich and famous, whose vanity or generosity could readily be called upon to support his museum.

As he stood aside, a gentle ripple of applause broke out among the invited guests. Jackson looked around him. He did not sense any potential conflict or apprehension.

Rahman Mansur cleared his throat audibly, and took the microphone.

"Thank you all for coming here today, to share the real pleasure which the formal opening of this exhibition brings to me personally. It also brings great satisfaction for the hard working and dedicated staff of the charitable foundation, which my organization established some two years ago."

Jackson glanced at several of his fellow guests. Eloquent and charming, it was not difficult to see how Mansur had achieved the global prominence that he had.

"It is an honour for me, therefore, formally to open this exhibition of ethnic art, as a reminder of the cultural diversity and integrity that exists in our world. All this will be lost, unless the industrialised world recognizes the threats that our poorer nations face."

Mansur spoke with conviction and clarity. There was little doubt that, whilst his early educational background was reportedly obscure, a sharp intellect complemented his entrepreneurial acumen.

The members of the press busily attended their note taking, as they waited for Mansur to continue. Jackson noted little sign of restiveness or disapproval. The guests had been carefully chosen.

"Our Foundation, based as it is on the success that the Globex group has been fortunate to achieve in its chosen fields, is dedicated to repaying the debt, which we all owe to the indigenous populations of the world. We aim to restore a sense of global community, based on a renewed understanding of those whose way of life is threatened by the developing world."

There was a respectful round of applause. Heads nodded in approbation. Jackson listened with growing uncertainty. The message that he was hearing echoed almost to the word the passionate sense of global responsibility of which his father had written. It was a creed that Jackson himself had espoused and in which he excelled in his studies at Oxford.

How, he wondered, did this fit with the aspirations of the hard-nosed client of Layton and Springer, which all those who had worked with him had come to recognize.

There was a pause as Mansur waited for the gathering to settle again.

"I wish the exhibition well. Its message is deserving of your support, for which I thank you. We look forward to seeing you all again this evening at the reception at the Ritz Carlton, which my wife and I will be hosting."

Mansur moved to the side of the podium. Jackson saw him receive a message from one of his aides. Within minutes, and with gracious compliments received from those nearest to the exit, Mansur and Herlov left in hurried conversation.

Hedizah Mansur was in London. Jackson had struggled to understand why thoughts of Mansur's wife had begun to trouble him. He had seen her just once at the funeral, a shy beguiling young woman with a gentle face and eyes that were deep with concern. Then there was the unexplained photograph on his desk.

He had looked again at the message board of Layton and Springer's internal website. Crosfield was making certain that the personal life of his, and the firm's, prestigious client was kept well in the forefront of the minds of his staff and fellow partners.

Jackson had little doubt that his lack of experience had left him with only an imaginary concept of the extent to which politics and intrigue necessarily dominated the internal agenda of any large organization. He felt himself somewhat naïve alongside the personal ambitions and self-motivation of his contemporaries.

He had approached the law on the basis of logic and integrity. The work that he had done on the *Globex Mariner* case revealed that he had much to learn if he was to make progress.

The words of Mansur were an empty charade. Jackson knew that now. Crosfield had wanted him there as his innocent eyes and ears. But he began to realize that what he had seen and heard was only the gloss on a bigger, deeper scenario, in which he had no role.

Somewhere however, in that scenario, there was a beautiful young woman, who seemed to have no part in the game which her husband, Michael Crosfield and others were playing out.

He made up his mind. It was instinctive and, he knew, irrational. But somehow he had to see Hedizah and talk to her. He suddenly felt a sense of overwhelming responsibility for her welfare. He felt cold. Perhaps he sensed a real concern for her safety.

When the reception ended, Jackson quickly made his way out of the museum and hailed a taxi. It seemed to take an age to navigate through the mid-morning traffic towards Piccadilly. The breezy conversation of the driver for once was of little interest to Jackson. He liked and believed in his fellow man. He wanted to know and share the concerns of others, but for reasons that he could not understand, he felt that for the first time in his life he was falling in love.

He jumped from the taxi and paid the fare.

"Good morning, Sir. Welcome to the Ritz Carlton."

The liveried porter smiled widely and nodded towards the richly decorated reception area. A neatly ordered events board in the foyer indicated that the Globex Foundation champagne reception would be held in the St James's Park suite at eight o'clock that evening.

Jackson walked up to the desk. He would have to lie. He knew that. But it might work.

"Good morning. I'm here to meet Mrs Mansur. It's about this evening's reception. We need to finalise a few details on the guest list."

The clerk looked momentarily uncertain. He walked to the opposite end of the desk and entered a small back office.

"I'm very sorry, Sir, but my colleague has just told me that Mrs Mansur has checked out. She left with one of her husband's associates a few minutes ago."

Jackson's expression must have shown his surprise. The face of the desk clerk looked concerned. He reached down, quietly withdrew an envelope from the pile of mail beside him, and leaned forward. He then looked sideways across the hallway. It was empty.

"Forgive me, Sir, but are you Mr Jackson?"

He nodded at the unexpected question. In an instant the clerk slid the envelope across the desk.

"In that case, Mrs Mansur left this for you."

Jackson turned away, pulled open the envelope and quickly extracted a sheet of crisply folded notepaper. He bit his lip as he read a short message that had been written in a neat feminine script. "Send me your mobile number, please. I'll call you as soon as I can. Hedizah."

* * * * * * * * *

Kuala Lumpur, Malaysia

The mist was beginning to rise as the sun crept higher over the tropical palms that lay either side of the track. The tall white minarets of the terminus building of Kuala Lumpur's main railway station were coming into view.

Jean-Yves Bertrand stood up and reached to the rack above his head. He pulled down his travel bag and made his way along the corridor to the connecting door. A queue began to form as passengers started to show their impatience.

"We apologize for the delay in the arrival of today's express from Singapore. We will be alongside the platform shortly."

The train slowed. Weather conditions over Malaysia's capital had caused the cancellation of the first flight of the day. The airline check-in desks had blamed the early seasonal mist for upsetting their schedules. The real cause, as Bertrand well knew however, was the continued burning of vast swathes of virgin rainforest upcountry and over the Malacca Straits in Sumatra and Indonesia beyond.

Like others on board, Bertrand had switched to the train. The journey had, at least, given him time to reflect on recent events, and how he now came to find himself carrying an international press card bearing the name of Luc Dutronc. It described him as a journalist employed on the overseas weekly edition of *France Today*.

Bertrand shuffled forward as the train creaked across an antique set of points before pulling into the station.

After his interrogation at Shark Bay, he had received a call at the country club in Kununurra where he had been put up overnight. He had been offered the job. A down payment in cash had been delivered to the club's reception, together with a note directing him to be in Singapore in two days' time.

He was to go to the Orchid Tea House in the Botanical Gardens and await a contact who would meet him at midday.

Bertrand had little time to be intrigued by the exotic arrangements that had been made. He was out of work and his back pay from the job at the sanctuary in Sabah had yet to arrive at his bank. It was less than likely that he would ever see it.

It hardly troubled him, however. As a legionnaire, he had long grown to accept that life was never his own. He could scarcely complain, since without the legion's arcane policy of secrecy, he would have found himself in jail for the murder of his mother's attacker.

It was strange. He had been so fond of his mother, had respected her so much, but now he could hardly picture her face.

Bertrand had made the rendezvous as instructed. A tall, attractive Australian girl made contact. She did not give her name or any other details, other than she worked for a regional newspaper.

His assignment required him to present himself that afternoon at the offices of the Far East Chamber of Commerce in the business district of Kuala Lumpur. He was to ask for a Captain Ranjit Mahmood, who would be expecting him.

Mahmood was the Senior Executive Officer of the Chamber's Maritime Piracy Reporting Centre. He had agreed to give an exclusive interview to *France Today*, for a supplement that the paper was running on crime at sea in the Twenty-first Century. European commercial and shipping interests had been shocked to learn of the extent to which organized crime was threatening safe passage across some of the world's busiest seaways.

The train finally stopped and Bertrand stepped down on to the platform. A searing wall of heat struck his face as he made his way to the taxi rank outside the ticket office. Crowds thronged the pavement. Vendors of local foods of all kinds jostled with shoppers and market traders.

Amidst the crowds, Bertrand could not help but notice the urgent demeanour of men, traditionally garbed, making their way to the mosque. The call for prayers had begun.

Within a quarter of an hour, Bertrand was making his way to the elevator lobby of a discreet six-storey building, nestling under the shadows of the giant Petronas Towers.

Captain Mahmood greeted him warmly. An Indian seafarer of long experience, he had come ashore to offer his expertise after a piratical attack on a vessel under his command. The incident had left the Chief Officer stabbed to death and a female radio officer abducted off the South Chinese coast.

"So, your European readers are interested in learning the problems that we face?"

Bertrand took out his notebook. Mahmood began to speak, quickly, almost passionately, about his subject.

"Modern day piracy is a highly organized criminal business in several parts of the world. In some cases the perpetrators are shielded by corrupt customs officials. In other cases, coastal governments engage in state-sponsored piracy. It's terrorism at sea. No different from attacks on innocent people on land."

Bertrand nodded as Mahmood continued, on what was clearly a well trodden path.

"It brings distress, danger and death to seafarers. You have to remember that a ship is a seaman's home as well as his workplace." He paused for a moment.

Bertrand wore his alias well. He looked down at his notebook. "What are these attacks aimed at? Are they directed at special vessels on particular voyages, or their cargoes?"

"There are patterns that we can follow, and even predict, but then again random attacks occur without warning."

Mahmood continued. "Hijacking of high value cargoes is the main aim, usually to order. They frequently target vessels carrying gas, oil and minerals. No prizes for guessing which countries in the Far East region are hungry for energy."

Bertrand said little. He allowed his host to recount yearly statistics, point to wall charts dotted with coloured markers and pass across his desk a series of confidential bulletins issued to the world's shipping and insurance industry.

Mahmood continued somewhat breathlessly. "It's war out there, you know."

"How do you mean?"

"Imagine an attack on an ocean-going tanker or a luxury cruise liner. Fast motor boats carrying men with modern automatic weapons approach the stern under cover of darkness. They climb on board with scaling ladders and ropes."

"Go on."

"The crew have few means to defend themselves. Generally they've no choice but to submit."

Bertrand nodded to Mahmood to continue.

"It's dangerous and uncertain. Who knows if the attackers are motivated by theft or if they intend to kidnap hostages for ransom?"

"Are you saying that you can't differentiate between so-called pirates and terrorists?"

"Precisely; who is to say that the demand for a cash ransom is made by a local warlord, a criminal syndicate or the local cell of a terrorist organization?"

Bertrand looked again at the man in front of him, speaking with such zeal. Mahmood's idealism was starkly at odds with the vicious world in which he had elected to work. He wanted to help, to save lives. The well-being of a lowly teenage deckhand far away from home and the welfare of his family were dominating issues for Mahmood. Bertrand was impressed. Such men were rare on his watch.

"Are any merchant ships armed?"

"Rarely, except those carrying nuclear waste from Europe for reprocessing in Japan. No one in their right mind would want to take on the fire power they have on board."

Bertrand smiled. He understood only too well.

"What about any other defences on board?"

Mahmood shrugged. "All round steel mesh fencing, automatic lighting, fire hoses and sonic blasters. That's about the best that the industry can offer but most owners fight shy of the cost of installing that kind of kit. It's expensive."

"Does it work?"

"Sometimes it does. Crews are getting better trained but we've still got a big problem with the unexpected."

Bertrand looked out of the window. The sun had broken through now. There was the growl of traffic below. Mahmood joined him.

"It gets worse. It's almost as bad as Calcutta."

Bertrand sensed a change of tone in the other man's voice.

"Home for you, Captain?"

His reply came quickly. "Yes, when I'm not here or chasing pirates round the globe."

Mahmood smiled in self deprecation. There was something that he was struggling hard to conceal.

Bertrand wondered if he should enquire further. Before he spoke again, the desk telephone rang. Mahmood was quick to answer. He listened intently then put down the receiver.

"As the British used to say, the best laid plans."

Bertrand smiled. "Don't worry my friend; we have the same expression in France."

Mahmood sought to excuse himself. "I'll have to leave you now. My director's calling from Jakarta. It looks like a new case."

Bertrand felt that he should learn more. He doubted that a true journalist would leave without further enquiry.

"Two final questions if I may?"

"Of course."

"First, doesn't the international community assist? NATO? The UN? Don't their navies intervene?"

"If only it were that simple."

Bertrand remained silent. Mahmood breathed heavily.

"The world's politicians never want to take risks where they can avoid it. It hardly need be said."

He paused for a moment to look down at a silver framed photograph on his desk. It showed a good looking young man in his mid-twenties. He was smartly attired in naval drills, with an embroidered cap and an impressive row of medal ribbons over the left pocket of his jacket.

Mahmood spoke slowly, as if trying to pick up the theme that he knew so well.

"National navies under international command are confined by their operational orders. They're out there to try to intercept terrorists or to check vessels for contraband, like carrying Iraqi oil when it was banned by the UN."

Bertrand sensed the change of mood. His reply was measured. "So it's unlikely that a naval vessel would intervene unless ordered to do so as part of some bigger operation?"

Mahmood replied hastily. "That's right. It's getting so bad, however, that sooner or later the western world is going to have to act. Dozens of ships have been attacked. But like everything, there's got to be money and resources made available."

The Frenchman watched Mahmood stand up and look at a ship's pennant hanging on the wall behind him.

"Indian Navy?"

Mahmood stiffened. "No, my friend; Indian Coastguard."

There was a moment's silence before Mahmood continued. "It was last year. A big vessel had been hijacked in the South China Sea. Her crew were cast off in the lifeboats. Her cargo was smuggled ashore and sold. The pirates had tried to change the vessel's name and appearance but she was tracked into Indian Territorial Waters in passage to Pakistan."

"Go on."

"We located her and I'm proud to say that, on this occasion, the authorities in Mumbai agreed to intercept the vessel and try to arrest the pirates."

Mahmood's eyes started to mist over. "My son led the boarding party …" His voice tailed away.

"I'm very sorry."

Bertrand shook the other man's hand. He had seen death in many forms. On this occasion he felt genuine remorse.

"I must leave. But may I ask you one last question?"

"Of course."

"Where, in your opinion, is the most dangerous part of the world for attacks on passing ships?"

"No doubt about that, the coast of Somalia. It's bandit country there."

Bertrand thanked Mahmood for his time and made for the door. Within ten minutes, he was seated at a corner table in an outdoor food mall in the next street.

"A beer, prawns and rice please. Do you have a public phone here?"

"Behind the bar."

She had told him not to use his mobile. He dialled the number that she had given him.

It was a voice recording.

"You have reached the phone of Ann Sutherland of the *World Economic Monitor*. Please leave your message."

Bertrand did so and returned to his meal.

CHAPTER THREE

The City of London, England

IT HAD BEEN A LONG DAY. THE members of Layton and Springer's Executive Board were becoming tetchy. Changed time zones and constant interruptions from mobile phone calls and zealous personal assistants were taking their toll. What was more, they had fallen well behind on the agenda and the afternoon session promised to be even more fraught. There was also a feeling of uncertainty and mistrust between partners, which had led to a series of hastily arranged alliances over the lunch adjournment.

The suite on the top floor of the firm's office building commanded fine views down the river, towards Tower Bridge. It was surrounded by a balcony terrace, embracing the most modern roof garden design. A marble fountain played a gentle spray of water over luxuriant ferns.

Michael Crosfield was chairing the meeting, as he had done for the last decade. The day was going badly, and he knew it. He gripped the balustrade railing. His face felt heavy. He looked pale, and grey lines underscored his eyes. He clipped shut his mobile phone and sighed.

"You look anxious, Mr Crosfield. May I get you a tea or coffee?"

The committee secretary, a trim, efficient woman in her mid-forties, had been with the firm for the whole of her career. It was her life. She was shocked at what she had heard.

"I'm OK, thank you. Let's reassemble, shall we?"

Grudgingly, the committee members returned to the oval-shaped conference table. Crosfield nodded to the secretary and the inner hallway door to the room opened. A tall blonde girl entered. The resigned looks on some of the older faces around the table showed that they had little enthusiasm for the presentation that the Head of Worldwide Marketing was about to make. It was anyone's guess as to which of the younger partners she was currently sleeping with.

Crosfield raised his voice to try to establish some form of authority to start the session, and tried to sound upbeat.

"I thought that it would be helpful to reaffirm our agreed mission statement, so that this can be included on our website bulletin board after the meeting. The marketing brochure will pick it up, when it is reissued tomorrow."

The presentation did little to lift the sense of unease.

Crosfield sought to summarise its conclusion. His voice sounded flat and uninspired.

"Ladies and gentlemen, I imagine that there is no disagreement then that the firm's profile depends upon our reputation for unchallenged principle and integrity."

He cleared his throat and continued. "Our dealings with clients and opponents alike are founded on the premise that our advice and conduct meet the highest standards demanded by our international clientele. It is to be matched by a fee structure that is transparent and responsible."

There was a moment's silence.

"So what's changed? I thought that such crap was merely a convenient way of keeping the legal press happy, whilst we did our very best to screw the clients for all we can get, by telling them that they're dead in the water if they don't do what we tell them."

The voice was that of the youngest member of the committee, who had arrived that morning from the firm's Los Angeles office. For an instant, there was a feeling that revolution was in the air, until Crosfield led a short round of applause.

"I couldn't have put it better myself. I knew that I could count on our newest recruit to show us the way."

The atmosphere seemed to lighten until an older man, a veteran of one of the firm's less glamorous departments, raised his hand towards the chair.

"Michael, I hate to sound negative after such a lively intervention from across the pond."

He paused for a moment, with a wry smile, as a further ripple of laughter carried around the room. His tone, however, was uncompromising.

"But, I have to say, Michael, that I, and I believe several others around this table, are very concerned to hear that the lawyers acting for the other side in the *Globex Mariner* case have referred the matter to the Ministry of Justice. We believe that they have also lodged a formal complaint at the conduct of this firm with the Legal Ombudsman's Department."

Crosfield replied brusquely. "You have every right to be concerned, if there was any substance in what has become a tiresome trail of unending innuendo and misinformation. But if you don't have the balls to act in messy cases, why don't you retire?"

Crosfield's bullish response had been characteristic of his conduct throughout the day.

The older man was not to be deterred. He continued politely.

"Whatever you say, Michael, the problems are becoming persistent. It's damaging the firm. You, yourself, saw the anonymous blog two days ago which said that Rahman Mansur had terminated our retainer. Our financial people are also getting concerned that there is no sign of payment of the bills which he owes. It's serious money."

Crosfield stood up and crossed to the other side of the room.

"Don't bloody well tell me how to run my client's account. I know what's owed and I know it'll be paid. As to the retainer, it's not been terminated and that's all this meeting needs to know."

There was silence.

"Michael, I don't want to fall out with you or anyone else here but you know as well as I do that the press has had some unkind things to say about you and Rahman Mansur. I think that we have a right to be concerned."

"You have that right and I have the right to run my business my way."

Crosfield snatched up his papers.

"I have to leave now anyway. I've got an appointment outside the office."

Crosfield strode down the corridor, took the lift to his private office and closed the door.

He dialled a local number in East London.

"I'll be there in an hour."

Within ten minutes Crosfield's Bentley Corniche was easing its way northeast, out of the City of London, towards the main motorway route to East Anglia. He drove quickly, once he had reached the turn off towards the Essex Coast. The traffic was light and he made good time towards Newton Quay. The village was situated at the head of one of the many creeks, snaking inland from the North Sea.

Crosfield glanced at his watch, slowed the car and parked on the roadside. He got out, closed the door, and started to walk down an ill-defined path, towards an old grain warehouse. The building had been converted into weekend luxury apartments, complete with a discreet private yacht mooring, and an upstairs view over the dark marshes that almost cut the village off from the mainland.

It was cold. There was a stiff breeze blowing in from the estuary, and a damp mist hung low over the coast.

The meeting had gone as badly as he thought it would. He had hoped that winning the *Globex Mariner* case might get some uncomfortably close enquiries off his back. But he was in deeply now, much too deeply to do anything but fight and hope that his usual luck would return. Somehow he was not so sure.

Of course, there had been little doubt as to the outcome. Mansur's people had managed to suppress the report of the Saudi coast guard enquiry. They had also made sure that the local investigatory authority was suitably compromised, with a mixture of bribes and threats.

A tame expert witness, with an impressive record in the maritime industry, but with a need to service a lifelong drug dependency, had been quite relaxed about perjuring himself in court, for the right price.

As for the judge, Crosfield had told Mansur that he would have to make his own approach. Crosfield did not want to know. There were too many eyes and ears in the corridors and chambers of the High Court, for an instantly recognisable City solicitor to traverse incognito, particularly with the mission he had in mind.

When Crosfield read the Justice Ministry announcement in the *Legal Gazette*, which announced that Mr Justice Henry Wilkinson would be taking early retirement and moving to live in Cyprus, he assumed that the necessary arrangements had been duly made.

Crosfield checked his direction. They had told him to head for the church tower and follow the path down to the old harbour, where he would find the entrance to the apartments.

He paused for a minute. His hands began to feel damp and he felt the first chill trickle of perspiration down his back. Crosfield knew what they would be wanting. It would be payment in full or a cast iron guarantee, neither of which he was presently in a position to deliver. His first nagging doubts had started when he read that the trial judge intended to retire, after the case had been heard.

Mansur had agreed that Crosfield's success fee would be credited to his personal nominee account at a bank in the Isle of Man. It had not yet arrived. He had tried in vain to find an opportunity to raise it with Mansur at the Geneva meeting. Subsequent calls to check the position had also gone unanswered.

He had no cash to offer and no collateral. What was more, he knew only too well that, despite his violent bluster to the contrary, his firm's own fee account was still outstanding. Only Crosfield knew that hidden within the reams of computer printouts lay the hundreds of hours of time, which he had invented, and the outlays needed to secure favourable evidence from the key witnesses involved.

Time was short, too short. The regulators and their acolytes would have a field day once they got their feet through the portals of Layton and Springer's ornately decorated reception.

Crosfield rang the bell. The entrance porch to the converted warehouse was subtly illuminated by two shaded lamps, which he could make out through the tinted glass porch.

The door was opened by a bull necked man, with a shaven head, pallid complexion and an unpleasing scar on his left cheek. As he entered, Crosfield felt the man's hand between his shoulder blades. He was shown into a ground floor sitting room, with curtains tightly drawn.

Low table lamps highlighted the silhouetted form of two young girls, standing naked in the middle of the room. Several men watched as the girls played out their routines.

Crosfield saw their faces; pretty, submissive and terrified.

"Trouble you, does it Mr Crosfield?"

The speaker rose to his feet. Ralph Lennard had gone far. He had progressed rapidly, from East End haulier and scrap metal dealer to chairman of one of the coveted inner ring of companies that controlled the London International Derivatives Exchange.

"I said, Mr Crosfield, does it trouble you?"

Crosfield looked at the taller of the girls, now straddled across one of the men, who had moved to the sofa. Eastern European by birth, she was no older than fourteen.

He said nothing. As he turned round, a door slammed in an adjacent room, and a girl's shrill scream echoed around the apartment.

Lennard smiled. He flicked a remote control to switch on a wall-mounted home cinema screen. Crosfield shifted his eyes and as he did so felt the back of Lennard's right hand crash against his jaw. He fell to the ground. Lennard stood over him with a wide grin, making sure that the weight of his right foot was brought down on the fingers of Crosfield's outstretched left hand.

"Funny, you don't seem to like what we have here. Most of my City friends enjoy it."

"You're sick, Lennard."

"Maybe, my friend, but the girls are happy. Look at them. Just think what might have happened to them if we'd left them at home."

Lennard grabbed the younger of the girls and held his hands round her neck.

"You owe me, Mr Crosfield. You know that. I know that. It's ten million dollars at my last count. You have fourteen days."

His grip on the girl tightened. Her dark child's eyes looked imploringly at Crosfield, as if somehow, he might, for a moment, alleviate the humiliating and terrifying hell in which she found herself.

"Get up, Crosfield. I don't want to see or hear from you again until my money's here and on time."

Crosfield staggered to his feet, cradling the fingers of his left hand in the palm of his right.

"Now get out."

The man who had let him in moved into the hallway. Crosfield dragged himself towards the door.

"Before you go, *Sir*, there's something else you should have. Just to show I'm serious."

Crosfield paused, breathing heavily, as the pain from his fingers crept up his arm.

Lennard thrust out his hand and stuffed two photographs into the breast pocket of Crosfield's dishevelled grey pinstripe suit. Crosfield struggled to remove them. He looked down at the images.

"You bastard, Lennard. If you touch her I'll…"

"I don't think that you're in any position to make threats."

The door slammed behind him. The clouds were low and it was starting to rain. A grey dusk was settling over the damp foreshore.

Crosfield carefully fanned out the photographs. The first showed the happy smiling face of a young girl of about thirteen years with long blonde hair tied back in a bow. Her head was supported by two soft cushions and her body propped up caringly in a wheelchair, specially designed for children with crippling muscular disorders. The second showed the entrance to a private sanatorium, situated beside a forested lake in Austrian Tyrol.

Crosfield muttered under his breath, as he stumbled back up the path towards his car.

"Anna."

He spoke her name slowly. Only two people had known where she was and one of those was dead. Crosfield spat out the blood that was beginning to congeal on his lips. He knew that he now had no alternative. He had foreseen what might occur and had made his preparations. Somehow, seeing Anna's picture made things simpler. He was irretrievably committed. It had to be done, and soon, to meet Lennard's deadline. Crosfield switched on the ignition and headed back to London.

* * * * * * * * *

Central London, England

Jackson heard the telephone ring as he entered the hallway of his apartment. As he reached the receiver, the answering machine clicked in. He listened, vainly hoping that it was the voice of Hedizah Mansur returning one of the several calls to her mobile that he had made since receiving her note at the Ritz Carlton Hotel.

His mind had raced in so many directions over the last twenty-four hours that he had no idea which way to turn. He had taken time out, during his research away from the office, to try to find out all he could about the strangely beautiful woman who had come to dominate his thoughts.

There was surprisingly little to learn beyond what the Layton and Springer's internal web board contained. There was an urbane announcement of the marriage of the firm's most prestigious client, Rahman Mansur, to a glamorous, unknown girl from a remote North Indian provincial town. It said that Mansur had befriended and rescued her from poverty and deprivation.

There were photos of the couple, after their wedding, at a multi-faith religious chapel in Paris. There were also shots of their honeymoon cruise, in the Mediterranean, aboard the luxurious *Globex Seaquest*, the group's ocean-going flagship yacht.

All that Jackson could discern was that a young woman had been seemingly swept into an alien world in which, despite her evident beauty, she looked wholly ill at ease.

How he had become an observer, albeit by proxy, to the life of this young woman both excited and frightened him. The unsolicited photograph on his desk and the note with her mobile number seemed surreal.

And there were other unsettling matters. Why had Crosfield been so blatantly dismissive of the innocuous report that he had tendered on his attendance at the Globex Foundation reception?

There was sporadic talk in the office, amongst the young associates. Some said that all might not be well in the firm's relationship with Rahman Mansur and that the last meeting of Layton and Springer's executive board had broken up in disorder. Others asserted that Crosfield's formerly unassailable position, as Senior Partner, had been challenged.

Jackson looked around the tiny kitchen. Supper alone with a microwave ready-prepared meal could wait. He poured himself a fruit juice and sat down.

He thought back to the press conference, at the Law Courts, which Crosfield had handled with such apparent confidence, only a few days before. Again, it may have been only rumour, but someone close to Crosfield's private office was heard to say that the *Globex Mariner* case was now the subject of further judicial scrutiny.

Jackson clicked on the remote to catch the news. There was a feature on the environment, industry and the position of the world's disadvantaged, left behind by the digital age. He thought of the funeral and smiled to himself at the childhood memories of the winter snows below Les Deux Croix, where his father lay buried. A picture of his mother came into his eyes. He felt alone, very alone.

He turned off the programme and walked to the narrow window. The streets below were busy with early evening shoppers. A white van was drawing up. The driver quickly ran up the steps of the apartment building. Within seconds the intercom sounded and Jackson went across the room to answer it.

"Courier delivery, for Mr Jackson."

"It's Jackson speaking."

"I need a signature please, Sir."

Jackson closed the door to his apartment and took the stairs to the lobby. He opened the front entrance, signed the delivery docket and took the package. As the vehicle quickly drew away he noticed that neither the package that he was holding nor the delivery van displayed any commercial logo.

It was beginning to get dark and it had started to rain. The light from the street lamps either side of the apartment building reflected on the damp pavement. Involuntarily, Jackson found himself looking both ways along the street before closing the entrance door, coding in the security number and making his way upstairs.

Once inside the apartment he carefully opened the small brown package. There was no identifying name or address on the outside. Jackson slowly unsealed the envelope and gently prised up the flap. He then carefully extracted the clear plastic cover of a single DVD and held up the envelope. There were no other contents.

Placing the DVD on the desk in the corner of the room, he switched on his laptop computer and walked across to the window. It was raining harder now. He drew the curtains, bent down over the desk and inserted the DVD. The screen illuminated quickly. There were no introductory commercial details and, as the opening seconds passed, Jackson's instinct was that what followed had probably been downloaded from a mobile phone.

The first images appeared. The sky was clear and there was bright sunshine. Across what appeared to be a stretch of sand was a chain link security fence and beyond it, the blue of the sea or a lake. The camera swung across a large sign, displayed in Arabic script and in English. It stated that the premises were the property of the Royal Saudi Arabian Customs Service, that entry was prohibited to all except authorised personnel and that any intruders were liable to be shot.

Beyond, on the landward side, the camera moved to an open warehouse area, surrounding a jetty and a wide concrete landing slip. A guard tower, with powerful arc-lights, lay immediately to the right of the high entrance gates.

Several blind seconds followed before the camera moved to the wharf, where a squad of some six or seven uniformed staff were unloading a steel framed lighter that was lying alongside a powerful-looking tug. Smoke was pouring from her funnel.

A gantry crane had been rigged on the lighter. What seemed like sizeable items of marine debris were being swung ashore.

Several blind seconds followed before the camera focused in from closer range on several larger items that had already been discharged. The images were clear and sharp in the brilliant sunlight. There was no mistaking the twisted bow of the remains of a ship's lifeboat, nor the tarpaulins that were covering several lifeless forms beside it. There was also no mistaking the name on the forward starboard bow of the lifeboat. Without doubt, it was from the *Globex Mariner*.

Jackson watched the images playing out in front of him with a mixture of incredulity and fear. There was a further period of several seconds before the images resumed.

It was darker now, and Jackson could make out the lights on the guard tower, illuminating the area. The succeeding images were jerky and erratic, as the camera holder struggled to peel back the nearest of the tarpaulins. The security light swept overhead.

As soon as it was gone, the shadowy picture revealed the head of a corpse. There were two bullet holes in the side of the skull that lolled towards the camera.

Jackson felt a cold sense of nausea in his stomach and began to perspire. He felt that he was dreaming and tried to disassociate himself from what he had seen.

Suddenly, his nerves tightened. His body shook uncontrollably at the clatter of his mobile phone. Unsteadily he picked up the unit and folded back the receiver.

"Hugo Jackson, please."

The caller was a well-spoken male, who made no attempt to disguise his voice.

Jackson hesitated and answered slowly.

"It's Jackson speaking."

"I believe that you received a package earlier?"

"I did, but who is this please?"

"My name is irrelevant. More importantly, have you seen the disk?"

Jackson looked towards the screen. He had halted the images. There were clearly more to come. He wondered what he should say.

"Yes. I've watched some of it, but I have no idea what it has to do with me and why it was sent to me in the first place."

There was a pause.

"Someone needs to know the truth. Let's just say that your name came up."

"I am afraid that I don't understand."

"I think that you should know. There's more, much more."

Jackson straightened and walked to the window. He pulled back a section of the curtain and looked down, as if to reassure himself that he was not being watched from outside.

"Whoever it is I'm speaking to, you should be aware that I have nothing to do with the *Globex Mariner* case, if that's what this is all about. The trial is finished. It's over."

"We know that. Your talents were better deployed elsewhere."

"Are you joking?"

Jackson was about to terminate the call but the caller persisted.

"Forgive me, a warped sense of trench humour. My wife always told me off for never taking anything too seriously."

The caller seemed to draw a deep breath, as if in self admonition for his earlier levity.

"Listen to me, Hugo. What's happening is serious, deadly serious. I'm afraid that you're in the middle of it, whether you know it or not."

Jackson replied as firmly as he could. "It makes no sense. I think that you and your people may have made a mistake."

The caller was persistent. "Believe me. There's no mistake, and I can prove it to you."

Before Jackson could respond again, the caller's tone changed from casual confidence to sudden anxiety. His closing words were delivered breathlessly.

"Meet me in exactly one hour at the Blue Anchor in Ferry Road, Docklands. There are documents that you should see. I'll have them with me. I'll be waiting in the last booth on the right as you go in. Be careful."

The line went dead. Jackson looked at his watch and sat down at his desk. He unpaused the computer and distantly watched the images roll on.

There were floodlit silhouettes of figures in chemical protection suits and masks examining the charred remains of metal drums and steel rimmed containers. The men were picking over the debris with extreme care.

The last image, before the camera closed out, showed temporary plastic screens being erected around the site. Jackson could only guess at the meaning of the stencilled warning notices in Arabic script. However, there was no mistaking the images that accompanied it. The message was only too clear. The area was at risk from nuclear contamination.

The screen faded and Jackson stood up. He checked the location that he had been given.

He felt compelled to meet the mysterious caller. Incomprehension, fear, almost a sense of expectation persuaded him that he had no alternative.

However irrational it might seem, Jackson's instinct told him that what he had seen and heard was somehow connected to Rahman Mansur. If that was right, it meant that any steps that he took might bring him closer to an understanding of what he felt for Hedizah. He needed to find out.

Taking the stairway to the ground floor lobby, Jackson let himself out into the street. Within five minutes he was on an underground train heading eastwards to Bank Station in the City of London, where he would change on to the Docklands Light Railway. He hardly noticed as the stations slipped by. As he approached his final stop, he could see the tall towers of Canary Wharf, brightly illuminated against the darkness and the heavy rain.

Jackson pulled up his collar and quickly covered the short distance to the crossroads that led to Ferry Road. The streets were wet and a low mist was beginning to form over the Thames quayside, less than a quarter of a mile away. He turned the corner and halted abruptly.

Two police cars and an emergency ambulance blocked the street. Paramedics were bent over a figure, lying prostrate across the pavement. A police motorcyclist was speaking into his radio and a curious crowd of onlookers was gathering.

An unprompted voice addressed Jackson, as he stood watching the scene. A sense of nervous expectation started to creep up his spine.

"Hit and run apparently. Driver never stopped. About ten minutes ago they said. Poor bugger never stood a chance, did he?"

Jackson did not wait to hear more. Avoiding the police cordon, he made for an alley that ran alongside the pub, to which he had been directed. He spotted the riverside entrance and entered. The booth by the door was empty. Standing beside it was a briefcase.

The bar was busy with customers craning to get a better view of events on the other side of the building.

Jackson saw his chance. He quickly grabbed the briefcase and ran out. As he did so, a card slipped from under the handle. He snatched it, and peered down in the half light. It gave a name but no contact details: "George Wilson (Lt Col. retd), Security Consultant."

Jackson headed towards the river. He needed the cover of a dark corner along the riverside to pause and think. Within minutes, he was seated, breathless, in a shelter alongside a Thames mooring.

He clasped the case closely. As he did so, his mobile phone rang. He answered slowly and hesitantly.

"Hugo Jackson."

He knew instinctively who the caller would be. There could be no doubt.

"This is Hedizah Mansur."

* * * * * * * * * *

Villefranche, France

The television images were all too familiar. Torrential rain swept down over a desolate hillside. A wooden road bridge, spanning what had once been a gentle stream through the village, hung down at a crazy angle. A cascade of swirling blackened water rushed beneath its crumbling spars.

Uprooted trees, the remains of makeshift buildings and the twisted wrecks of battered vehicles littered the foreground. Higher up, a landslide of mud and rocks had scythed its way through what, a few hours earlier, had been a thriving marketplace. The debris had, almost providentially, halted itself a short distance before the entrance to the local temple.

Distraught families wept. Priests sought to comfort the bereaved and bless the dead. Bodies lay roughly covered, where they had fallen, babes in arms, young children and their parents.

The rough land, over which generations of farmers had strived to raise their livestock, and to encourage a meagre harvest, year on year, lay wasted. The few fruit trees that remained stood twisted and stark, against a grey sky. Animals lay dead and bloated.

The reporter cowed against the wind. Next to him stood a young man caked in mud, wearing the insignia of Les Medecins sans Frontières.

Hedizah Mansur switched off the set. She held her head in her hands. Tears flowed freely down her cheeks. She stood up as the door to her bedroom opened. It was Sophie, her confidante and friend, over the last months.

"Is it very bad?"

Hedizah nodded her head. She swallowed hard.

Sophie crossed the room. She held Hedizah's head against her shoulder, as she started to sob.

"I remember it so well."

Sophie tried to comfort the young woman, whose arms were now around her neck.

"It was my village. I know it."

Hedizah had heard the first report, several hours before, of an earthquake in the remote north east of the Punjab. She could see, from the later images, that the village that lay destroyed had been her early home. As a young girl, she had been happy there. Despite their rural poverty, there had been warmth and love, devotion and sincerity in the extended family home.

Then the epidemic had come, and everything that she held dear had gone. Her life had changed. Love had been replaced by cold indifference in the proxy family who had taken her in. There had been a brief interlude of friendship with the teaching nun. Then came a bond of enforced servitude, as the sham of her enforced marriage to Rahman Mansur became a daily reality. Sophie had seen what had become of the beautiful young girl who had arrived from afar. Worse, she had watched her unhappiness turning into fear and despair.

"Please let me help."

Hedizah shook her head. She took Sophie's hands in her own.

"Thank you, Sophie. I'm where I am. I have to accept that. Maybe there'll be a way out. I don't know."

The older woman looked at Hedizah. She knew that nothing was normal in the house. There had been visitors who she had not seen before. Mansur had scarcely left his office since his return from London. She could not understand why Hedizah had come back before him, and why in the company of Max Herlov.

Hedizah spoke quietly. "You had better go now."

As Sophie left the room, Hedizah walked across to the bedroom window. The sun was beginning to dip behind the cliffs, casting a long golden shadow over the still Mediterranean waters. She looked towards the terrace and the mooring below. She had been right. It was the same as the day before. Several men were patrolling the garden, as it sloped down to the foreshore. She shivered, despite the warmth of the late afternoon sun.

There was the sound of footsteps in the passageway outside. Instinctively, she pulled down her loose fitting jumper over the top of her jeans. Mansur had insisted that she wear only western style clothing, despite the fact that when the occasion arose he was ready enough to assume the traditional trousers and robes of his native Kurdish lands.

The door opened.

"You look upset." Mansur's voice was flat and unemotional.

Hedizah looked up at the tall, imposing figure, as he entered. She felt cowed in his presence. He seemed to have denied her any feelings of her own. It had all happened so quickly. She seemed to have lost all sense of direction in her life and, at times, the very will to live.

"Of course I'm upset."

"You're very beautiful, even when you're sad."

Hedizah turned away. Mansur stood over her. He almost spat out his words.

"You had nothing. Who knows what would have become of you, if you had stayed on in India. You had no family, no money and no future. I have given you that."

She fought back the tears and faced her husband. "You wanted me so you bought me. That's all."

Mansur gripped her shoulders. "You have everything you need. That is what you should consider; wealth instead of poverty. Without me, you'd have had to sell your body to feed yourself. That's what I've saved you from."

Hedizah could not reply.

Mansur released his grip, crossed to the window and looked out.

Hedizah's voice was soft, almost inaudible. "What's going on? I feel a prisoner here. Why are those men outside?"

"It's business. That's all."

Hedizah ignored his reply. "Can't you understand what you have done to me? I'm trapped here, imprisoned."

Mansur said nothing, but Hedizah persisted.

"You want me. Then you leave me. You force me to your bed. You have no compassion or care for me. Why do you keep me here? Is this what happened to your first wife?"

Mansur spun around, grabbed Hedizah by the neck and shook her. He lowered his head and almost spat out his words. "That's no concern of yours."

Hedizah was becoming hysterical. She wrenched herself free and screamed out, "And what about your children? Where are they? Do you have any feelings for them?"

Mansur raised his hand to strike Hedizah but stopped himself. "Don't mention my first family again. I warn you, Hedizah. For your own good."

Suddenly the atmosphere changed. Mansur stepped back and lowered his hand.

Hedizah could not stop herself.

"Why are there always so many secrets? Why can't you at least share something with me? Why can't you show me that you care about me? That you care about something other than your business?"

Mansur's voice displayed his rising anger. "Because that's what matters. That, and the need to succeed. To succeed in a cause I believe in."

Hedizah spoke slowly, almost resignedly. "And does that justify how you treat me; as an acquisition, a new asset in your empire?"

Mansur was unrepentant. "You're here because I want you here. That's all you need to know."

Hedizah looked at Mansur. Her moist eyes were deep with anxiety and incomprehension. She pulled herself away and carefully picked up the television control unit. The French international news channel headlines were being repeated.

"We return, now, to the story of the devastating earthquake in Northern India and to our reporter, at the scene in the Punjab."

"What's this?" Mansur's surprised tone was genuine.

"Watch, please." Hedizah almost implored him to do so.

The camera focused on the young dishevelled journalist whom she had seen earlier.

"The scene is one of death and devastation all around me. Those that have survived are clinging to life in the shelter of the temple, one of the few buildings here to survive. Government sources say that food, tents and blankets will be airlifted into the area. So far, however, this has proved impossible, owing to dense fog. Flying conditions are presently impossible for helicopters. The Government is also calling for international medical aid in an effort to head off disease."

Mansur stood back, and eyed Hedizah with contempt. "Why are you showing me this?"

Hedizah's eyes did not leave the screen. She started to sob. "Because that was my village. It was my home, the only place of real happiness in my life."

Mansur smiled wryly. "So you want me to take pity on you, in addition to keeping you in luxury. Is that what you are asking?"

Hedizah turned. He cheeks were streaming with tears and her voice was beginning to break.

"I'm asking for nothing for myself. But look at what you have seen. You have money, influence and resources in the region. You could help. If I mean anything to you at all, I beg you to do something for those that have survived and for the memory of my family. Please."

Hedizah's dark eyes were filled with tears of sadness, frustration and resignation.

Mansur took hold of her again. This time his face was white with anger and his grip was painful.

"Listen, you stupid little fool, what do you think that a broken down village and a few hundred dead peasants mean to me? They're irrelevant, pathetic. Disasters have always happened. It's life's way. What matters is power."

Hedizah fought to free herself. "Please let me go, you're hurting me."

Mansur released his grip but this time brought the back of his right hand hard against Hedizah's mouth. She fell heavily. A dark weal started to form on her upper lip and a thin trickle of blood began to trickle down her jaw. She tried desperately to push herself away but he held her down by her wrists.

His face was only inches away from hers. He almost spat out his next words. "People are here to make money. When you have money, you have influence. When you have influence, you have power. I have power. More than you will ever realize."

Before Hedizah could speak his mouth was over hers. He pulled open her jeans. Her screams were stifled as she vainly fought to resist him. It was over in seconds. He stood up, looking down at her pitilessly. She gasped for breath and groaned with pain.

"Now perhaps you'll remember what power means."

Mansur stood up, and, without looking back, left the room.

Hedizah struggled to her feet, and tried to regain her composure, when the door opened.

Sophie bent down, and held Hedizah's head in her arms. She spoke gently.

"He called again for you."

Hedizah wanted to cry out but no sound came. She could think of nothing but her recollection of a short conversation with a man she had seen just once, and who now seemed her only hope of salvation, even of survival.

* * * * * * * * *

Dubai, United Arab Emirates

"Ronnie Simpson?" Jean-Yves Bertrand's voice was tinged with tired exasperation.

"Who's asking?" The response was not encouraging.

"I'm looking for Ronnie Simpson, the proprietor of Desert Tours and Safaris."

"You've found him, mate."

Bertrand looked at the makeshift caravan office and glanced back down the dusty track. It had been a rough drive.

"You're a hard man to find."

"Maybe, but I prefer it that way."

The two men stood apart, each wary of the other. The wind was beginning to whip up the dust from the track and from the undulating sand dunes and scrub beyond. The sky was clear and the dry heat unremitting. Bertrand felt the back of his neck start to chafe and pulled up the collar of his jacket.

The other man took off his sunglasses and nodded towards the caravan door. "Let's go inside."

The interior was almost as bleak as the outside. Several faded posters advertised the thrills of wadi bashing in a four wheel drive, the romance of a desert sunset and the chance to photograph rare antelope.

Bertrand looked out through the partly shuttered window. He spoke slowly.

"It's pretty quiet. How's trade?"

Bertrand turned to face the stocky, square-shouldered man in his mid-thirties, with fair hair, and a tanned complexion, dressed in a dirty safari shirt and shorts. He spoke casually.

"Any chance of you introducing yourself and telling me why you're in my office, telling me my business is crap?"

Bertrand smiled. "No offence. Jean-Yves Bertrand. I'm pleased to meet you."

Simpson reached across to the refrigerator. "Want a beer?"

Bertrand pulled up a chair. He smiled as he spoke. "Best Aussie brands available out here?"

The Australian replied swiftly. "Only if you pay for it. I stick to what I can get under the counter, in the souk."

"How's that?" Bertrand's question was genuine.

"There's plenty of trade if you know where to find it. Most of the tourists stick to the duty free and the bazaars, where they can get happily ripped off."

Bertrand paused before speaking again. "Been long in Dubai?"

The Australian looked hard at the Frenchman. "About a year."

Bertrand said nothing. Simpson closed the refrigerator, pulled off the lids from two cans and handed one to Bertrand.

"Thanks. Good health."

"Cheers, mate."

The two men fell silent. Bertrand spoke first. "What brought you here?"

The other man's reply was swift but uncertain. "I needed a change."

"You look as if you found it."

Simpson smiled and nodded. "True. No company. No stress."

Bertrand grinned back. "And no customers by the look of it."

The Australian leaned back on his chair. "So you found me. Suppose you tell me what you want."

Bertrand put down his beer. "I'm looking for a man, with the right kind of experience, to work with me and my employers on a specific project. Enquiries suggest that you could be such a man, and that you might be interested."

The Australian looked straight at Bertrand. "That depends on what is required."

Bertrand's tone hardened. "You had a good record in the military, a captain in the Australian SAS, good service in New Guinea and the Solomon Islands, decorated for undercover assignments in Afghanistan. Impressive, if I may say so."

Simpson stood up and carefully placed his beer on a pile of dusty files.

"It was good soldiering while it lasted. It's over now. There's too much interference by time-serving government pen pushers."

Bertrand continued quickly. "Is that why you quit?"

Simpson looked down and spoke softly. "Partly, but it was mainly because I got sick of getting spattered with the blood and brains of my mates so that some politician with a bent for foreign excursions could make his name at our expense."

Bertrand spoke more softly. "Still bitter?"

"No point. Just eats you up in the end."

The Frenchman picked up his beer and swallowed hard. "I know how you feel."

The two men fell silent once more. It was Bertrand again who spoke first.

"Ever been married? Kids?"

Simpson sighed. His reply came slowly. "I tried once. Hardly much of a life for a soldier's wife, sitting at home and waiting for the knock on the door."

His face tightened. "I think that I loved her, but I never really got the chance to tell her. They sent news up with the mail one time. She'd killed herself. Too much to bear, the note said, never knowing if she'd see me alive again."

"I'm sorry."

"Thanks." The Australian spoke quietly. "I never thought that it was fair to try again. You?"

Bertrand shook his head. "They didn't encourage it and made sure that we stuck with the bordellos in camp."

"Foreign Legion?"

The Frenchman nodded.

"I met some of your guys, when we had a joint op in Iraq, before I got sent up to spit lead at the Taliban."

Bertrand finished his beer. "Got anyone now?"

The Australian opened the pocket of his shirt and brought out a crumpled photograph. He handed it to Bertrand.

"She's pretty."

"Yes, she is. Somalian. Her name's Runah. Her husband and son were tortured and killed by some warlord faction up country. She managed to flee here. The Swiss ran a mercy flight. She was lucky to get on it. She's got a half-brother in Djibouti. He'd just finished at university when all hell broke out. He was lucky too."

"You sound concerned."

Simpson smiled. "I suppose I am."

He paused, as if trying to reconcile himself to an unexpected emotional attachment.

"We help each other."

Seconds passed, as he sought to find the words that he needed. "Two broken souls in a broken world you might say."

The Frenchman smiled warmly. "I'd like to meet her."

"You will later. We can go into town, but you've still not told me what you want from me."

"Shall I drive?"

Bertrand pulled out the keys to his vehicle. "We can talk as we go."

Simpson nodded. Bertrand held open the door.

"Before we go, I need to know if you're willing to leave her. There's a job to do. You'll be well paid but I don't need to explain the risks."

Bertrand paused and looked straight at the other man, before continuing. "I also need to know if Runah can arrange for me to meet her half-brother."

Simpson looked around the caravan. It was untidy and unwelcoming.

"I tried to make a go of a job that didn't involve shitting my pants every time I went to work. I wanted to give her something. Something we could live on, perhaps in time, work on together."

Simpson closed the door and looked at the empty car park, the battered sign and the desert beyond.

"Perhaps there's a lesson here. Best not to chuck over the job you know."

Bertrand smiled at the other man. He had meant what he said.

"Could you do it one more time for Runah? If the terms were right, could you risk it?"

Simpson replied quickly. "Would you or your people give her security? If I wasn't here, she'd have nothing. At least we could live on what this place brought in. Until now."

Bertrand started the engine. "And if you didn't make it back?"

The vehicle began to pick up speed, lurching erratically over the rock-strewn track. It was some two kilometres to the main coastal highway back to the city.

Simpson spoke slowly over the roar of the engine. "We never thought it could be permanent. She needs to be safe, that's all."

Bertrand reached inside his jacket as he drove. He brought out a sealed package and handed it to Simpson.

"I'm told to tell you that, whatever happens, the same amount again will be paid to you, or to Runah."

Simpson kept his eyes firmly on the track ahead as the dust kicked up beside the truck. He spoke without looking at Bertrand.

"I'll help you if I can. I only hope that your people are doing something worthwhile with their money. It's one thing to take a bullet in the crutch for the sake of the flag and the guys back home, but the money's a non-starter, if it's just to prop up some bastard who's fleecing his own people."

"Are you looking for a noble cause, my friend?"

"No. I'm only looking for some kind of assurance, that if I end up where I've seen my mates go, at least I'm with the good guys, for once."

The vehicle slowed as they approached the intersection. Bertrand looked across as Simpson swung the truck on to the highway. His words came slowly. "I asked myself the same question. That's why I'm here."

Simpson took his right hand off the wheel and held it out. Bertrand shook it warmly. Several minutes passed before Simpson spoke again.

"We keep going for about ten kilometres. We've got a small apartment in a village a short distance off the road, near the coast. It won't take us long."

The two men fell silent once more. Simpson eyed Bertrand as if waiting for an opportunity to get an answer to a question that had been troubling him.

"You mentioned Runah's half-brother. Any reason you want to tell me?"

Bertrand answered quickly. "What I know is, he works part-time for a lawyer in Djibouti. His name is Emil Douchert. He's a French expat. I met him once, I think in Chad. As I recall, he was somehow kicked out of France and was trying to survive as best he could."

Simpson looked at Bertrand, who continued in the same vein.

"We need him. Whatever his background, he is one of the few men who can gain us entry into Somalia, for what we have to do."

Simpson nodded and turned his head back to the road ahead. They drove on. A few minutes later, Simpson slowed down and pointed across the highway to a tiny cluster of dwellings along the shore.

"It's that building over there. As you can see, it's hardly much to look at, a crumbling ruin, but it's home for us."

A tall, slim woman, in her early thirties, shielded her eyes from the sun and pulled a scarf over her head.

The vehicle stopped and the two men climbed down. As they walked towards the girl, Bertrand took the other man's arm and spoke in an undertone.

"I thought that I should tell you. Douchert is not only our key to getting into Somalia, he's probably the only man who can get us out again alive."

Simpson walked over to Runah and held her tightly in his arms. She cradled her head against his shoulder. The breeze blew her scarf away as she lifted her head towards Bertrand. He smiled.

Her eyes were dark and distant, her face fine-boned, her manner dignified and gentle. She clung to Simpson as he turned to introduce Bertrand. Her long robe splayed out.

Simpson held her hand gently. He motioned Bertrand to follow him towards the house.

It was cool inside, a refuge from the late afternoon heat, fanned by the offshore breeze.

The Frenchman looked around at the meagre interior and caught Simpson's eye. "I'll leave you now."

Bertrand made towards the door. "Let's talk tomorrow. Can I come back in the morning?"

He watched as Runah smiled and gazed up at Simpson, towering above her. She replied, slowly and warmly. "Join us for coffee, Mr Bertrand. We'll both look forward to it."

Bertrand nodded and left. Simpson would join him. He was sure of that now. He only hoped that he would not keep Runah waiting too long for his return, or worse.

Chapter Four

Leipzig, Germany

The bar was at the end of the street. It was situated on the ground floor of a drab, early sixties apartment block, built at the height of the powers of the communist government of the German Democratic Republic. An experiment in collective living, it was said. The sweet smell of cooking gas and coking coal hung heavily in the late afternoon air.

Crosfield felt the air chafe roughly in his throat. He coughed painfully. Looking to his right he saw several men standing in his way, grey, surly and unwelcoming. Every wall within sight was thick with graffiti, some dating to the fall of the Berlin Wall, others railing against every injustice that the new millennium had brought forth.

It was starting to rain. Crosfield pulled up his collar and picked his way across the broken pavement, carefully avoiding the remains of a burnt-out car.

The group of men shuffled towards the single entrance to the bar, a wooden framed door with cracked panes of glass and rough boarding. Crosfield did not wish to appear more of a stranger than he was. He followed the group inside, as the rain fell more heavily and started to splash up dirt and mud from the narrow entrance steps. He looked at his watch. He was early, and had some fifteen minutes to wait. Having ordered a beer, Crosfield settled down at a table next to the window. Despite the grime on the glass, it gave him a clear view down the street.

He felt tired, depressed and frightened. Events were moving too quickly now. They had given him an ultimatum. He had expected that but they had found Anna. It had never occurred to him that anyone could have located her, or would want to.

The bar proprietor put down the beer and stared at Crosfield.

"I'm waiting for someone. He'll be here shortly." Crosfield's voice sounded hollow.

"I know." The gruff reply came quickly. "He's just telephoned to check that you were here."

Crosfield felt cold in the pit of his stomach. He looked around. The room was devoid of warmth. His eyes ranged over faded film posters of a past era. On each wall was a notice giving details of how to claim social security benefits. The government in Bonn seemed anxious to impress its erstwhile impoverished neighbour. Explicit photographs tacked to the back of the door advertised every kind of sexual service. Crosfield felt sick, and took a long swig of his beer.

He had wanted wealth from the first, not necessarily for its own sake, but as a means whereby he would never have to depend on others. He had cheated and bullied his way to the top of a renowned City of London law firm.

But that had not been enough. He had become fixated with something else, the power that wealth could bring, and the people that held it. For reasons that he never knew, Rahman Mansur had sought him out. A series of secret meetings followed. Crosfield saw in the urbane, ruthless Byzantine entrepreneur all the attributes that he needed, to further fuel his own ambitions.

Mansur had power, wealth and an international business empire. What he lacked, however, and what he urgently needed, as Crosfield soon discovered, was respectability.

Successful as his ventures into mining, energy and shipping had been, there were debts to pay, compromises to make, opponents to outflank or remove. Suddenly, there was a series of specific leaks to the world's press, allegations to answer and an unexplained campaign, investigating his background and methods. Bankers and backers were restive. Barriers that had once proved easy to overcome now required different means to assail.

The reputation and integrity of a prestigious law practice, with a gilt-edged clientele to match, was what Mansur's organization required. Crosfield had grasped the opportunity and Layton and Springer acquired a new client.

A series of seemingly legitimate transactions had provided Crosfield with the means both to secure the position of senior partner and, at the same time, to ensure that at every turn Mansur rewarded him handsomely, in cash or kind.

But Crosfield knew that he had got greedy. He had overplayed his hand in the *Globex Mariner* case. True, he had succeeded in extracting Mansur from a disaster, which might have finished them both, but the price that Crosfield demanded to sabotage the enquiry and mislead the court had been too high.

As had been made clear at their meeting in Geneva, just days before, Mansur was not going to pay.

Crosfield knew that he had also gone in too deeply in the risky world of trading futures in the world's precious metals. They meant what they said. Unless payment or collateral was forthcoming, Crosfield would be dead in the ground, and probably Anna too.

He had never loved a woman. He never wanted to. It had been easy to satisfy his needs, wherever and however he required. But Anna was his daughter, the consequence of a chance encounter with a teenage waitress in Munich, long since disappeared.

Soon after her birth, she was diagnosed with cerebral palsy. Crosfield had felt genuinely saddened at the child's plight, and had provided financial care and support. So far as he could, he loved Anna. When he visited the sanatorium, it was almost a respite from the bizarre and dangerous labyrinth that he had created for himself.

Then there was his sister. They had never been close. As a young girl, she had been an idealist, devoutly Christian, a carer and a teacher. They had gone their separate ways. Her death from cancer disturbed him, but little more.

He had vaguely promised to establish a dedicated charitable trust to secure the future of the hospice that she had established, but had never done so. He agreed, however, to take on her son at Layton and Springer.

He thought that, by so doing, he might be able to distance himself from the investigative tendencies of his nephew's journalist father. He did not really know Richard Jackson and he needed to be sure that the columns of the *International Economic Monitor* remained ignorant of the true nature of his own and Mansur's ambitions. The skiing accident was perhaps fortuitous. As for Hugo Jackson, it remained to be seen whether he became a threat or an asset.

Crosfield looked at his watch and then peered out of the window. Suddenly, the room seemed cold. He turned and felt the stubby barrel of a snub-nosed automatic pistol in the back of his neck.

He wheeled around. The bar was empty now. The group of men had gone. The barman had closed the door. Crosfield was staring into the lined face of Max Herlov. He was about the last person on earth that he had expected to see. He felt his stomach retch and bile rise in his throat.

"You look pale, Mr Crosfield. I'm sorry if I surprised you."

Herlov withdrew his weapon, and slipped it into the inside pocket of his dark leather jacket. Crosfield tried to stand but Herlov pushed him back into the chair.

"Weren't you expecting me, or was it difficult to find our meeting place?"

The tone of Herlov's voice was as uncompromising as it was condescending. All colour drained from his cheeks. Could Herlov know? Why was he here?

Crosfield's mind raced through the events of the day. He had flown to Berlin under an assumed name, using the second of his three British passports, and then paid cash for a single rail ticket to Leipzig. He had rented a car at the station, using a forged Belgian licence, for the drive to the run-down suburb where he now found himself.

He looked at Herlov. His expression was impassive. Crosfield felt his bowels about to open, as cold fear shot up his spine.

"Don't worry, Mr Crosfield. You made it here. That's all that matters now."

Herlov's tone had changed again. For an instant, Crosfield wondered if, somehow, there might be an explanation. If there was not, they would kill him. He knew that.

"You haven't actually met Pytr Majec, have you?"

Herlov's voice suggested that there might be a glimmer of hope. Crosfield stood up and looked at the second man. He was taller than Herlov, with a powerful build and broad hunched shoulders. Crosfield estimated that he was in his late forties. He had thinning dark hair and a brutish pasty-coloured face, with a livid scar on his right upper cheekbone. His thin narrow eyes viewed Crosfield with a combination of threat and wariness.

"No, we haven't met, but we know each other, don't we?"

Crosfield was struggling to regain some form of composure. It was easy to see why Majec had chosen the meeting place. The porous borders of Eastern Europe had allowed unrestricted access to men like Majec, who needed to keep on the move. Herlov had told Crosfield that Mansur had hired Majec in the wake of the *Globex Mariner* disaster. Crosfield knew from the moment he learned the fate of the ship that urgent steps were needed to forestall any local enquiries. Mansur had not been slow to follow his advice.

Majec had come, with a reputation for selling himself and his men, to the highest bidder. As the old Yugoslavia descended into bloody chaos, they had willingly participated in whatever form of inhumanity their paymasters had decreed.

Now, as was all too clear, Crosfield knew that his own fate depended on this man carrying out the desperate plan that he had conceived. It was to pay off those who would, as was evident, allow him no leeway. The net was tightening.

But, if it was right that Max Herlov, with his own background of intrigue and violence in Chechnya, had identified Majec as meeting the needs of the moment, why was he here? Had Majec told him of what was intended and, if so, what did this mean for Crosfield? Alternatively, was Mansur's trusted aide playing a different game, one of which his employer was unaware?

The bartender reappeared.

Majec spoke without looking up.

"We all need a drink; vodka three times."

Herlov paused as the three men sat down. He spoke slowly. "As I see it, Mr Crosfield, you need us both to help you."

"Go on."

"Pytr Majec told me what you intend to do."

Crosfield said nothing. He was faint with terror. It was what he feared most, but almost what he was expecting.

Herlov continued. His tone was light and disdainful. "You didn't seriously think that he would keep it to himself, did you?"

The two men laughed mockingly at Crosfield's discomfort. The three glasses arrived. Crosfield downed his drink in one.

Herlov was enjoying himself. The ingratiating instinct of the bully had had to be suppressed in Mansur's presence, but now he could give it full rein.

"I said to Pytr that, if the price was right, I saw no objection."

"What do you mean, Herlov? What do you know and what does Mansur know or suspect?"

Crosfield tried to stand but Herlov restrained him. His tone was unchanged. "You sound as though you don't trust us."

Crosfield's voice was breaking. "Tell me where you are coming from."

"Easy, my friend, we can help you."

Herlov's reply was more than Crosfield could stand. He jumped to his feet and grabbed Herlov by the throat. Shaking with fear and anger, Crosfield surprised the other man, who staggered backwards, only for Majec to bring his right fist into the small of Crosfield's back and force him to the floor.

Herlov recovered his balance and flung himself down on to Crosfield's limp form. He pressed his face close and spat as if in contempt.

"Pytr and his men will do what you've asked. They'll move when the money's in the account they've nominated. How you get it there is your problem. As to what I know and what I'm doing here, you're the clever lawyer, you figure it out."

Herlov jabbed the fingers of his left hand into Crosfield's neck.

"Time's running out for you, Mr Crosfield. I hope that you'll not be foolish enough to back off now, for all our sakes."

Within seconds, Herlov and Majec were gone. The bartender walked over to Crosfield and placed a second glass of vodka on the table.

"Drink it. Call me if you need me. I know these men."

The man dropped a name card and walked away.

* * * * * * * * * *

A village near Aix-en-Provence, South of France

Hugo Jackson was running scared. He had known the physical fear of heights in his early days in the mountains with his father. Like others, he had overcome it with time. He had similarly overcome the terror of his first parachute jump with his university officer cadet cadre.

But this was different. It was a cold, detached, unremitting fear that had not left him since the failed rendezvous at the Docklands pub only days before. He realized now, if he had not done so at the time, that what he had witnessed was no accident. He reread the cryptic report in the evening paper.

Fatal accident outside Docklands tavern

> *A middle-aged man was knocked down and killed by a passing car in a hit and run accident outside the Blue Anchor pub in Ferry Road, Docklands last evening. A police spokesman said that the victim who, as yet, has not been identified, was seen entering the building about five minutes beforehand. A customer, who spoke to our reporter on condition that his name was withheld, said that he saw the deceased sit down, as if waiting for someone. Several minutes later, according to the same witness, the man received a call on his mobile phone. He was then seen to rush to the main door. Another witness, who again spoke on condition of anonymity, said that an oncoming car seemed to swerve, before mounting the pavement. The man was pronounced dead at the scene by the ambulance crew. A briefcase, thought to have been carried by the deceased, has not been recovered.*

Jackson folded the paper and put it in his pocket. The late afternoon sun was still warm. He glanced at his watch and replaced his glasses.

Having waited for some five minutes on the riverside quay, Jackson had run towards the next station on the Docklands Light Railway. When he arrived, he found that there had been a breakdown. He was fortunate to find a passing mini cab, which dropped him beside Liverpool Street Station in the City of London. There he had deposited the briefcase in a left luggage locker, where it had remained until earlier in the day.

Having returned to his apartment, Jackson decided to continue as though nothing had happened. He spent the next day in the office.

It was in the evening, as he sat alone in a quiet bistro near his apartment, that he received the call. A female voice, speaking in French, told him that she could arrange a meeting with Hedizah Mansur. He needed only to confirm his agreement. She would call back with the details.

He had made an excuse to his manager at Layton and Springer. Could he take two days' leave, to attend to unexpected family business, arising from the administration of his late father's estate. He had lied and he disliked it, but he was not in control of his life.

Others were, seemingly, directing a plot in which he was fast becoming the principal protagonist, but the prospect of meeting Hedizah had almost forced the bizarre events of recent days into his subconscious.

A sense of unreality had taken hold of him at the thought of seeing the young woman with whom he knew that he had irrationally fallen in love.

But reality had returned. He had retrieved the briefcase and taken the morning Eurostar train to Paris and changed on to the TGV to Aix en Provence. Then, as he had been directed, he had driven a hire car to the place where they were to meet.

He left the briefcase unopened until he had parked the car in the yard at the rear of the hotel. The case was unlocked. Jackson removed and opened an unsealed brown envelope. Inside was an ordered set of papers, contained in a slender ringed file with coloured markers against what appeared to be certain key documents.

Jackson looked around him. There was one other vehicle parked in the yard, a blue two-door Renault commercial van. It appeared to be empty but it was difficult to be sure as it was partly hidden by the shade of a large bougainvillea bush. Jackson decided to press on with the documents.

The first section of the file contained copies of a complex series of drawings. The text on each was close-typed in what appeared to be Chinese-style characters. The drawings appeared to comprise a set of blueprints for construction of a specific piece of equipment or machinery.

Jackson turned the pages. As he did so, the true reality of what he was seeing began to become clearer. The succeeding sections of the file could more readily be discerned as certificates relating to the origin and composition of a range of components.

Then came the documents with the coloured markers. This time there was no mistaking the form and content of what he saw. Extracting these carefully from a plastic envelope, he found himself looking at a set of bills of lading on an English language printed form, containing typed insertions on their face.

These documents unambiguously stated that fifty sealed steel containers, packed with equipment and machinery parts, had been shipped aboard the motor vessel *Globex Mariner* at the North Korean port of Kyomipo, for carriage to the southern Red Sea.

Behind the bill of lading were matching sets of invoices, policies of insurance and bills of exchange. All were headed with the titles of different departments of the Ministry of Transport, Pyongyang.

Jackson gasped involuntarily as the total value of the cargo became apparent. One hundred million dollars, payable on delivery at the final designated inland delivery point.

He continued paging through the file. The next marked section contained a lengthy document typed in English and headed 'Confidential Loading Instructions'. It comprised a coloured set of symbols, designating the cargo as the highest category of dangerous and hazardous goods that the International Maritime Authority recognized.

Jackson put down the file on the seat beside him. His head and body felt numb with the realization of what he had read. Cold fear and incomprehension at his position, and how he had come to be where he was, began to grip him. He also knew that within minutes she would be arriving.

He made to replace the file in the briefcase and close it but, as he did so, he noticed another document folded into the sleeve of the case. He removed it carefully.

It was evident that this document comprised only the first page of a much longer dossier. The rest was missing. It bore the heading of the Enforcement Directorate of the International Atomic Energy Authority, Vienna. Its title stated unambiguously that it was a Confidential Investigation into the reported carriage of unauthorised nuclear and fissile material aboard the motor vessel *Globex Mariner* from North Korea to an unknown destination in the Middle East.

Pinned to the back of the page was a coloured photograph. Jackson recognized the background instantly. It was the terminal facility that he had seen on the DVD. In the foreground was a stretch of perimeter wire fencing, from which hung the torso of a figure wearing desert camouflage fatigues. It was slumped forward. The arms were bound back. There was a gaping wound across the back of the neck, from which the remains of the head remained grotesquely suspended.

Jackson had seen enough. He thrust the document and the photograph into the case, snapped it closed and pressed it under the driver's seat. Opening the car door he gasped for air. His stomach retched.

Glancing at his watch, Jackson could scarcely believe that he had been sitting in the car for fewer than ten minutes. The sun was beginning to settle over the low hills towards the coast, casting long shadows across the town square. His mind was unable to grasp the events of the last few days and the way in which he had come into possession of such extraordinary material.

Whatever its provenance, however, and assuming its authenticity, what Jackson had seen was evidence of events that implicated the senior partner of Layton and Springer and its most celebrated client in a global conspiracy of breathtaking proportions.

Not only that, but if, as the papers suggested, a disaster had overtaken the *Globex Mariner* there had, at the very least, been a deliberate and calculated deception perpetrated on an English Court of Law or, at worst, the complicity of one of the country's most senior judges.

He walked slowly towards the café where they were to meet. The clock on the Romanesque church tower, on the opposite side of the square, struck five o'clock. Its slow resonant sounds calling the villagers to mass seemed to Jackson, for a moment, to make the world stand still. It was an everyday sound that had been heard and welcomed for generations. It was also a stark and real contrast to the chaos that the last few days had inflicted on him.

The final peal of the bells died away. A group of women in grey shawls and men in dark coats hurried towards the entrance to the church. Then he saw her, walking slowly and calmly towards him from the church porch.

Hedizah Mansur was taller than he imagined. Her dark hair was swept back under a scarf, and she adjusted her sunglasses to meet the glint of the late afternoon sun. She had an easy relaxed gait, her slim figure reflected in a loose fitting jumper and jeans. Her arms swung slowly at her sides. For a young woman with such radiant good looks, she seemed wholly disinterested in the sidelong glances that she received as she stepped under the coloured awning of the café and approached the table where Jackson was sitting.

He stood up almost involuntarily and stretched out his hand. She took it. As she did so, he felt a warm strong grip that lasted longer than he had dared to hope.

Jackson moved round and nervously shifted a chair. She sat down and took off her sunglasses. He had never imagined gazing at a face of such exquisite beauty and charm. Soft dark brown eyes conveyed strength yet showed vulnerability. A fine sanguine skin and a gentle mouth revealed a shy but sensuous smile.

Hedizah removed her scarf and shook out her hair. Seconds passed and neither spoke. She looked into Jackson's eyes and slowly pushed her right hand across the table.

"Please, Hugo."

Jackson responded more slowly than he would have wanted. He took her hand and held it firmly, stroking her fingers as he did so.

"Hedizah, I'm sorry, but I hardly know what to say. I've never seen or met anyone like you before. We're here meeting as complete strangers and yet I feel that over the last few days I've almost come to know you."

Hedizah took his hand and looked down.

"Why should you? You have nothing to reproach yourself for. We're here because of things that we do not understand and people whom we do not know."

For a moment Hedizah relaxed, almost like a schoolgirl on her first date, when she finally gets to know the name of the boy who has been glancing at her every day on the way home.

Jackson smiled back. Despite everything that had happened, he was in the company of someone who he had first seen only a matter of weeks before, when any kind of meeting between them could hardly have been contemplated.

Hedizah moved closer. She thought back to the message that she had left him in London, at the instigation of a woman who had anonymously called her beforehand. The same woman had called again and spoken to Sophie. It was after the realization that it would be impossible for her to continue with Rahman that she decided she had to run the risk and see Hugo Jackson.

The caller had confirmed the arrangements, leaving another message with Sophie, when it was known that Mansur would be leaving, at short notice, for an unscheduled meeting, somewhere in the Middle East.

Hedizah had previously thought that the unassuming young Englishman might perhaps act as some kind of covert counsellor or guide. Now that she had met him, she knew at once that what she had found was someone who would not merely offer sympathy and support, but the love that she so desperately craved.

The two looked at each other almost shyly. Several other customers in the café eyed them, intrigued. The proprietor decided to leave them alone.

Now she was there, beside him, Jackson was almost conscious of his mind seeking to discard, almost to erase, the memory of everything that he had seen and read. He had no idea how he was going to proceed or how he was going to act, but somehow none of that mattered.

The warmth of her presence, the stark beauty of the young woman beside him, who had come into his life in the most extraordinary way, was all that he could absorb, or wanted to.

Whatever the risks that they might both have to run, fate somehow had brought them together for this moment. Nothing had prepared Jackson for the sudden depth of passion that he was beginning to feel for Hedizah.

He also had no means of knowing how she regarded him, after a rendezvous which had somehow been planned by another and which neither could have anticipated.

Jackson felt embarrassed, uncertain how to proceed, but the only thing that he knew for certain, in the maelstrom into which he had involuntarily been propelled, was that he wanted desperately to make love to Hedizah.

Whatever the risks to them both, he wanted to seize the moment, almost as though making love might be nothing more than a passing passion, prior to a permanent adieu.

He felt transparent, gauche perhaps, chivalrous in a peculiar kind of way. Nothing was making sense.

Hedizah stood up. She took his arm and put her head on his shoulder.

"Let's go inside, Hugo."

The two made their way into the hallway of the adjoining hotel and the staircase that lay beyond. They looked at each other shyly. Hugo squeezed her hand and they walked slowly up.

Neither could have seen the man in the Renault van slowly wind down the driver's side window, take several rapid images on his mobile phone and then turn down a side street beside the hotel.

Within seconds, the images had been sent to the email address that he had been given, and he had accessed his own online bank account. The payment was there. His job was done.

* * * * * * * * *

Golan Heights, Israeli-Syrian border

Rahman Mansur glanced across at Herlov as, once again, the Humvee lurched precariously towards the precipice below them.

"Nothing to worry about, gentlemen, I assure you. The roads up here are all shot to pieces at this time of year."

The driver turned and gave his two passengers a less than confident grin.

"The trouble is, we have to keep our lights down. They know we're coming but you never can tell. It's badlands here. There are too many trigger-happy punters, on both sides."

Mansur said nothing. The casual drawl of the young South African did nothing to conceal his anxiety. Their destination, a tiny deserted village along an inhospitable section of the Golan Heights, lay some two kilometres distant. Their rendezvous was to be a concrete blockhouse, unmarked on the maps of either the Israeli or the Syrian border troops, manning the sector. The commander of the nearest United Nations peacekeeping force, a company of Ukrainian conscripts, had been only too happy to surrender the ground, against a vague undertaking that his troops would not be shelled.

The vehicle struggled upwards. It was still an hour before dawn. Mansur looked out. It was grey, cold and beginning to snow. He tried to settle back in his seat but it was worn down. Whichever way he turned, his back chafed against the straps of his flak jacket or the metal rims of the frame.

Herlov looked determinedly and impassively out of the opposite window. If he was feeling the same degree of discomfort and anxiety as Mansur, he didn't show it. The climb was steeper now. There was the distant crump of mortar fire.

"Routine. It happens every day. I got used to it when I was stationed up along the Angolan border."

The South African's breezy tone was beginning to wear thin.

"Not far now. Behind the next ridge and we'll be there. You'll be in time for breakfast, or whatever."

There was no response.

Mansur regretted the need for the meeting but it was inevitable. The *Globex Mariner* disaster had seen to that. They had been patient, more so than he had had any reason to expect, but the call had come, as he knew it would.

The loss of the vessel and her crew had been an inconvenience, but the loss of her cargo was devastating.

Herlov had done well to find Pytr Majec at short notice. They had managed to disrupt the local investigation sufficiently enough to defend the law case in London and deflect the inevitable press enquiry. But, as Herlov had consistently reminded him, in reality all that Mansur had achieved was a stay of execution, whilst a replacement cargo could be found and more secure shipment arrangements made.

"Almost there."

The vehicle slowed in the hazy gloom as it approached a set of steel shuttered gates between sandbagged emplacements.

Not for the first time, Mansur had wondered at Herlov's seeming reluctance to proceed.

He could not fault his ruthlessly efficient skills as a quartermaster, honed in numerous dirty conflicts, of which Mansur was only too aware. But there had been a change. Herlov had become distant. He had shown no lack of respect, Herlov was too shrewd for that, but Mansur could not rid himself of the instinct that his long-serving aide might have another agenda.

He had accepted Herlov's word that a meeting with Majec in Leipzig had been necessary to ensure that there were no loose ends, before the next vessel sailed from Piraeus. But his sources had hinted that there might have been another man at the meeting. They could not be sure.

Mansur's mind then quickly flashed back to the scene with Hedizah. When he saw her for the first time, he wanted her. He saw that her beauty would be an enduring asset, when the time came for him to return. Until then, he needed her to live wholly on his terms.

Hedizah had had no choice but to come with him. He had seen to that. But something was different now.

With both there was cause for concern. Was it Herlov whose loyalty needed to be tested, or was it Hedizah who, somehow unbeknown to him, was looking for an affinity elsewhere?

Mansur continued to stare out of the window as they drove slowly through the security gates. The Humvee ground to a halt. It was getting light. Several arc-lights cast a shadowy beam through the mist to reveal a grim concrete bunker ahead of them.

"Journey's end, the ride's over. Good luck."

The driver jumped down and held open the doors for Mansur and Herlov to step down from the vehicle. It was damp, cold and gloomy. Snow from the previous night's storm lay untidily on both sides of the rough path that led to the windowless concrete structure ahead of them.

"Come inside quickly."

An orderly, wearing the drab fatigues of an Israeli infantry regiment, ushered the two men inside. His instructions followed swiftly. "Leave your jackets and weapons here."

Mansur and Herlov removed their protective gear. Herlov placed a Glock automatic on an upturned metal ammunition box. They were shown into a low-ceilinged room with minimal lighting, a steel table and several rusted folding chairs.

The orderly saluted and closed the door, taking up his post immediately outside, an Uzi machine pistol cradled against his right shoulder.

There were two other men in the room. The oldest was wearing a rough fleece jacket, baggy camouflage trousers and American high combat boots. He approached the two visitors.

"Good to see you both again. Sorry about the venue and the early start."

He stretched out his hand to Mansur and Herlov in turn. Colonel Lev Barshok's handshake befitted that of a veteran Israeli paratroop commander who, over the two previous decades, had lived and fought over the very ground on which they were now standing.

The other man emerged from the shadows behind the table.

"I've no doubt that you remember Major Assad Rawazi of the Syrian internal security service."

Mansur had every reason to remember the man who now approached him. He wore an olive green uniform, with burnished brass buckles on his webbing belt and well-shined black boots. They had met, in a similarly dark room, behind an old coffee shop in central Damascus some nine months before. It was then that Mansur had first explained what he intended to do, and sought the reaction of those who might be inclined to give him the covert support that he needed.

Rawazi had struck a hard deal as the price of passive Syrian cooperation. He had made it plain that his terms were non-negotiable. One such term was that others, who might be adversaries, needed to be involved.

In the arcane and murky world of Middle Eastern counter terrorism and espionage, such meant that Rawazi's counterpart in Israel would also need to give his approval. The balancing interests of sworn enemies, and the wheels of communication, demanded the sharing of critical intelligence, even when the public face of conflict was only too evident.

A second meeting had been arranged, less than a fortnight later, in an outer suburb of Beirut when Mansur and Herlov had met Barshok for the first time. Within a matter of hours, they had agreed Mansur's proposal. Each had made it plain that their approval had a price. Mansur would not only share the technology secrets with both, but the privilege of so doing came at a cost of fifty million dollars to be shared equally by the states of Israel and Syria.

Mansur had come too far to be in a position to decline. Herlov would facilitate the speedy provision and transfer of the funds. They would utilise a series of offshore financial instruments that the western world's banks were only too prepared to underwrite in exchange for significant fees. The banks in turn would ensure that those fees would be adequately shielded from their financial regulators.

The *Globex Mariner* had sailed with her cargo. When the loss of the vessel became public, Mansur's Levantine sponsors had gone to ground. Somehow, Herlov had managed to procure a term in the banking arrangements whereby the payments to Barshok and Rawazi would only be released on right and true delivery of the *Globex Mariner* cargo. That had not occurred and no payment had been made.

Mansur knew only too well that neither man would countenance the same arrangements again. This time Mansur would be paying, up front and in full, before the first crates of cargo were loaded on the *Aegean Dolphin*.

"Let's all sit down."

The Israeli officer's tone was affable yet unmistakably firm. "Coffee?"

The others nodded. Barshok poured a thick sweet brew from a heated field flask. He looked at Rawazi. "Shall I begin?"

The Syrian smiled. "Diplomacy after the bullet, Sion's way as ever. Go ahead, Colonel. We both know what's on offer."

Barshok pulled up a chair and looked at Mansur.

"So, with the diplomatic niceties out of the way, tell us your proposals, Mr Mansur. Tell us, again, how you intend to force an unwilling world to grant independence to the Kurdish region. Tell us how you intend to succeed, when our friends in Ankara and Washington would cut your throat if they knew what was intended. And of course, please reassure us that this time we will be paid, as we thought we had agreed."

Barshok and Rawazi looked at Herlov with a combination of disdain and menace.

"We gave you the benefit of the doubt, Mr Herlov. We assume that there is no misunderstanding. When the vessel sails we shall expect payment. Do I need to make myself clearer?"

"We understand, Colonel. The circumstances were different last time, as you well know."

Mansur spoke quietly as if trying somehow to deflect the accusation away from Herlov, when they both knew that it was he, Mansur, who had prevailed on his bankers not to make the payment.

Barshok looked at the man seated opposite him. The payment, as they both knew, was an irrelevance. It amounted to little more than a balancing of the books between adversaries. More was at stake.

He respected Mansur for what he was trying to achieve. He understood Mansur's ambition to create an independent homeland for an ethnic group that wanted a territory that it could call its own, and boundaries that protected its language, culture and religion.

The Kurds needed a change from centuries-old conflicts that had seen their people persecuted, their homes destroyed and their land despoiled.

After all, was Mansur's aspiration for a Kurdish homeland any different to what his own country had striven to achieve – what had driven him and thousands like him through the heat of battle and the scourge of daily terror?

Barshok believed in the ideal of the Jewish state. He also believed that the Palestinians, too, deserved their freedom and independence, but not over the torn bodies and broken souls that their brutal violence had created. There had been too many families bereft, too many friends lost. There was no easy answer. There never had been.

Rawazi must have mirrored Barshok's own thoughts.

"Syria has always been friends with our brothers in Iraq. We have no issue with the aims that you have. But, if you succeed, you will need recognition and diplomatic support in the region, whatever the Americans and the Russians may agree above your heads."

He paused for a second before continuing. "We should not forget, of course, our Turkish brothers. They, at the end of the day, will be only too anxious to live with a new regime, if the world will quietly forget their own inconvenient history with the Armenians."

Mansur had heard the demand before. He knew what it meant. Syria would want access to Kurdish oil wealth, with its attendant local security of supply. There would be more rhetoric in the same vein, a collective entitlement to ever-diminishing energy resources in the region; not only gas and oil but water also.

Mansur spoke slowly. "I understand what you say, Major. You have made your position clear. But these are issues for the future. You will have to trust me."

Rawazi replied quietly. "Mr Mansur, we are prepared to back your plan. It's up to you to make it work. If it does, we all benefit. If it does not, we'll survive, as we do at present. However, for you my friend, if you fail, there'll be few places to turn to."

The body language of the old colonel suggested that his patience was wearing thin.

"Gentlemen, enough ideology if I may say so, with no disrespect. Major Rawazi is right. Mr Mansur, you need to assure us that what went wrong with the *Globex Mariner* will not see history repeat itself."

Herlov glanced at Mansur, as if seeking approval to respond. There was a moment's silence. The Israeli and the Syrian looked at each other with resignation, world-weary contestants in an undeclared continuous conflict, which each knew neither could win.

Mansur nodded. Herlov spoke deliberately. "Of course, it will be different this time. We too have a strategy."

"I hope you do, Mr Herlov, for all our sakes."

Mansur looked coldly at the Israeli soldier. Herlov continued. "We've sourced the material from Tehran."

There was an awkward moment's silence.

Herlov spoke almost in apology. "It's close, but it was all we could do."

"Go on."

Mansur nodded to Herlov again, bidding him to continue.

"The consignment will be loaded at a secure airfield, a hundred kilometres north of Tehran, once the order to sail the *Aegean Dolphin* from Piraeus is given. We've arranged for loading, in one lot, on to a chartered heavy-lift aircraft, that flew in from Taipei several days ago. The casings and transit crates were manufactured in southern China and concealed in containers shipped to Kaohsiung. They were then trucked at night to the airport."

Mansur was looking down at the rough table. The other two men said nothing. Herlov continued in a measured tone.

"The aircraft will then fly with the equipment to a military airbase close to the port of Tripoli."

The Syrian shifted his position. His expression was unchanged. "Sorry. Please continue."

Herlov cleared his throat. He was beginning to get a bad feeling about the meeting. Mansur continued to avoid his eye.

"The *Aegean Dolphin* will load the equipment, transit the Suez Canal, pass down the Red Sea and wait for further orders off the coast of Yemen."

Herlov stopped abruptly.

"And then?" Barshok sensed Herlov's slight hesitation.

"We are still negotiating the discharge and on-carriage with our friends in Basra and Karachi. We hope that we can go for Basra and run a road convoy up to the north. With no foreign troops wanting to fight there are people who can secure the route to Mosul."

"Is that all?"

Before Herlov could respond, Mansur looked up. His reply was crisp. "Trust us, gentlemen. Remember, we all need to make this work. This time we won't fail."

"And we're sure that you won't."

Barshok stood up and stretched out his hand to Mansur and Herlov in turn.

"Will you signal the vessel from here?"

Herlov nodded.

Barshok called in the orderly from outside. Instructions were swiftly given to send an encrypted radio message to the master of the *Aegean Dolphin*. His orders were to sail from Piraeus within twenty-four hours, and to proceed to Tripoli, Libya, to load the cargo that had previously been nominated. The master was instructed to acknowledge the message and to confirm his intended departure time within six hours.

Barshok looked dispassionately at Mansur and Herlov. He spoke slowly, as if sensing that what they were attempting would need luck of the highest order to succeed.

"Thank you, gentlemen. I assume that we may expect your payment and your further news?"

"You will." Mansur's reply was confident.

Barshok ushered Mansur and Herlov out of the bunker. The meeting had lasted less than an hour. A watery sun was rising over the distant Mediterranean coast to the east. It was still bitterly cold as the two men pulled on their jackets and climbed back into the Humvee.

The South African driver appeared from nowhere. As they started the descent, Herlov fingered his mobile phone and checked his watch. He had one hour to send the agreed text message to the master of the *Aegean Dolphin*. It was a message that only he and the master knew would be sent. It would say that instead of proceeding directly to Tripoli, the vessel was to slow steam fifty miles off the south coast of Malta and await Herlov's further orders.

* * * * * * * * * *

Djibouti, Gulf of Aden

The warm mid-afternoon breeze gently ruffled the flags that bedecked the roof of the old French administration building, in the centre of the city. The newly painted white brickwork and green shutters of the Hotel de Ville stood out, in contrast to the drab exteriors of nearby shops and offices.

Bertrand turned his head at the low growl of the helicopters that were to precede the military parade. White uniformed gendarmes stood to attention, as a military brass band played the national anthem of the independent state of Djibouti and, out of deference to their continuing defenders, a rousing version of the Marseillaise.

The crowd strained to catch sight of the squadron of armoured vehicles processing slowly up the palm-fringed avenue from the port. Bertrand looked above his head. Scarcely concealed sharpshooters had taken up positions on the flat roofs of the apartments and warehouses that bordered the route.

Sporadic clapping began as a contingent of local camel-borne infantry, richly garbed in green and white cloaks, trotted by. A company of French foreign legion paratroopers followed, distinctive in their red berets and desert fatigues, marching to the sinister sounds of their slow death march.

Bertrand felt an involuntary twinge of nostalgia, as his old unit passed by. It was quickly dispelled by his memory of a decade or more of dirty wars in the dark wastes of Africa.

An array of ageing military vehicles followed. The crowd started to become restive. The band paused, for an instant, as a display of fireworks lit up the sky. Spontaneous, if sporadic, applause broke out as two ornately dressed trumpeters played a short fanfare.

The President of the Republic stepped up on to a raised dais in front of the old town hall. Political and diplomatic platitudes followed, which did little to raise the enthusiasm of the crowd. People began gradually to drift away.

Bertrand wondered if the citizens of Djibouti were aware of the threat to their fragile freedom. As a tiny state at the head of the Gulf of Aden in the Red Sea, with porous frontiers bordering on the lawless lands of Eritrea, Ethiopia and Somalia, little could be guaranteed. Whether the continued presence of the French military would be sufficient to deflect the encircling scourge of extremism remained to be seen.

The President's short adulatory address was over. Bertrand had seen it before. It was the same story, a leader elected by a dubious franchise, and maintaining power by a series of uneasy alliances. This was no different.

The formalities concluded, the President turned away from the crowd to confer with several government members, before making the short walk back into the old town hall, accompanied by a phalanx of bodyguards.

Bertrand was interested in the only man on the dais not attired in some kind of distinctive uniform. The man Bertrand was seeking was about sixty, grey haired and with a pallid complexion. He wore a faded white tropical suit and a western Panama hat, with a silk band, that seemed strangely at odds with the resplendent headgear of the others on parade.

The man shook hands with the President, made his way down from the dais and across the square towards the old administrative quarter of the city. Bertrand followed, at a distance, making his way through a series of Moorish cloisters and narrow alleys. Some five minutes later he emerged into the bright sunshine and entered a small square with an alabaster fountain ringed with palms. Bertrand watched as the man glanced over his shoulder and stopped at the door of a two-storey building in the far corner.

The windows on the first floor were all shuttered, and there were several heavy iron grilles at ground floor level. Above the outside entrance porch, the faded tricolour and insignia of the former French-run customs service could still be seen.

The door was opened quietly and the man entered. Bertrand looked at his watch. He waited five minutes and placed his newspaper under his left arm. As he did so, another man on the opposite side of the square nodded unobtrusively and walked back into the shadows of a nearby souk.

Bertrand had found the right address. He rang the bell and glanced at the unpolished brass plate beside the door. Several minutes elapsed before a young boy in his late teens released the inner bolts and peered out.

"Maître Douchert is not in the office today. It's Independence Day, a holiday."

Bertrand smiled. "You must be Masoud."

The boy frowned.

"Runah's half-brother?"

A nervous smile crossed the boy's face, but he did not release his grip on the door.

"I'd like to see Maître Douchert."

The boy said nothing.

"Now, my friend, please, I know he's here."

The boy seemed unable to move. Bertrand gently pushed the door inwards.

"Don't worry. It's all right. I saw Runah in Dubai only a few days ago. She's fine. She misses you."

The boy lowered his head. Bertrand pretended not to notice the tears that filled the boy's eyes. Bertrand entered an ante-chamber with a high ceiling. A fan played slowly above his head, an array of carpets covered the floor and several wicker framed chairs, with faded cushions, made up the reception area.

The boy stood uncertainly in front of an office door. Bertrand nodded and the boy knocked. There was an audible scraping of a chair, before the door was pulled open.

"I told you, Masoud, not to let anyone into the building."

The boy stood aside, as the man saw Bertrand.

"Who are you? I told the boy I'm not seeing anyone today, client or no client."

Bertrand said nothing.

"Please leave now before I call the gendarme."

Bertrand walked past Douchert into the office. He spoke slowly. "We need to talk. It's Emil Douchert, isn't it? You won't remember me but we met once in a past life many years ago. My name is Jean-Yves Bertrand."

"I don't remember you. Please leave."

Bertrand ignored him and sat down beside the desk. Douchert walked to the other side. As he passed, Bertrand could not fail to notice the brandy on his breath.

"Mâitre Douchert, please sit down. I need you to help me."

The other man remained standing. "I have a law practice to run and I'm not taking appointments today."

"I know what kind of practice you run. The same as you did in Chad. Do I need to say more?"

Douchert's face drained of colour as he pulled his chair up behind him. Bertrand stood up and closed the door. He turned to face Douchert and looked around. The desk in front of him was in disarray. Files were strewn untidily on the floor and the computer screen was streaked and dusty. Outside, an air conditioning unit whirred intermittently. Several unwashed glasses stood on a side table, propped against the wall, beneath a battered and grimy plastic window blind.

"It's not much, Monsieur, is it? But it's all I have. I live and work in this place. There's nowhere else to go."

Bertrand felt no animosity to the sad, somewhat broken, figure who sat in front of him. He almost felt genuine sympathy. He had seen it time and again, men alone as they grew old, separated from home, by time and events.

For an instant, Bertrand saw himself as he might have been. For him the Legion had become his home. For years it was his security. For Douchert, the path had been different but perhaps, not as different as he imagined.

The older man spoke slowly. "As you're clearly not going to leave, may I offer you a cognac? Or there's coffee if you ask the boy."

"No thanks."

Douchert cleared his throat, but his voice still sounded hoarse. "How do you know me? I should warn you to be careful."

Bertrand leant over the desk and looked at the grey face of the man on the opposite side.

"Never mind that now. Please listen to what I have to say and what I want from you."

Douchert stood up and took off his jacket. He hung it roughly on the back of his chair and pulled a bottle of cognac from one of the drawers in the desk. Perspiration started to run down his neck and chest. His right hand shook as he poured a long measure into a well-fingered glass.

Pushing his chair back noisily, Douchert started to pace the room restlessly, as Bertrand outlined his requirements. He listened, still pacing the room. When Bertrand had finished he bent over him.

"It's impossible. No one would sanction this."

Bertrand said nothing. Douchert reached for the bottle again. He looked at Bertrand. His voice was cracked, yet somehow defiant.

"As soon as you leave, all I have to do is call the Head of National Security and you'll be kicked out. Believe me, I have power and influence here."

Bertrand stood up and held Douchert by the collar of his open shirt.

"Listen. You have no choice but to do what we ask. If you don't agree, your paymasters will find out all about your track record here."

Douchert retched uncontrollably.

"Enough. OK."

Bertrand started to release his grip. He had no wish to hurt Douchert, but without his cooperation, he and Simpson would not be able to cross the border into Somalia within the time frame that he had been given.

"Please sit down, Mâitre Douchert, and tell me what I need to know, and where I can find these people."

Douchert's eyes began to glaze over. Bertrand pulled Douchert towards him.

"Tell me now. Please."

The lawyer spoke quickly, almost deferentially. "The boy, Masoud, will take you there."

Bertrand turned away. He reached into his jacket and brought out a sealed envelope.

"Take it as a down payment. I'll call you, when I'm back."

Bertrand opened the door. The boy was standing, pale faced, outside.

"Mâitre Douchert will be OK, Masoud. But I need your help, for Runah's sake as well as mine."

Ten minutes later, Masoud was leading Bertrand down a further maze of alleyways, in one of several souks, surrounding the old port trading office. The boy looked back, stopped, nodded to Bertrand and pushed open a narrow door, into what appeared to be a tiny coffee house.

Bertrand drew a deep breath. For an instant, he felt the pang of a soldier's nerves before an operation. This was the moment of truth. He knew it. The whole project depended on the right result from this meeting. He wondered again why he had taken the job and why he had been asked. He needed employment, that much was certain, but as to his motive, he was now not so sure.

Masoud whispered urgently. "Quick, mister! Quick, come in."

Bertrand had rehearsed in his mind what he needed to say. He thought back to the meeting in Kuala Lumpur and the information that he had subsequently gleaned.

As he now knew, the threat that he had made to expose Douchert to his friends in government had next to nothing to do with his professional indiscretions.

It had, however, everything to do with the fact that Douchert had established himself as the conduit through which ransom sums, amounting to millions of dollars, had been paid to free vessels seized by so-called pirates off the Somalian coast for the last twelve months or more.

Only Douchert knew that the amount of commission that he retained was far in excess of what he had agreed to pay to his protectors in government, as the price of their consent. The kidnap and ransom industry had, it seemed, become a snake with several heads.

It was into this shady world of death, threat and deception that Bertrand now entered.

A tall man with a ragged beard and grubby flowing robes entered the room. He told Masoud to leave and nodded to Bertrand, motioning him to sit down.

"Coffee or juice?"

"Neither, thank you."

The man smiled at Bertrand and spoke quickly. "So is your business money changing? Or, as Masoud has brought you to me, perhaps it is something else?"

Bertrand replied in a matter of fact, soldier's tone. "They tell me that you work with Emil Douchert, that you have friends, contacts in Somalia, who know the coast and can be relied upon to act on and obey your direct orders."

The other man leaned forward, still smiling broadly. "Is that what they say?"

The Frenchman replied firmly. "Some people I know, people that I trust, have told me so."

The older man sat back on his chair. "Monsieur Bertrand. I recognize you for what you are. You know the rules. You know the boundaries. You know the risks. Otherwise you wouldn't be here."

The atmosphere eased. Bertrand reached into his jacket pocket and placed a packet on the table.

"A down payment for what we would like you to do."

The other man's erstwhile benign expression hardened for a moment. "Wait here."

He left the room through a curtained door. Bertrand was left alone.

A few minutes later he returned, with another younger man, who approached Bertrand and stood over him. His tone was condescending.

"You know that some of the dollar bills are counterfeit?"

Bertrand shrugged his shoulders and replied blandly, "They were collected from the state bank just now. Emil Douchert fixed a special appointment before the bank opened. It was the least that he could do for me."

The two men slapped Bertrand on the shoulders and burst into raucous laughter.

"They know it, we know it. It happens every time. Somebody in the bank does the switch. Nobody cares, because we make sure that nobody knows."

Bertrand grinned. "It's your little secret, I suppose."

"Yes, Monsieur Bertrand, but one which I assume you will keep."

"Of course, if you insist."

The men opposite him noticeably relaxed. "Let's talk. Tell us what you need."

After a quarter of an hour, the three men stood up and shook hands. The older man with the beard concluded the meeting.

"Two weeks, you say. We'll be ready. You can trust us."

"I hope you're right."

Bertrand smiled at Masoud, who had waited in the alley outside.

"It's over for now. Tell Maître Douchert that he'll hear from me shortly." He handed Masoud several banknotes.

"Take care. Perhaps you'll see Runah again soon. Let's hope so."

Bertrand made his way slowly back through the crowded streets towards the Hotel de l'Orient, an establishment that had seen its heyday when passengers from the great liners of the past stopped off in Djibouti to experience an alien world of bazaars and intrigue.

He glanced at his watch. He was in time. He and Ronnie Simpson were to meet at five.

Bertrand entered the faded hallway, collected his room key and strode briskly up the short winding staircase.

The room door was open. There was blood on the wall by the washstand and there was no sign of Simpson.

Chapter Five

Chilton, Cotswolds, England

JACKSON LOOKED OUT OF THE WINDOW. The late summer sunset cast a touch of gold over the mellow stone houses of the village of Chilton, standing at the foot of the Cotswold Hills. The shadows lengthened beneath the tall spire of the church opposite. The village green, sloping down to the river, was almost deserted, except for a party of children returning home from the last bus of the day.

The lane was quiet. He would have seen the arrival of any afternoon visitors to the guest house that he had checked into earlier in the day. He had left London after completing a morning's research at the national archives. It scarcely seemed feasible that he was still attempting to work an apparently normal day, after the dangerous helter-skelter that his life had become.

Jackson had no idea how, or why, someone had taken such extraordinary trouble to put into his possession knowledge and evidence that made him privy to a conspiracy of worldwide significance. But what he did know was that his life would never be the same again and, whatever else might befall him, he wanted Hedizah to be at his side. He could not rid his mind of the image of her beauty and the passion that they had shared.

Jackson was also beginning to realize that the hand of Rahman Mansur was inextricably linked to issues of judicial cover-up, the perversion of the course of justice and perjury. Furthermore, the trail of enquiry was pointing more and more closely to the higher echelons of the law firm that employed him.

He did not know who was behind what had been leaked to him so deliberately. He wondered whether Michael Crosfield himself had been involved, but, if so, why and for what end? Was there perhaps some other source inside, or outside, Layton and Springer, that was using him as a means to expose the firm's senior partner and its most prestigious client?

He had also asked himself another question. Overcome as he was with his love for her, how could he know for sure whether Hedizah was a willing or reluctant player in the cast of characters that were surrounding him.

What he needed was to get away, to try to think and to rationalize, if that were possible.

He hated to think of it, but had Hedizah encouraged him to make love to her, as her husband's proxy, for no reason other than to find out how much he knew? Or, was it the act of a young, lonely and frightened girl, who had seen in him an ability to love and to care?

Whatever the reason, Jackson had experienced a sensation that he could not and would not discard. The sensuous nature of their lovemaking, cloaked with all the dangers that it entailed, was almost as nothing to the realization that he needed to be with Hedizah for the rest of his life.

They had left the village in France separately, each with their own thoughts of intimacy and destiny. There was no definable path forward, no means that either could see that would or could take them into the future together. Somehow, for reasons that neither understood, that prospect did not seem so foolish.

There was also another reason for him to leave London, and for which he needed a different environment.

How was it that the *Newsweek* television programme had been able to persuade Mansur to take part in a public interview? Why, at this of all times, had Mansur consented to allow outside access to his reclusive empire? Why was he willing, at least according to one critic's advance review, to permit the viewer a rare insight into his life?

Jackson pulled the curtains across the tiny cottage window of the guest house and clicked the remote.

The camera made a wide sweep of distant hills and a village with low dwellings set amidst date palms and a winding stream. Then, as quickly, the camera reverted to the studio desk.

"We are fortunate today to be able to bring to you an interview with the secretive entrepreneur, Rahman Mansur. He is a man whose enterprises are known worldwide but who has cloaked his success and enterprise in a web of anonymity. He has agreed to speak to our freelance reporter, Ann Sutherland, at an undisclosed location in northern Iraq."

Jackson drew a sharp breath. He had never met Ann Sutherland but he recalled her knowing questions at the High Court press conference. He also knew that she had worked, with his father, on investigative articles for the *World Economic Monitor*.

Strangely, Jackson was not surprised at, what seemed, yet another coincidence in the events that were unfolding around him. He wondered, not for the first time, whether his best course was to continue to lie low. In the absence of any better option, he had little choice.

An attractive young woman, with headscarf and long dress, introduced Mansur in a soft, understated Australian accent.

Rahman Mansur was, without doubt, an impressive looking man. He was tall and broad-shouldered, with a strong rugged face, moustache and a thick shock of wavy grey hair. He had the air of a desert warrior but, behind his dark eyes, a ruthless cunning and abrasive confidence was plain to see.

Mansur sat opposite his interviewer across a low table draped with a finely woven cloth. Two traditional Arabic coffee cups and an ornately tooled bronze flask stood at one end. The backdrop was a sparsely decorated room lit with low oil lamps. An open window allowed the morning sunshine to reflect against the room's white walls.

The interview began.

"Mr Mansur. This is the first time, so far as we are aware, that you have agreed to an interview with the western media. Most people will ask why, and why now?"

Mansur answered quickly and urbanely. "We all know that the world is changing. It is changing faster than at any time in the past. New technology has opened frontiers that only a decade ago would have been thought of as fanciful. My organization, the Globex group of companies, is playing its part in these changes. Much has been achieved. We considered that we should recognize this by enabling a wider public to learn something of what we do."

Jackson felt himself impressed by the fluent and all too plausible introduction. He knew, from others, of Mansur's formidable intellect. It had taken him from an undisclosed and obscure background to academic success at the University of Harvard and later, at the Massachusetts Institute of Technology.

"What challenges, Mr Mansur, are facing you in the light of the changes that you refer to?"

"There's no secret in this, Miss Sutherland. Climate change is an acknowledged fact. A decade from now every major producing country will face critical shortages of raw materials, energy sources and water."

The interview continued at the same pace.

"But how does your response differ from others? After all, governments the world over are themselves struggling to face and resolve this very crisis."

Mansur showed no hesitation in his reply. "They are, as you say, struggling. International accord comes at a price. A series of compromises can be grandly proclaimed, at an international conference, but may be shown to be virtually meaningless when the delegates return to the real world at home."

"How then, Mr Mansur, do you and the Globex empire consider that you can succeed when in your view governments worldwide are condemned to failure?"

Mansur's confident tone continued. "By the creation of a multi-national network of technological expertise, that can offer global industry a secure longer term resource for their energy needs in the Twenty-first Century."

For the first time, the interviewer showed a sense of irritation.

"Do you really believe, Mr Mansur, that one organization can provide that resource? Is it achievable or even realistic?"

"Please don't underestimate me, Miss Sutherland. Believe me. It needs an organization such as mine to take a long-term view of our resources, minerals, oil and gas, water and the means to transport them. Unless these critical issues are focused in responsible hands, I fear for the future, I really do."

The interviewer decided that a change of course was needed.

"We will just have to wait and see Mr Mansur, as I am sure you will agree."

There was a short pause before the next question.

"May I ask you about other aspects of your life?"

Mansur nodded.

"We know little of your early days, before you went to the United States to study and before your first venture. That, I believe, was the purchase of the bankrupt Transoil Corporation in Chicago and its transformation into a leading gas supplier under the Globex banner?"

"It was."

"Are you prepared to tell us more about your childhood and early days?"

Mansur smiled. "There is little to say, other than that I was born and raised, in poverty, in a village not far from here. I have tried to recognize, at every turn, the need to remember what others suffered and still do."

"How do you achieve that, Mr Mansur?"

"I do so primarily through the charitable foundations that we have established across the world. As you are aware, they aim to cover humanitarian needs, and the preservation of ethnic, cultural and artistic diversity in the countries where we work."

There was a further pause. The interviewer glanced down. The camera closed on Mansur. The viewer sensed that there was to be a further change of direction.

Jackson's mouth felt dry. His hands and neck were cold with perspiration.

"It has been suggested, Mr Mansur, that your recent marriage to Hedizah, your second wife, was a determined gesture on your part to deflect growing concern about your business methods and political aspirations."

A fleeting but lasting image of Hedizah appeared on the screen. She was dressed in an elegant red and green silk sari, bedecked with dramatic jewellery of the finest pedigree. It was her wedding day in Paris. Jackson noticed everything and nothing, except her dark, sensitive, faraway eyes.

Mansur replied equably. "I married Hedizah twelve months ago. I met her during a business visit to the Punjab where I was establishing a new business unit. She was young and beautiful. I had been alone for too long, after the death of my first wife in childbirth."

Mansur looked hard at his interviewer. "That was many years ago and that is all I have to say."

There was a further, more awkward, pause. Jackson pushed himself upright.

"Do you have any further questions, Miss Sutherland?"

"I do, Mr Mansur, if you are prepared to answer them."

"Please continue."

Ann Sutherland checked her notes again.

"It has been suggested that, to override local opposition, often from the very people whom your foundation seeks to protect, you have used strong arm methods and employed individuals of dubious background."

The screen switched to show a man, in Serbian paramilitary uniform, with a group of heavily armed men abusing a young woman and her children. The face of Pytr Majec was unmistakable.

"Mr Mansur, these people were Albanian refugees. The film was shot in Kosovo. May I ask if you recognize this man?"

The denial was quickly forthcoming. "I have never seen him before in my life."

The screen switched, as quickly again, to the bomb-blasted skeletal remains of what had once been the proud central square of a fine historic city. A man was pictured, crouching on his knees, arms tied behind his back and his head bowed. Seconds later his brain exploded as a pistol round was fired from point blank range, by a smiling executioner.

"This is Grozny, the capital of Chechnya, ten years ago."

Mansur looked at the face of Max Herlov on the screen and said nothing. This time the tone of the question was harsh and direct.

"I assume that you deny all knowledge of this man also?"

"I do. That is correct."

Mansur was going to give no ground. He could sense where the next question was coming from.

"May we turn to one other event with which your organization has been associated, the loss of the *Globex Mariner* with her cargo and crew in the Red Sea? There have been rumours that, somehow, this vessel was linked with your known political sympathy for a free state of Kurdistan. It has been suggested that there may have been weapons and explosives on board destined for freedom fighters in northern Iraq. Would you be willing to comment on this?"

Mansur's face hardened. His eyes looked bleakly at the young woman sitting on the opposite side of the table.

"Miss Sutherland. I have been patient with you. This question is based on rumour, innuendo and a strange lack of understanding for one representing such a respected publication."

Mansur's tone was reproving but unemotional. He continued with the skill and confidence of an advocate, closing his final speech and sensing that the verdict of the jury had swung in his client's favour.

"As your own journal reported, this unhappy and tragic matter was recently the subject of a judgment in the respected courts of the United Kingdom. Any wrongdoing on the part of Globex was strenuously denied. The judge agreed with our case. That is the end of the matter."

Ann Sutherland forced a smile, as if she sensed that the answers which he had given were sufficient to prove the contrary.

"A final question, if I may, Mr Mansur."

Mansur's expression was unsmiling. If he was hoping to end the interview, his face did not show it.

"Please."

The eyes of the two met before Ann Sutherland spoke again.

"If the opportunity arose to arm and equip the region of Kurdistan with advanced weaponry to support its claim for independence, what would be your position?"

For the first time, Mansur raised his voice, with a hint of contempt. "This is more hypothesis and speculation on your part, Miss Sutherland. My record and that of my companies speaks for itself. Our business is industry and commerce on a global scale. We have no interest in conflict. If, one day, my homeland becomes independent I will rejoice like thousands of others. But my dream and theirs will come by peaceful means. Thank you."

The presentation ended with a final camera sweep across the mountains of southern Turkey and a distant shot of the peak of Mount Ararat, far to the east.

Jackson stood up and switched off the television. His love for Hedizah seemed overwhelming and the obstacles in his way equally so. There was a call signal from his mobile. He pulled it from his jacket. There was one message. Would Hugo please contact Michael Crosfield on his return to the office? He should prepare for a possible overseas assignment. Details would be provided shortly.

* * * * * * * * *

Djibouti, Gulf of Aden

Alix Wenger looked into the mirror and adjusted his tunic. The crisp white drills and gold braid had survived his hasty packing. He made an approving final adjustment to the double line of brass buttons, and his row of medal ribbons. There was a sharp knock. An orderly put his head round the door.

"The brig's ready, Sir."

Wenger stepped out of the watch officer's cabin and walked along the corridor leading to the bridge. He quickly descended the narrow stairway to the main deck. Within a minute, he was seated on the Captain's boat, heading for the main pier, less than half a nautical mile distant.

He tucked his cap under his arm, settled back in his seat and narrowed his eyes as the vessel's bow swung into the face of the early morning sun.

Not for the first time, Wenger had wondered at the wisdom of following the family tradition and making his career at sea. His grandfather had been a destroyer captain in the Second World War and his father the master of ocean-going cargo vessels operating from the port of Bremerhaven. Now he wore the uniform of a First Lieutenant of the navy of the Federal Republic of Germany.

The slim grey lines of the frigate from which he had just disembarked were now hidden from view by the vast bulk of a United States landing support vessel. The tiny brig turned against the tide as the waters eddied around the exposed landing steps below the old French Naval Academy building.

They would be landing in a few moments. Wenger could see the early sun glinting on the burnished swords of the welcome party on the pier. He thought back over the last twelve hours. It was only the previous afternoon that he had been enjoying a sailing excursion with his wife and two young children on the waters of the Alster Lake, a few kilometres from the family home on the outskirts of Hamburg. They had landed at a quiet islet for a picnic lunch when his mobile rang. It was the Ministry of Defence in Bonn.

Wenger was in command of a unit of special service police commandos, trained to respond to threats to German interests overseas in the commercial maritime sector. The unit was on constant standby. The orders that he received had surprised him. He was to meet his team, at a secluded and disused civilian airfield near Kiel, about one hour's drive north of the city. There, they would board an unmarked aircraft with full kit and would be conveyed to a United States base, north of the port of Djibouti in the Red Sea. They would be met by a helicopter from the German naval frigate, *Emden*.

Once ashore, he was to attend a reception being hosted by the local German Consul, who would give him his operational orders. It appeared that the reception was a diplomatic initiative to record that control and command of the United Nations protection flotilla, which was headquartered in Djibouti, had now passed to the German Navy.

Wenger knew that the flotilla routinely deployed two frigates and a destroyer in the Gulf of Somalia, ostensibly to curb piracy attacks in the area. In reality, the objective was to forestall the seaborne transfer of terrorists and their equipment from the troubled lands in the north to a supposed safe haven in the lawless wastelands of the Horn of Africa.

He also knew that the Admiral previously in command had been quietly removed from his post. CIA field officers, operating covertly in Hargeisa, an age-old mountain-top city in the west of Somalia, had discovered that a blind eye had been turned to a recent attack on a French-flagged container vessel by armed raiders. The vessel's Captain and Chief Officer had been murdered. The reasons were unclear but there had been rumours of contraband goods being sold by naval personnel in the local souks of the city.

"Good morning, Lieutenant."

Wenger was jolted from his momentary recollections by the jaunty voice of the German Consul, dressed in a smart tropical suit and Panama hat with red ribbon.

"Welcome to Djibouti. My name's Karl Stedman. I'm the local consul here, shipping agent, interpreter and home for lost tourists, that sort of thing. Anyway, they tell me I'm to escort you to the reception. All very secret they said."

Wenger smiled at the pleasantly eccentric manner, so beloved of the expatriate, long lost to his home country and happily, if resignedly, immersed in the ways of the local genre.

He shook hands with Stedman and spoke crisply. "You have my orders, I understand. My men are embarked, as instructed."

Both men looked seaward, at a sudden gust of wind. The *Emden* had swung at anchor and the German flag on her stern was now clearly visible.

Stedman replied in the same excitable tone. "Well, not exactly, there's been some chit chat among the powers that be."

"Meaning?"

Stedman's response was good-natured. "It's all a bit irregular, a bit outside my brief. But you chaps are probably used to it."

Wenger grinned again. "But you have my orders?"

"Yes, of course. There's a Frenchman here. His name's Jean-Yves Bertrand. He's in charge, they tell me. Don't worry. You'll meet him at the reception."

A tall, uniformed officer, from the local gendarmerie, ushered Wenger and his voluble companion towards a balconied terrace, with a white awning that overlooked the bay and the distant rocky coastline beyond. There was a sound of animated conversation and the chink of cocktail glasses.

Wenger glanced about him. There was the usual round of guests to be expected at a diplomatic maritime reception; young naval attachés from foreign embassies with their consorts, local businessmen and an array of hangers on, all looking for commercial opportunity, intrigue, seduction or all three.

Wenger quickly spotted the commanding officer of the *Emden*, a tall, grizzled seafarer nearing retirement, to whom he had reported earlier in the day. He had made Wenger only too aware that, whilst he would offer the support of his vessel and the other two vessels in his flotilla, he had scant regard for the undercover assignment proposed.

He also evidently had little sympathy for a junior officer who had descended on his ship with a bunch of hardened desperadoes, however disciplined they might be.

Wenger gave a half smile in the Captain's direction and received a curt nod in reply. He suddenly felt his sleeve tugged by his companion, who motioned him towards two men who were standing apart from the group, both dressed in civilian suits.

"Over here, my friend, where your destiny awaits you."

Karl Stedman seemed to be relishing his brief intrusion into a world that he knew must exist, but of which, at least outwardly, he had never been a part.

"Mâitre Douchert, it's good to see you as always. Are you still keeping an eye on our lords and masters, and making sure they stick by the letter of the law?"

Wenger glanced around as the reception got into full swing. Champagne and canapés were proffered by starch-coated waiters on silver trays. Women tried to feign indifference or desire in response to the attentions foisted on them, and the flags of many nations gently swayed in the sea breeze.

Less than 200 kilometres away, ransomed and blindfolded hostages might be pleading for their lives at the whim of a local warlord.

"Lieutenant Wenger. May I introduce Emil Douchert, a local lawyer, who knows more of what goes on here than the President, I venture to suggest."

"Thank you, Mr Stedman."

Douchert looked tired and jaded. Dark lines underscored his eyes and his cheeks were pallid and grey.

There was a moment's silence as Wenger looked expectantly at the man to whom Douchert had been talking. Stedman spoke quietly. "Lieutenant, I believe that I should also introduce you to my colleague, Jean-Yves Bertrand. Like you, he too has only recently arrived here."

Bertrand stretched out his hand. "I'm pleased to meet you, Lieutenant."

Another moment of silence followed. Stedman cleared his throat.

"If you don't mind, gentlemen, I should be going. We've got a family occasion, my daughter's birthday, you know. Monsieur Bertrand, may I leave Lieutenant Wenger with you?"

"Of course."

There was an unexpected clang of a ship's bell and the sound of a bugle from the roof of the academy. The Master of Ceremonies called the guests to order.

"Ladies and gentlemen, may I ask for your kind attention, and your momentary quiet, to hear the welcome speech from our esteemed President, to be followed by our Head of National Security. Thank you."

"My apologies to you both, but I also have to leave now." Douchert bowed his head to Bertrand and the young German, and made his way quietly to a staircase leading down to the pier. As he did so, he nodded to another guest who had just arrived. His eyes motioned him in the direction of the two men to whom he had been speaking. They would meet, as arranged, in one hour's time.

Bertrand and Wenger listened to the official welcome speeches and then took the opportunity to slip away to a far corner of the balcony. Neither was aware that the man to whom Douchert had spoken was standing with his back to the wall, only a metre below them.

"So, Monsieur Bertrand, I am told that I am to look to you for my orders."

Bertrand smiled. "That's right but, of course, as usual, we are only the men on the ground. I'm old enough to be your father but I expect that you know what I mean."

Bertrand had no reason to feel at ease, however. A phone call, in the early hours, had informed Bertrand that Ronnie Simpson was alive and was being held in a farmhouse near Bosasso in the Puntland region of Somalia. The caller told Bertrand that Simpson would be freed when Bertrand arrived with a further sum of United States dollars amounting to twice the figure that Simpson had brought with him. In the meantime, he could rest assured that his other requirements were being carried out.

Bertrand looked at Wenger as they moved slowly away from the main body of guests towards the outside balcony. Wenger was half his age, married perhaps with a young family and a solid career ahead of him, if such was ever possible.

Bertrand bore no grudges. There had been no point and, more particularly, no time.

Only once had Bertrand come close to what he thought might be something different. An assignment had taken him and his platoon covertly into Zimbabwe. He had met a woman, blonde haired, sun tanned and careworn. She was tired beyond her thirty-five years, working out her days on a small farm property. She had shared the homestead with her husband, until he had been killed in the final days of Rhodesia's last bush war.

Now she was dead too. He had heard word from a Belgian journalist, working in Lusaka, that she had been counted amongst the victims of a tribal land grab, inspired by the very workers that she had employed.

Then his uniformed days were over. Now, maybe, he was closing the ring.

The next hours in Djibouti would determine whether the drama in which he had become a central player would reach a successful climax or, yet again, leave a trail of innocent bodies for the scavengers to pick on at will.

"Is something wrong, Sir?"

"Nothing, Lieutenant, thank you."

"You seemed a long way away."

"Sorry."

Wenger gave a half smile. He sensed that, behind the timelines on the face of the man who he had met only minutes before, lay a sense of awareness, a new beginning, even a mission. But then, as his wife had so often told him, he would never make Admiral, because he could never kick a man when he was down.

Wenger and Bertrand looked out over the harbour. The late morning sun glinted on the water. Bertrand spoke slowly and clearly. He told Wenger that, however irregular the contents of his orders were, he had to trust him. If all went awry, there would be a routine denial of involvement by all concerned. Only, this time, Bertrand would not allow it to happen.

Wenger felt that he was right. Bertrand had done other people's bidding for years. Now he had something he needed to do for himself, perhaps something to prove. But, maybe, there was more to it than that.

The two men shook hands. An orderly dutifully returned the young lieutenant's cap. The Captain tried to avoid his glance as Wenger strode down the staircase towards the pier and the waiting brig.

As he did so, the man whom Douchert had passed earlier started to move away from the bottom of the stairway. He had been able to listen to every word that Bertrand and Wenger had exchanged. He walked quickly towards the gated entrance to the port area and paused opposite the entrance to the old customs shed. Bertrand watched him go and wondered.

Emil Douchert had been a necessary risk. He knew that. However, without his local knowledge of the means to gain entry into the forbidden zones of Somalia, nothing could be achieved.

For certain, Douchert had seen an opportunity, as he had done before, but Bertrand realized that whoever Douchert had procured to seize Simpson would not dare to kill him.

They were dependent on Douchert as their paymaster. The demand would be negotiable. Bertrand would bide his time. He would get Douchert his cut. Then he would see. If things changed, Bertrand was quite aware of what he would have to do.

He watched the man speaking on his mobile. What Bertrand could not know was how much of what he had learned Douchert would pass on, and to whom.

* * * * * * * * *

The City of London, England

Crosfield surveyed the design of the private meeting room attached to the office of the senior partner of Layton and Springer in the City of London. No expense had been spared in outfitting the room, in the most modern style, to suit the demands of the slick international clientele whom the firm hoped to attract and retain.

Soft refracting lights, glass cabinet tops, minimalist fittings and modern artwork contrasted with the dark traditional oils and heavy oak furniture that once evoked notions of board room security and reliability. A slim table-top plasma screen stood discreetly concealed behind an opaque glass console. The constant chatter of emails, financial indices and instant worldwide news offered him little comfort.

Crosfield looked out of the wide balcony window towards St Paul's Cathedral and the river. He could see the morning sun glinting on the tall glass towers of Canary Wharf. Once, such a skyline had seemed almost welcoming. It had been part of a challenge, part of the deception that had seen his rapid rise to the principal seat of power in the law firm that had become his life.

He wondered whether that life might yet allow him some refuge from the events that were threatening to destroy what he had achieved, however that might have been accomplished.

As his chauffeur drove that morning from his apartment in Clifford's Inn towards the City, he once again read the text message received from Ralph Lennard the evening before.

Somehow, Crosfield had hoped that the rough treatment that he had endured at their recent meeting on the Essex coast would become a memory, an incident frozen in time that would not in the end have any impact on the delicately balanced edifice that his world had become.

Until a short while before, he had, successfully it seemed, been able to juggle personal ambition, conflicts of interest, deception, fraud on his partners, and even a blatant distortion of the judicial process.

He had even been able to play the markets successfully with client funds and his firm's money without, it appeared, risk of exposure. But things had changed.

Now, opposite him, sipping water from finely crafted glasses bearing the firm's logo, sat two pale-faced unsmiling officers from the Investigation Executive of the Justice Department.

The two men had been waiting for him in the firm's reception. He had to thank the quick thinking of his secretary for showing them into his private meeting room, before any unwanted attention was aroused. The fact that they had come had not, in reality, surprised him.

Both men bore the expressions of state servants, enjoying the exercise of power over independent professionals who, given the opportunity, Crosfield suspected, they might have wished to emulate.

Crosfield made up his mind to treat his two potential inquisitors as time-serving bureaucrats, with a trivial agenda and ability to match. In truth, he knew that he had much to hide and no means of knowing how much time or leeway he might have to prepare his defence.

The older of the two men introduced himself and his colleague. He explained their presence in a disconcertingly urbane and reasonable way.

"Mr Crosfield, we realize that our presence here may be an embarrassment to you and your partners. This is actually the first time that either of us has been called upon to step inside the office of such a well known and respected firm."

Crosfield spoke guardedly. "Thank you. I appreciate your discretion."

The man opposite him continued in the same helpful vein. "We have, routinely, to say that this is only a preliminary interview. We have no objection to your having your own legal representative with you, if you wish to do so. We are quite happy to wait."

Crosfield found himself ill at ease with the reasonable approach that had been adopted, at least up to that point. He replied politely, "That won't be necessary at this time. Thank you. Would either of you like coffee or tea?"

"Water will suit us fine, thank you."

Crosfield knew, however, that in all probability the verbal fencing had only just begun. Years of experience of negotiations had taught him to recognize every nuance of tone, every conversational feint, however slight, that an opponent might let slip, intentionally or otherwise.

There was a moment's silence as the younger man extracted a crisp, newly bound publication from his briefcase. He looked at his colleague before turning back to face Crosfield.

"Again, it's routine only, but we have a statutory duty to hand to everyone who we interview a copy of our terms of reference under the new Justice Act that came into force last year."

Crosfield replied quickly and confidently, "I know what it provides, but thank you anyway."

The older man cleared his throat. "Mr Crosfield. We are in a difficult position. Something's happened. The matter has been referred to the minister. His permanent secretary suggested that we ask for your views, off the record, if you have no objection."

Crosfield felt an involuntary trickle of cold perspiration in the middle of his back. These men were not the dullards that he had taken them for. He nodded his assent.

A few moments later the older man withdrew a single folded sheet from his suit jacket pocket and laid it on the table.

"Please take as long as you need to read it. We are quite happy to sit outside for a few moments."

He stopped almost in mid-sentence as if assessing Crosfield's likely response. Before Crosfield had time to pick up the paper he continued, but this time his tone was different.

"If we do leave the room, Mr Crosfield, we'd rather you didn't use the telephone, if you don't mind."

Crosfield remained silent for several seconds before replying. His throat felt dry. "That won't be necessary."

He knew, if he had not suspected it before, that he now needed to exercise extreme care. His instincts told him that the two men opposite him had time on their side, which he did not.

His interviewer pushed the sheet of paper towards him.

"Please take a moment to consider the text. It's the final draft of a press release which, subject to the Cabinet Secretary's approval, we intend to issue at midday today."

Crosfield picked it up. He was conscious that they were watching his every move. He was also conscious that the blood was draining from his cheeks as he slowly read the printed text.

Tragedy at country house
High Court Judge found hanged

A Scotland Yard spokesman confirmed that last evening the body of Sir Henry Wilkinson was found hanging in the barn of his country home, Oakington Manor, in the village of Grendon, near Newbury. Initial enquiries revealed that Sir Henry, a Judge of the High Court, had returned home from London earlier in the day. The body was found by his wife, who is being comforted by friends. The couple had two children, a son who died of leukaemia at the age of nine, and a daughter who was reported to be flying back to the United Kingdom from a teaching post in Italy. A note, whose contents have not been disclosed, was found with the body. A police spokesman said that no one was being sought in relation to the death and that foul play had been ruled out. Friends, who spoke on condition of anonymity, remarked that Sir Henry, who was the Master of the local Hunt, had seemed depressed over the last few weeks. It appeared that the judge had asked for leave of absence, following his ruling in a recent controversial case in the London Commercial Court. The case involved the disputed loss of the vessel, Globex Mariner, which was owned and operated by a company controlled by the industrialist, Rahman Mansur. Rumours that the Justice Department has been requested to investigate the conduct of the trial were denied by a representative of the Department, who declined to answer further enquiries.

Crosfield looked up.

"I'm very sorry to read this. We all had the greatest respect for Sir Henry."

The two men were staring at him. Crosfield cleared his throat. It was clear that they were expecting him to speak.

"There's no doubt that it was a difficult case. There were many unfounded allegations raised against my client. They were all unreservedly dismissed by the Court. In a high profile matter like this, the stress on the judge is considerable."

"Quite so." The older man nodded as if in agreement.

Crosfield felt unable to stop himself. He was flushed, but he felt cold. His palms were damp, as he nervously fingered the paper. He knew that they were watching his every move. He continued less than confidently.

"We held a special press conference after the trial. There will be no appeal. As far as I am concerned the judgment is final. My client was exonerated from any responsibility for the tragedy that occurred."

The reply from the younger man was not what Crosfield expected. "Indeed Sir, they were. We have a transcript of the press conference here. It's quoted in a report in the most recent edition of the *World Economic Monitor*. You've doubtless seen it."

Crosfield fought hard to maintain his composure. He had to keep a disdainful profile but the game was being played in a skilful way.

"Gentlemen, as I have stated, I, and I am sure likewise many of my partners, am saddened by the report of the judge's death, in such tragic circumstances. I have, however, no specific comment to make on the press release beyond what I have just said."

"Thank you, Mr Crosfield. That is very helpful."

Crosfield imagined that the interview was over. The two men eyed him impassively, as he fought to control the random thoughts and images that seemed to race before his eyes.

How much or how little the Justice Department really knew about the conduct of the *Globex Mariner* case somehow no longer seemed to matter.

He found himself almost taking comfort from what he had said to Mansur at the recent meeting in Geneva. Whilst he had procured perjured evidence to deceive the Court, perversely he had nothing to do with the financial arrangements which, he assumed, that Mansur had agreed directly with the late Sir Henry Wilkinson.

Crosfield almost had to stop himself, absentmindedly, reminding his interrogators that he had at least not gone so far as to bribe a High Court judge himself.

He grasped the edge of the table and stood up stiffly. "Gentlemen, I'm not sure if I can assist you further at the present time?"

The older of the two men nodded to his colleague, deliberately folded the paper containing the press release and inserted it into his jacket pocket.

"Not for the moment, Mr Crosfield."

There was a pause as they turned away. "We can see ourselves out. Thank you for your time."

The door of the private meeting room closed. Crosfield wiped the perspiration from his hands as he walked slowly into his adjoining office. It seemed uncharacteristically quiet, even for eight fifteen in the morning.

He sat down and picked up the private and confidential envelope that had arrived in the office earlier. It was an overnight courier packet from the United States and contained a personal letter from the Senior Partner at Shulster and Tyler Inc., Chicago, the auditors of Layton and Springer's entire professional operation.

The letter said, quite simply, that it was a matter of regret that the auditors for the present year were unable to sign off the firm's accounts in their present form. To do so would place the auditors in breach of their obligations of compliance with the financial and regulatory authorities in both the United Kingdom and the United States. The reason was that there were significant time, cost and expense irregularities with regard to the firm's accounting relationship with the Globex group of companies in general and with regard to the numerous files relating to the *Globex Mariner* case in particular. A meeting to clarify matters was requested, in London or at the auditors' documentary centre in New York, at an early date. This meeting would additionally be attended by the auditors' attorneys from Houston.

Crosfield took off his jacket. His shirt was damp with perspiration, his face and cheeks drained of colour. He had been expecting that one day the circle would begin to close.

Whilst he knew that he had to face each one of the threats that faced him at the same time, his instinct told him that even at this stage he still had to identify the quarter which posed the gravest risks. He believed that he could buy time with both the Justice Ministry and the auditors.

But, however much time he could buy in the professional arena, there was no such opportunity to forestall the demands of Ralph Lennard. His position was crystal clear. Either Crosfield paid his debt, within an ever-narrowing time frame, or he would be dead.

Crosfield had no choice and no room for manoeuvre. The risks of initiating his plan were great. The risks of not doing so were even greater.

He had reflected on the reason why Herlov had appeared at the meeting in Leipzig, when he had been expecting only Pytr Majec to be there. He would never know but would have to trust his instinct that somehow and for some reason Herlov had divided his loyalties. Crosfield could only hope that he had guessed correctly. He picked up his mobile.

"Herlov. This is Crosfield. You are on. Call me when you're ready to trade."

There was a pause and a sharp intake of breath before Crosfield received the confirmation he needed. He then pulled on his jacket and left his office. His secretary and personal assistant looked up.

"Where's Hugo Jackson?" he asked her.

"He's at an all day conference at Counsel's Chambers."

"Tell him to meet me at my apartment at eight o'clock tonight. I've something for him."

* * * * * * * * * *

The Aegean Sea

The vessel edged her way southwards against a stiffening breeze. Her bow began to roll and pitch unevenly. The port of Piraeus was already an hour's steaming astern, as the helmsman sought a course out into the southern Aegean Sea.

Already, the sunset far to the west was casting long shadows over the rocky crags of the Peloponnese peninsula, on the starboard side. To port, the vessel would shortly pass Cape Sounion and the islands of Poros and Hydra, before turning on to a heading to the south west. At a steady speed of some ten knots, this would take her to within a short distance of the rendezvous off the island of Malta in a little less than forty-eight hours.

Georgios Milakis stood on the bridge wing of the *Aegean Dolphin*. He looked towards the two holds, forward of the vessel's accommodation and engine room. There was no doubt that the shipyard fitters had done a good job. They had effectively rebuilt the ageing vessel. The decks and hull had been strengthened, the engines and steering gear overhauled, and the bridge had been outfitted with the latest navigational aids and communications equipment.

Bold lettering on the recast hull showed the vessel's newly painted name and port of registry, Monrovia. The vessel's certificates, which had been handed to Milakis by the local agent in Piraeus, showed that the *Aegean Dolphin* had recently been transferred to the Liberian Registry. Classification documents had been signed off, confirming that the vessel met all relevant international standards for operational safety and seaworthiness.

Notwithstanding this, Milakis felt uneasy. He walked to the steering platform, checked the chart table and nodded to the helmsman. The sea state was getting rougher. He opened the intercom to the engine room and called for a reduction in engine revolutions.

Milakis knew only too well that he had no legal entitlement to command the *Aegean Dolphin*. Technically, he still held the master's ticket, which he had obtained from the Greek Ministry of Marine some ten years beforehand. But it had been suspended, pending the outcome of an inquiry by the Government of Cyprus into alleged smuggling offences committed on a previous vessel, of which he was the captain.

He had agreed to turn a blind eye to a hidden consignment of narcotics when the vessel had left her Colombian loading port, bound for Marseilles. The French customs had been waiting. His arrest, detention and release on bail pending an appearance before an investigating criminal magistrate had meant several months' enforced unemployment on his home island of Paphos.

Milakis had needed the money that he had been offered. A casual affair in a distant port had resulted in an acrimonious and expensive separation from his wife and erstwhile childhood sweetheart. The two children, whom he adored, now refused to see him. Maintenance and alimony payments had rendered him almost bankrupt.

Then they had located him in a seaside bar, where he had been working long hours as a waiter to meet the cost of his meagre board and lodging. The initial cash payment figure was non-negotiable. It was clear, however, whoever was offering it knew that it would be sufficient to buy him out of the financial morass into which he had drifted.

A reward for success, he was told, would also be available. The terms offered seemed disarmingly straightforward. On delivery of the cargo that the *Aegean Dolphin* was destined to carry, appropriate arrangements would be made to ensure that the French criminal action and the Cyprus inquiry would go no further. His master's licence would then be quietly restored.

Milakis told himself that he had little choice but to accept. At the time, he had no cause to regret his decision and, within a week, he had taken command of the *Aegean Dolphin*, whilst she completed her outfitting at the dockyard in Piraeus.

He knew that the risks that he ran, sailing as an unlicensed sea captain, were considerable. If those who had sponsored him failed to comply with what had been agreed, his position would doubtless worsen. He was, after all, a fugitive from justice. What was more, the authorities would have little difficulty in locating and attaching the cash fee, which had already been paid. If that occurred, his criminal bankruptcy would surely follow.

But it was only after arriving on board that he began to realize that he had been blind to the reality of what lay behind the cash and other inducements that he had so willingly accepted. The orders that he received were contained in a sealed envelope. He should expect sailing instructions from an agency office located in St Croix, in the United States Virgin Islands by an encrypted email sent to a dedicated computer in the Captain's office, adjacent to the bridge.

He was, additionally, entitled to accept verbal orders, given by telephone, by two named individuals, whose identity details had been programmed into the ship's main telephone receiver in the communications room. One of the two listed was Max Herlov, who was described as the owner's personal representative.

Confirmation had been received on the following day. The vessel was to sail three days later, leaving on the late afternoon tide. He was to make passage to Tripoli, Libya, where a specific cargo was to be loaded. It was this cargo that had necessitated the special refurbishment of the vessel.

Milakis had traded to Tripoli before. The old extremist regime had long gone. The port, on his last visit, had provided an opportunity for shore leave and the chance to relax in the Italian quarter.

This time, however, it would be different. The vessel was to announce her arrival by radio, on a military frequency, and to await inward clearance to a berth outside the normal commercial area of the port. Only when all cargo had been loaded, securely checked and sealed by shoreside personnel, would the vessel receive outward clearance and details of her onward voyage.

Milakis had begun to feel uncomfortable. He realized that what he had signed up to might be something far more sinister than the illicit carriage of narcotics. His anxiety had increased when the crew list and seaman's books had been brought aboard. He had scanned the names and nationalities. At first glance all seemed normal enough. There was a Ukrainian chief officer, an Indian chief engineer, Greek junior officers and engineers and a Filipino bosun and deck crew, some twenty-five in total. Then, he read the dozen or more additional names listed as supernumeraries. Their documentation was authentic and had apparently raised no concerns with the port authorities. But when the first of those listed came on board and introduced himself as Pytr Majec, Milakis' concerns were further heightened.

Majec told him that he and his team would have charge of the vessel's security in port and at sea. Captain Milakis would be responsible for the vessel's safe navigation and nothing more.

The vessel's crew were at all times to adhere to any instructions that Majec's men might give. They had specific orders. Any non-compliance would be met with an appropriate response. The Captain should understand that there was no question but to accept Majec's on-board authority.

When Majec's team embarked the day before sailing, Milakis realized that he and his fellow seafarers, were, without doubt, about to become prisoners on their own vessel. He had an uneasy feeling that they might all become hostages, in the hands of men whose looks and demeanour would brook no argument.

Later the same evening the gates of the dockyard had been sealed. Majec had supervised the loading of his team's personal kit and equipment. Milakis, his officers and crew had been confined to their cabins.

As soon as the vessel had cleared the Piraeus customs zone, Majec had ordered his team to break out their weapons. From then on, each of the command and operational centres on the ship was controlled by at least two heavily armed men.

Milakis walked out to the starboard bridge wing. He looked at the burly man who stared out towards him. Swarthy, thick-set, with a protruding face and an unpleasant scar across his close shaven head, he cradled an automatic pistol against his left arm.

The seas were calmer now, and Milakis called down to the engine room, asking for an increase in speed. He then checked the chart table and began to lay a new course for the navigating officer and the helmsman.

The evening sea spray and breeze would normally have refreshed him, but despite the warm glow of the early evening sun, he felt cold.

Milakis had heard rumours on the Piraeus waterfront, before he had come on board. He had needed to waste a couple of hours before collecting his port security pass and had done so in a cheap bar, on a narrow side street, leading down to the harbour. He had no appetite for the naked girls who played out their daily routine of pole dancing and exotic rituals before a dreamy audience of lonely sailors and inquisitive tourists. However, he could not help but overhear bar talk regarding the death, in unexplained circumstances, of a surveyor named Stelios Kyriakos. Kyriakos, it was said, had been inspecting a second-hand vessel, completing refurbishment, at a yard outside the main port area. On leaving the vessel he had fallen down a gangway on to the quay below. It was a strange fate for a man who had spent his life on ships.

The post mortem details had been withheld and, according to informed sources in the press, a marine police inquiry had been initiated. A spokesman had announced that investigations were continuing.

Later, Milakis had seen the dead man's name on the vessel's certificates. He had no means of knowing what had befallen him after he had signed them, but the evidence of what had occurred subsequently left him with little doubt.

Then, there had been the short and urgent call from Max Herlov, who had changed his orders. The vessel was to steam towards the island of Malta and await further instructions, before proceeding to Tripoli for loading. Immediately following that call, Majec had left the vessel.

Milakis was trapped, through his own fault. He knew that. It was not greed that had led him to agree the terms offered, but somehow a desire to set things right. Now there seemed no way out. He had made a belated attempt to salvage his own wellbeing. Perversely, it had put him in fear of his life.

Then, shortly before sailing, a package had been handed to him by the ship chandlers, who were delivering fresh food and water supplies for the vessel's voyage.

He had opened it in the privacy of his cabin. The package contained 100,000 new United States dollar bills and a state of the art satellite phone. There was an accompanying note telling Milakis to conceal the phone in his cabin and await instructions.

The note bore a tiny insignia at the top left-hand corner. Milakis had done his national service with the Greek naval intelligence department on an island in the eastern Aegean. He knew from colleagues, seconded from elsewhere, that the insignia was the trademark of the Israeli Secret Service.

Chapter Six

Diyabakir, Turkey

MAX HERLOV FELT HIS AGE. HE STARED into the mirror. His face looked grey, tired and insipid. He leant down over the grubby washbasin and splashed the discoloured water over his cheeks. It did little to refresh him. Grabbing a well-used towel, he dried himself as best he could, and prepared to step out of the bathroom to rejoin the meeting that had started some twenty minutes beforehand.

He knew that Mansur had been watching him. It was never obvious but somehow his boss was making it known, quietly, perhaps even surreptitiously, that all was not well between them.

Herlov had worked for Mansur for the past nine years. In that time, he had seen Mansur's organization grow into a global conglomerate, listed on the world's major financial exchanges with energy, mining and shipping interests covering the five continents. He knew that Mansur's methodology was brutal, uncaring and corrupt. Mansur had hired Herlov and men like him to ensure that, when coercion was needed, it would be applied, ruthlessly and efficiently. Herlov knew that he had, in reality, exchanged one job as a hired mercenary, for another.

But, then again, he had spent too long working as a hired hand in the chaotic and bloody battlegrounds of Chechnya, and elsewhere in the ailing Soviet Union. He had needed to leave before either his luck ran out or he had begun to enjoy the killing, the degradation and the torture for its own sake.

He had seen it happen to others, self-styled soldiers of fortune, with no allegiance, no past and no future. It had happened to Pytr Majec, whom Mansur had willed him to employ, against his better judgement.

Majec was a man for whom the excesses of the Balkan conflict had become a daily drug, fuelled by a cult of endemic violence and brutality, wherever and upon whomever it could be inflicted. Now Herlov had played a hand that included Majec. He had gone to the meeting in Leipzig to see whether what he had suspected was true. He had been right, but the risks would only increase if he fell in with the plan that Crosfield had hatched. But that had been only part of the problem.

He had realized, months before, that Mansur had aspirations for political power and influence. These went far beyond the business edifice that Herlov had helped him to create. That was why he had insisted that Herlov accompany him to the meeting with Barshok and Rawazi. Mansur needed their acquiescence, even if the price of acquiring it had increased substantially.

In reality, Herlov had hoped that the near disaster of the *Globex Mariner* would have dissuaded Mansur from a second attempt. He had noticed that Mansur seemed unwaveringly certain that he could control events, or at the very least, distance himself from what had occurred.

If the *Globex Mariner* case had been lost, the press campaign that would have followed would have left Mansur bankrupt, alone and most probably dead at the hands of his own people or others. The meeting in Geneva had shown that Mansur was willing to dispense with the services that Crosfield and his firm had provided. Herlov recognized that Crosfield, like himself, was a ruthless opportunist. He had, however, provided Mansur and his organization with an unchallenged cloak of corporate respectability.

Herlov was sure that Mansur had made an error, possibly a fatal error, in trying to repeat the venture. The *Globex Mariner* cargo might already have given Mansur the political muscle and power to support an independent state of Kurdistan, with himself as its head. But it had not.

Now Mansur was going to try again. It was a mistake and Herlov had told him. In doing so, he had indirectly raised Mansur's suspicion as to Herlov's intentions and his loyalty.

There was sharp knock on the door.

"Are you OK in there?"

The voice was that of one of the three members of the Kurdish Independent Council, whom he had met earlier in the day. They had responded to Mansur's call to arms, and to his invitation to the strategic and tactical meeting that they were now attending. The agenda required no less a decision than how, where and when the nuclear triggers were to be delivered, how the final assembly of short-range battlefield rockets was to be undertaken and where they were to be deployed. The timing of that deployment would determine the terms that were to be demanded from the United Nations to commence negotiations on the formation of the independent state of Kurdistan.

"I'm on my way."

Herlov slid back the latch on the door. The man was waiting outside and eyed him uneasily.

"Sorry, I got sick from the car drive. I'm getting too old for all of this."

He shook the man's hand and gave him a meaningful grin. Together they walked back into the murky parlour room where Rahman Mansur and the two other men were waiting.

Cigarette smoke and the smell of sweet coffee hung heavily in the air. After the failure to deliver the *Globex Mariner* consignment, the men facing Mansur were demanding answers and guarantees.

Herlov had been surprised at how, almost for the first time since he had known him, Mansur's ruthless confidence appeared, at least to Herlov's eye, to have momentarily deserted him. Whether the others had noticed Herlov could not be sure.

Mansur had seemingly struggled to give credible assurances that the scheme and the timetable for delivery of the replacement shipment on the *Aegean Dolphin* left nothing to chance. He had tried to overcome their doubts by insisting that Herlov recount every detail of the vast financial commitment that Mansur had undertaken to secure his aims. Times, dates, risks, threats assessed and avoided, had all been explained.

At the insistence of those present, Herlov, with Mansur's consent, had disclosed key documents and information, details of which, until then, had been known only to Mansur's closest associates.

The three men scrutinised the material and plans that Herlov provided. Mansur assured those present that technical excellence had been achieved and security assured, to such an extent that only he was aware of the final intended port of discharge. He would expect the on-carriage arrangements to the secret rendezvous point in northern Iraq to be undertaken by experienced agents of the Kurdish Council.

Herlov wondered whether Mansur was relying too much on old allegiances that might no longer exist. He had disliked the changed arrangements and the late switch in the venue of the meeting. It had been due to take place at a well-organized location in Mosul, under the guise of a conference on future oil and gas output from the oilfields of Kirkuk. Instead, the meeting had been moved to a coffee shop in the untidy town of Diyabakir, in the foothills of the badlands of southern Turkey and the border with Iraq.

Strangely, Mansur had seemed unperturbed. He had made the payment agreed at the meeting with Barshok and Rawazi to secure Israel's and Syria's consent to the operation. He felt convinced that publicity, generated by the television interview, had deflected media attention from the fate of the *Globex Mariner*. He had, he believed, even demonstrated a sense of human frailty, almost a sense of romantic destiny, by openly discussing his marriage to Hedizah.

And yet, when he had been pressed on the details by the council members, Herlov perceived a change. Herlov suspected that it might have been caused by the dawning realization that the political will of those whose support he needed to achieve his ultimate goal was starting to wane.

The oldest of the three addressed Mansur in measured tones.

"We continue to share your goal. Kurdistan needs you. The people need the independence that has been denied them for too long. They want to right the years of wrongs and betrayal afflicted on them."

The statements made at the start of the meeting had been genuine enough, the culmination of years of frustration, politics, plotting, insurrection and murder. Mansur listened impassively.

"But times are changing," the man continued. He paused for a moment. "On the ground it's no longer the same. There is more wealth in the average family. There are new jobs in the oil industry, new technology and, for the first time, freedom from the mania of the Saddam era."

Herlov saw no change in Mansur's expression.

The leader of the delegation continued. "The young see things differently. They want to travel, use the internet; they want freedom to make love. The old customs are changing. They don't want to listen to the tales of old men with even older weapons living in the hills, to free a land from an oppression that, to some, seems like history."

Mansur responded dismissively to the doubts that had been expressed.

"Gentlemen, we have come too far to turn back. You will have to make your decision, where you stand, when the moment comes. In the meantime, I am going ahead. I have no other option."

Mansur nodded to Herlov. The other men stood up and bowed their heads. The meeting was over. They all knew that it had been a failure.

The council members remained behind and, having shaken hands, Mansur and Herlov left. As they walked down the narrow alley outside the coffee shop, Herlov could see that Mansur had come to a decision.

"You did well with those documents, Max. I assume that the dates were all changed as we agreed."

"They were."

The two men stopped in the midst of a busy crossing where the alley from the coffee shop emerged into the town's main square. Herlov realized that Mansur might now have other plans, but it was too late for him to change his mind.

He had given new orders to the Captain of the *Aegean Dolphin*. Pytr Majec had left the vessel before she sailed. He had taken Michael Crosfield's call and was acting on it. Herlov had decided that he needed a way out, for himself. He did not wish to be alongside Mansur if, as he felt sure might happen, events overtook the *Aegean Dolphin*, just as they had with the *Globex Mariner*.

Mansur spoke, as if in response to Herlov's thoughts.

"They need to convince me that they are still behind me. If they're not, I've another buyer for our consignment. He's willing to pay all that we've spent, and more, to get his hands on what I can offer."

They waited for the traffic to slow and made their way through the throng of traders and stall holders.

Perhaps he had acted too soon. Herlov didn't know.

"Max. We'll see each other in France in two days. By then, the vessel will be in Tripoli. We'll have time when she's loaded and making passage down the Red Sea to decide the next move. What do you think?"

Herlov looked across the sea of faces in front of them.

"I hope that I can still trust you, Max. Your loyalty means a lot to me."

Suddenly, Mansur was lost in the crowd, having pressed a piece of paper into Herlov's hand. He opened it slowly. It was a copy of the cash receipt in euros made out in the name of Ulf Karsten, the alias that he had used, when hiring the car in Leipzig for the meeting with Majec and Crosfield. He looked at it and wondered whether this was Mansur's way of reminding him of where his true loyalty should lie. Herlov threw it down and walked on.

* * * * * * * * *

Paris, France

Jackson stared at the faded plaster on the roof above his head. Beside him, with her head resting on his left shoulder, Hedizah lay naked. A duvet, half-pulled across, revealed her dark, sensitive and moist body. She had swept back her long hair. Jackson's right hand caressed the soft skin of her face as he moved towards her again.

She was quite beautiful. Her body was young, shapely and her need for passion almost unknowing. They had both felt the desperate need once more to consummate a relationship that had enveloped them, as if from nowhere.

But each realized, only too keenly, that whatever ecstasy lay between them had, and could only have, been founded on secrecy, deceit and danger. Jackson saw in Hedizah an almost spiritual soul, gentle, beautiful and serene. Hedizah saw in him compassion, strength and kindness. Each found in the other qualities that both hoped would secure their life together and their future, wherever that might lead them.

Jackson took Hedizah in his arms and the two were as one. This time her grip would not let go. He turned towards her. Her eyes began to close.

Images of her past life fleeted across her subconscious. Events had moved so fast.

In the quiet of an afternoon, in a French village hotel situated in the hills above the Mediterranean, they had made love for the first time. She knew then that her life would never be the same again.

Jackson stirred. She pressed herself closer.

"Hugo. Hold me, please hold me." Her voice was soft but imploring. "I'm frightened for you, for both of us, so frightened."

She felt Jackson's arm around her.

"I keep seeing you for the first time, and I keep feeling that I may lose you."

Jackson smiled. "It's the same for me, Hedizah."

"I'm sorry. Outside the church, after your father's funeral, you looked so sad but somehow so dignified in your grief. I saw your eyes, your face. It was kind and strong."

Jackson stroked her forehead. Hedizah continued to speak, quietly, earnestly.

"Forgive me. Even on that sad occasion I wanted you, wanted to be with you, even though I didn't even know you. It makes me feel guilty."

"There's no guilt to feel. You looked wonderful."

They both smiled.

"You say nice things to me, Hugo, and I know that you mean them. But where are we to go? I want nothing more than to be with you but I don't know how long we can see each other like this."

Jackson's jaw tightened. "I know, Hedizah. If only I could say that I had the vaguest idea of a solution. I worry for you all the time when we are apart. I worry because of our love for each other. But most of all I worry about Mansur. What could happen and what he would do if he found out, to you, my love, and to Sophie."

Hedizah pressed herself closer. She raised her head on her hand and looked towards the shuttered window, beneath the sloping roof of the tiny attic in which they found themselves.

"Without Sophie we would not be here. She's risking everything to bring us together."

Jackson looked across to Hedizah. Her eyes were moist.

"I know how much she means to you."

There was a pause. Hedizah's words were almost inaudible. "It's as though she has a mission. She has seen so much unhappiness. She lost her own love. I know she believes. She prays. There's something spiritual within her."

Tears began to flow down Hedizah's cheeks. "She reminds me so much of the sister in the convent. She wanted nothing for herself and nor does Sophie. I think that she would do almost anything to see us happy together."

She began to sob. "It makes me feel so very humble, almost ashamed."

Jackson took her hand. Hedizah sat up. Her dark body was trembling with anxiety, emotion and tenderness.

"Hugo. There's something that terrifies me, but I don't know what it is."

"My love, I'm as frightened as you, but also more frightened for you. I love you, Hedizah. I want to promise you that we will be together, in the future, safe and sometime soon. Only I don't know how."

"You can't know how, Hugo. I just want to feel that, somewhere, there is a way forward, that there is someone to believe in and something to look forward to, for both of us. Does that sound foolish?"

"No, of course not, we have to have hope."

Hedizah eased herself towards Jackson. Their bodies met again in an agonizing desire to show to the other how strong their physical and emotional spirits had become. They needed to share the present. They saw a future that had no certainty, and a recent past that had thrust together two strangers from worlds apart and yet somehow intertwined.

Jackson stroked her eyelids as she groaned gently and her body curled up beside him.

He looked around at the room. They were like countless others before them, anonymous characters passing through the ever changing population that day and night thronged Paris' inner city backstreets. But theirs was not a vain search for whatever pleasures or vices might be sought out. They were there as refugees, however temporary, from a kaleidoscope of events that had cast them together.

In less than an hour, Hedizah would meet Sophie. Furtively and discreetly they would make the return train journey to the south of France. They would arrive late in the night, knowing that Mansur would be returning in the early hours of the following morning. Sophie had learned that he was meeting Herlov at eight o'clock in his office at the Villefranche property.

Jackson had turned a blind eye to the message on his email saying that Michael Crosfield wanted to see him at his apartment in London that same evening. He had replied to Crosfield's personal assistant, saying he had been delayed by the need to track down documents requested by Counsel, whose chambers he had attended the previous day.

Now he was to meet Crosfield the next evening, at a venue to be advised. He lay back as he listened to Hedizah breathing. She was asleep. There was little time, for either of them.

It was difficult to accept that in the cascade of events that had occurred, Hedizah had become so much a part of his life that not seeing her, not being with her, was unthinkable.

If there was one certainty in the maelstrom that had swept over him, it was that he had to find a way for them to survive together, to live their lives with each other.

He had needed not only time but advice as to the direction he should take, without risking all that he was now committed to.

After watching the television interview, he had made up his mind. Instead of driving directly back to London that evening, he would call at his old college in Oxford. If his former tutor were available he would ask to see him.

He thought back to the interview that had taken place fewer than forty-eight hours beforehand.

Dr Alan Jenkins had known Hugo since schooldays. He had been a contemporary of Hugo's father when they were both at Oxford over three decades before. Jackson knew that Jenkins had assisted his father with research and had co-authored several articles in the *World Economic Monitor*.

He was an academic who had not become divorced from the real world. It was rumoured that Jenkins routinely advised the British Foreign Office on strategic issues and that he occasionally worked for the Secret Intelligence Service.

Jenkins had met Jackson at the bottom of his staircase in St John's College's inner quadrangle. It was dark when Jackson arrived. The two men sat in Jenkins' study, with only a desk light for illumination. Jackson had immediately noticed how quiet the college was. He had forgotten how medieval walls and heavy gates could create an illusion of isolation from the seeming hostility of the world outside.

But he was not looking for an escape. He was not looking for self analysis or counselling. A proven climber and high altitude skier, he was not confessing to a loss of nerve or looking for a way out of his predicament.

Over coffee late into the night, Jackson described to his mentor the strange and arcane series of events and happenings that had occurred since his father's death and burial in Switzerland less than two months before.

Dr Jenkins had betrayed no emotion. He said little other than to verify dates and times. He asked about the whereabouts of the documents relating to the *Globex Mariner*, which Jackson had secreted in the self storage lock up.

Jackson was able to recount the principal details without difficulty.

It was agreed that Jenkins would travel to London on the following day and collect the documents, with a key that Jackson would retrieve from his apartment. He had spoken kindly to the younger man.

"I don't quite know what you are expecting from me, Hugo."

Jackson's reply was almost laconic. "I'm not sure either. But the situation is a bit complicated to say the least."

Jenkins could not resist making a mild jibe. "And that didn't take account of your falling head over heels in love with Hedizah Mansur, my friend."

Both men had grinned.

"More coffee?"

"Please."

The older man had stood up and poured the coffee from a steaming jug. He walked across the room and placed it on a tray beside a stack of student essays.

"If there was a script here, Hugo, if someone had been writing the parts, you and, I suppose, the lovely lady, have stepped outside it. You might perhaps have added a twist to the plot that the author wasn't intending."

Jackson's response was surprisingly light-hearted. "Meaning, I assume, that the person or persons unknown have taken very deliberate steps to put me in a position to expose this whole business, but they didn't, understandably, expect me to place my head so readily in the lion's jaw."

The levity of Jackson's tone had not been lost on Jenkins.

"You have put the case as succinctly as I would expect from a Layton and Springer trained legal associate."

"Thank you. I doubt that I deserve that."

The two men had fallen silent. Jackson looked at the seeming security that the academic's study outwardly offered. He knew that his only course was to press on. His own and Hedizah's life depended upon it.

He spoke slowly with confidence and genuine conviction.

"I cannot bring myself to break off from Hedizah. I love her desperately. Even if I did not, I'm not sure whether the picture would change much, if at all."

Jenkins had leaned across and spoken quietly.

"The fact is, Hugo, that for reasons that have yet to be played out, the die is cast. It's a very brittle cage and a dangerous one, as you know only too well."

Jackson had said nothing. Suddenly, Jenkins' amiable voice hardened.

"Don't rattle it, Hugo. Let events take their course. You have no alternative. Believe me."

He had eyed Jackson with the look of a man advising a young protégé for whom he felt responsible. It was a feeling that had come to haunt him, time and again, as he had grown older and students had left his charge.

"I'll collect the documents tomorrow and review them. They'll be safe with me. In the meantime, keep your appointment with Crosfield."

Jackson had stood up. "Thank you."

"Be careful and be silent, Hugo. When the time comes, you know where to find me, if you have to."

The two had shook hands.

"By the way, I don't suppose you have met or spoken to Ann Sutherland, have you?"

Jackson had turned his head. He was puzzled and not a little surprised.

"No. Should I have done? All I know is that she's a reporter for the *Monitor*. She was at the press conference at Court and, as you know, presented the interview with Mansur on television last night. Is it important?"

"Not really. It was a mere enquiry. That's all."

Jackson recalled the interview word for word. He would follow his mentor's advice. The meeting with Crosfield was set for the day following his return from Paris.

Hedizah stirred. He held her gently. They both knew that it was time to part. She crossed to the bathroom and as she did so Jackson noticed a folded paper being pushed under the door. He walked to the door and picked it up. It was a telephone message for Hedizah from the concierge taken some ten minutes before. It read simply that the caller would be arriving home shortly and was looking forward to her return. It did not leave a name.

* * * * * * * * * *

A village near Hargeisa, Somalia

Bertrand threw himself behind the low earthen wall in front of him. As he did so, the dry rocks to his right were splintered by the impact of several rounds of high velocity rifle fire. Fragments of rock and shrapnel flew randomly across what passed for a tiny farmyard. He felt a shard of metal graze his cheek and the first trickle of warm blood.

Things had gone wrong, badly wrong. Now he was in as unhealthy a position as he could ever recall, with the simple task of retrieving a mission which, within the last twenty-four hours, was coming close to disaster.

Soon after returning to his hotel in Djibouti and finding that Ronnie

Simpson was missing, a message had arrived, delivered by a nameless street boy, saying that Simpson was being held in Somalia. Bertrand had reminded himself that Douchert had warned him that all might not be what it seemed.

A contact phone number was given. Bertrand should call within the hour. Much was at stake. He should be under no illusion. If he failed to call, Simpson would die. It was that simple.

Bertrand had thought of Runah and the young boy at Douchert's office. He remembered Simpson's long goodbye in Dubai, the sad longing eyes of the young girl who saw in him her only hope of some kind of safety in her life. Bertrand had changed all that, with his promise of a bounty when the mission was accomplished. Perhaps it had always been the same.

Bertrand knew that any trip into the heart of a lawless war zone had its risks. Carrying over a quarter of a million United States dollars single-handed into an area ruled by warlords and bandits merely added to those risks. But they had planned.

They had needed local personnel to carry out the operation in a way that would pose the least risk of discovery. That meant personnel who had experience of the type of maritime criminality of which Bertrand had learned during his meeting with Mahmood in Singapore.

But, as they appreciated only too well, their strategy raised serious problems. Not least was the recruitment of men from a background where their only loyalty was to a local fiefdom and the only form of negotiation was the payment of hard cash at the end of a gun barrel.

The very hired hands that they engaged might have taken the lives of crew members on other vessels held for ransom. They might just as easily decide to betray their employers to a neighbouring clan or a rival, if a perceived advantage might maintain, however remote it might seem to an outsider.

Bertrand needed a man like Ronnie Simpson to go into the Somali hinterland. With the aid of contacts known to Douchert, it might be possible to find an intermediary. If terms could be agreed, however uncertain they might be to a western eye, they might find a group on whom Simpson and Bertrand could rely when the attack was to be mounted. But someone had got wind of the arrangements.

A single-engined plane had been chartered to fly Simpson incognito to a rough airstrip outside the port of Bosasso, from where Bertrand intended to launch the strike. It was an inhospitable, sparsely populated region in which it would be possible to lie low with arms and equipment. Simpson's task was to reconnoitre, make contact and report back.

Only Douchert was aware of what had been planned. When Bertrand had received the phone call from those holding Simpson, Douchert had denied all knowledge. Strangely, Bertrand had been inclined to believe him. Anyway, there had been no time to investigate further.

But Bertrand needed Douchert. He was probably the only man in Djibouti who had the ear of the Governor of the State Bank. Together, they possessed the ability to control the destiny of considerable sums of cash that clandestinely passed through the bank's treasury accounts.

When the demand for a quarter of a million dollars had been made, as the price of Simpson's life, Bertrand had done two things.

First, he had contacted his employers. Their authority was needed to the provision of collateral security from the State Bank, together with a guarantee to repay the cash ransom which Bertrand would need to withdraw.

Secondly, he had met Douchert to discuss the most secure means of delivering the cash into the right hands. A previous payment had mysteriously disappeared. Innocent deaths had followed.

Douchert had shrugged his shoulders. "It happens. This is not the Bourse in Paris, you know."

There would be time to deal with Douchert later, if necessary.

Time was short. Bertrand needed a new source of funds, secure transport into and out of Somalia, side arms for his own protection and support from an extraction team, if he could get it.

He called Alix Wenger on board the *Emden*. The young lieutenant would try to persuade his commanding officer to permit him to embark his commandos in the vessel's helicopter, under the pretext of a training exercise.

It was not the operation that had been sanctioned by the high command in Bonn. Wenger was doubtful if he could offer more than logistical support to deliver Bertrand into Bosasso and bring him back. He could supply a weapon for Bertrand's use but they had been ordered to open fire only when the main attack was launched. Bertrand would be left on his own.

Wenger agreed to contact Stedman, the local consul, who had welcomed him so expansively at the cocktail reception. He might be able to assist with the money transfer.

Minutes later, Wenger had called back. Within half an hour Bertrand was in Stedman's cramped office overlooking the commercial harbour. Gone was the loquacious manner that had clothed their first meeting. The consul listened intently to what Bertrand required.

As the local eyes and ears of his government in a sensitive region, he was well accustomed to representing organizations and individuals who needed quiet protection, without arousing the interest of the authorities.

He promised Bertrand that he would find a way. True to his word he did. The two men met again at a dockside coffee shop. Stedman explained that, provided Bertrand's principals could offer him the necessary collateral and guarantee, he would arrange for the cash to be delivered within the day.

Bertrand looked around the consul's office as he counted the notes. The national flag of Germany gave an official stamp to his low level diplomatic operations, but the remainder of the office testified to a workaday operation of an expatriate doing his best on alien shores.

Bertrand shook Stedman's hand. The notes were safely stacked in the holdall he carried.

"No trouble, my friend. We do it regularly. Vessels calling here need cash all the time. Crew wages, food and fresh water, something for the customs officers. It all happens the same way."

"I'm grateful. I'll call you when I get back. Wenger's got the permission he needed. I've at least got some transport."

"Take care down there. As you've seen, nothing's quite as it appears."

Bertrand had hardly needed the second reminder.

He ducked as several further rounds crashed into the timber above his head. It was less than twelve hours since he had bade farewell to Stedman and less than two hours since Wenger and his team had landed him from the helicopter, some three kilometres from the farmhouse. It was there that the handover was to take place.

Now he was alone. He had made the trek over the rough and broken terrain in good time. The house stood beside several skeletal trees, whipped into a sinister shape by the region's violent windstorms. There were two dry stone walls bordering a stone pathway leading to the main wooden door, which was shielded from view by a timber-roofed veranda.

The only outbuilding was the cattle byre in which he was now taking cover. They had instructed him to approach the building carrying the holdall. If there was any sign of others, both he and Simpson would be shot.

It was little comfort to Bertrand to know that Wenger's second in command was watching his every move, through long range binoculars, hidden in the craggy boulder-strewn hillside from which he had just descended. Whether Wenger would breach his orders and bring down fire to support him, Bertrand did not know.

Then, as he had approached the house, the still of the morning had been shattered by the staccato sound of incoming rounds crashing into the cattle byre, only metres from where he lay.

Beside him lay the holdall stuffed with the cash ransom called for, meticulously counted and checked with Stedman's assistance. Next to it lay the stubby shape of a Glock automatic pistol, a toy weapon against the high calibre rifle that was trained on his position.

Bertrand looked up at the blue sky and the yellow desert morning mist that had yet to clear. The sun was obscured by a film of cloud. Everywhere, the weight of the summer heat radiated up from the scorched ground.

He crawled awkwardly to his right to gain a wider view of the ground ahead, and behind him, if the need arose.

Unless they held their fire, or Wenger's men came to his assistance, Bertrand wryly admitted to himself that his prospects of a safe extraction were nil. He was pinned down.

Suddenly, again all was quiet. Bertrand could hear the distant sounds of animals, over the hill and out of view. Then in front of him there was the thunderclap of an explosion, the flash of phosphorous and a dense fog of black smoke.

Bertrand wrapped his arms over his head and eyes. For what seemed an eternity the smoke hung heavily, before the tiniest whiff of breeze started to blow it away. As it did so he lifted his head. Walking towards him with his hands held high was Ronnie Simpson, a bandage wrapped around his right arm. Behind him was a tall man in his mid-thirties in a long robe, bare-headed and brandishing what looked to Bertrand to be a short-barrelled shotgun.

"Monsieur Bertrand. Come out now, it's quite safe. Bring the money and put down your weapon. Walk slowly towards us and no one will be hurt. My men have been ordered to hold their fire."

Bertrand eased himself up. Awkwardly he picked up the bag and walked out of the cattle byre, throwing down the pistol in full view of Simpson's escort, now no more that twenty metres away. The sharp smell of phosphorous still clung to Bertrand's nostrils but the smoke was clearing now.

Simpson's guard nodded and pushed his captive forward. Bertrand placed the bag on the ground. The man stooped, opened it and shouted to the house for another of his men to come out. Then, lowering his weapon, he told Simpson that he was free. He spoke in a shrill distinctive voice in perfect English.

"Forgive me, Monsieur Bertrand. We apologize for causing you and your good friend here so much distress, but when he arrived and told us what you had in mind, we needed to be sure."

Bertrand walked towards Simpson. "Are you OK?"

"It's nothing that a beer won't cure, when you're next buying." Simpson's reply was not as confident as it sounded.

The other man approached. Bertrand saw that his face was pale, with a rough moustache and beard. Simpson stepped aside and gestured towards his erstwhile captor.

"Jean-Yves, I'd better introduce you to this bastard. His name's Douk El

Sanah. He's the leader of this merry band. He says that he and his people are at your disposal."

Bertrand looked into the man's dark eyes. They showed compassion, betrayal and a cold ruthlessness that Bertrand had seen before. The two shook hands.

"By the way, they don't want our money. At least not in the way you imagined. They're going to hand it over to a Catholic Mission Hospital down there."

Bertrand said nothing. Simpson continued. "Our friend will tell you all about himself later. But, believe me, he's no ordinary desert villain. Not many in these parts can shoot like him and have a degree from the States."

* * * * * * * * * *

Tresco, Scilly Isles

Crosfield looked at himself in the mirror. He looked pale, ashen and exhausted. Black smudges underscored his eyes and his cheeks were flushed. He felt himself breathing heavily. His chest continued to give him pangs of pain.

He switched on the shower and hoped that the piercing sensation of the hot water would improve the way he felt. But he knew it would not.

Taking a towel, he wrapped it around himself, walked on to the hotel balcony and sat down at a glass topped table. He poured himself a coffee. The hot breakfast that he had ordered sat untouched. The coffee did little to restore his resolve. His knuckles showed white as he gripped the low stone wall that separated his suite from the garden.

Beyond, clumps of ferns and grasses and several palms, encouraged by the warm subtropical climate of the island of Tresco, swayed gently in the breeze. A few early swimmers walked out of the sea on to a wide sweep of sandy beach.

He sought some relief in the atmosphere; a moment of respite from the self-imposed pressures that were now heaped down on his head. A hasty car journey from London, and an early evening helicopter to the Scilly Isles from Penzance had brought him to an island paradise. But it was a delusion, in the same way as the assignments and conferences over the years at other idyllic islands across the world had been. He had cheated on himself and on others. He had kicked his way to the top and had stayed there. He had connived with the likes of Rahman Mansur. He had also gambled and lost.

A bully he had been, and a creep when it suited. Now he was on the outside. He could feel the cold on the back of his neck, the clammy palms and a sense of naked fear. He felt like his fellow pupils at school, who cowered when he approached. He had seen similar despair on the faces of people whose interests had been cruelly destroyed by a combination of commercial pressure and the arrogance that a powerful legal team could deploy.

All that was behind him now.

He turned back into the suite and surveyed the two items of evidence that had caused him to run. It was nearly eight o'clock. Hugo Jackson would be arriving on the mid-morning helicopter. He had cancelled the meeting at his apartment and left a voice message for Jackson to text a designated number for instructions.

Crosfield picked up his mobile phone in his left hand and the letter in his right. He scarcely needed to remind himself of what they presaged.

The house telephone rang.

"Mr Crosfield. There's a message from the airfield. The helicopter left earlier than scheduled to avoid cross winds. Mr Jackson will be here within twenty minutes."

Crosfield grasped the confidential letter that had been hand-delivered to his private office the previous day. He had almost come to know its contents by heart.

It was unprecedented for the Lord Chief Justice of England to write in personal terms to the senior partner of a major London law firm, calling explicitly for his immediate resignation. But, as Crosfield well knew, he had been treading on deadly ground for too long.

He read the terse wording yet again. The comforting quality of the notepaper and its judicial seal served only to remind him of where he now stood. The letter stated that the Lord Chief Justice had been made aware of the outcome of the recent meeting between Crosfield and representatives of the Justice Department. It went on to say that, following publication of the press release concerning the death of Sir Henry Wilkinson, an anonymous source had contacted the City of London Police.

The source, it was said, had information and documents that would prove beyond doubt that the judge had accepted a significant bribe and had acquiesced in the suppression of critical evidence in the *Globex Mariner* case. The letter indicated that investigations were at an early stage and that police enquiries were proceeding. However, it seemed probable that allegations that had already been raised would be substantiated.

That was not all. The same source had revealed that steps had also been taken to conceal the nature of the vessel's cargo and her destination. This was now the subject of an international investigation headed by the FBI and aided by Interpol in view of the strategic issues involved. Furthermore, in view of the fact that more than one suspicious death had been reported on their soil, enquiries had also been launched by the Royal Saudi Arabian Security Service.

In the light of these issues, the Lord Chief Justice had been obliged to refer the whole matter to the Cabinet Secretary for review. The letter concluded with the cold suggestion that, in the light of the situation as it stood, Crosfield might wish to consider his position. It would be in the interests of all concerned if he were to report to the City of London Police at the earliest opportunity, surrender his passport and assist their ongoing enquiries.

Crosfield felt cold perspiration begin to roll down his neck.

The phone rang again. "It's reception here. Mr Jackson has arrived. Shall we show him up to your suite?"

"Yes. Bring him up."

Crosfield had scarcely planned how to open the meeting with Jackson. He only knew that it had to take place now and not later.

He replaced the letter on the table and clicked the video button of his mobile phone.

The grinning face of Ralph Lennard appeared on the moving image. There was a brief background view of sun-dappled Alpine peaks and verdant meadows on their lower slopes. Then the image switched to the terrace of the sanatorium where Anna was a patient. Two men were seen by her wheelchair, talking to one of her carers.

Lennard's voice-over was clear and to the point. Crosfield's handicapped daughter was well. Of course, nothing would happen to her but the time for payment was shortening by the day.

There was a knock at the door. Jackson walked in and stood uncertainly in the tiny hallway. He wondered yet again whether he should have come. He knew now, without doubt, that Crosfield was a primary player in the *Globex Mariner* conspiracy and he had seen the grim evidence that the case had thrown up.

There had been no opportunity to consult Alan Jenkins. He had been unavailable when Jackson had called. He was mindful of his advice not to rattle the cage. Perhaps agreeing to travel to a clandestine meeting with Crosfield was foolish in the extreme. On the other hand, as with everything else that had occurred, his instinct told him that not to go on would imperil Hedizah even further.

Whether his love had blinded his common sense he could not tell, but, reckless or not, he felt that he had no choice.

Crosfield sensed Jackson's unease, motioning him to the table on the balcony.

"Sit down over here, Hugo."

He was trying to sound affable. Perhaps it was as much to mollify the truth of what he was about to admit, as trying to overcome the uncharacteristic nervousness that he felt in his nephew's presence.

Jackson sat down and looked out over the balcony.

"It's a fine view."

Crosfield cleared his throat and spoke slowly. "You got my message then. Sorry it sounded a bit mysterious."

Jackson nodded. "No problem."

There was a pause, as if Jackson was expecting Crosfield to reveal the purpose of the visit that he had arranged. Crosfield seemed strangely reluctant to do so.

"Have you had breakfast?"

"Yes thanks. At the hotel before I left."

"Good. Can I offer you coffee now or a cold drink?"

"No thanks."

Crosfield pulled up a chair. "Hugo, I'm really not sure whether I should call this a family conference or a business meeting, lawyer to lawyer."

"Uncle or Senior Partner?"

"Precisely."

Crosfield looked out. Clouds were building up over the narrow island protecting the bay. "A storm soon I guess."

"The wind's freshening. It's time to take care, if you're a sailor."

The two lapsed into silence. Crosfield now made up his mind. He reached for the letter and pushed it across the table.

"I think that you should see this."

Jackson took the paper and adjusted his chair.

"I'm afraid it doesn't make attractive reading. It's scarcely a testimonial worth having, I regret to say." Crosfield intended to be sarcastic but instead sounded candid, almost apologetic.

Jackson looked up momentarily and began to read. It was as if he had been given a preview of Counsel's opening speech for the prosecution at a notorious trial at the Old Bailey. The letter laid out the charges plainly for the jury to see. The evidence would follow.

Crosfield was watching him. Jackson looked down, on the pretext of studying the letter again. He felt strangely detached from what he had read, although, from all he knew, there was nothing there that should have surprised him.

It was less than forty-eight hours since he had left his old college at Oxford, and less than twenty-four hours since he had received confirmation that Jenkins had collected the documents. Whether Jenkins was the unconfirmed source to whom the Lord Chief Justice had referred was a matter of conjecture. But, somehow, Jackson felt a sense of relief that the subterfuge that had brought such extraordinary evidence before him had seemingly come to an end. That material, whatever its provenance, was now squarely in the public domain.

What was not, was his relationship with Hedizah, a private passion set against the same background of brutality, treachery and murder to which the letter testified. Jackson looked up.

"You don't look surprised, Hugo."

"I'm not. Should I be?"

Crosfield stared at the younger man. "You guessed or were told?"

Jackson stared back. "Perhaps it was something of both."

Crosfield pulled his chair forward and looked down at the backs of his hands. "I suspected as much. There've been too many coincidences."

Jackson said nothing. Crosfield stood up and stared into the distance.

"It doesn't matter now. It's only a question of time."

Jackson's question seemed almost over eager. "Meaning?"

The tone of Crosfield's reply was resigned. "What's done can't be changed."

Again, Jackson felt that he had responded too quickly. "I'm not sure that I understand."

The reply came without rancour. "You don't need to. I've created this situation. Maybe someone will catch up with me, but not before I've done what has to be done."

Both men fell silent. The clouds had thickened and a dark sky loomed overhead, as the storm started to sweep up the Atlantic approaches. "Let's go in."

Jackson involuntarily stood aside to allow Crosfield to enter the room. The balcony door closed. Rain had already started to cascade down the glass. The two stood and watched. The sun-dappled tropical garden of minutes before was deluged by a flood of rainwater.

Crosfield had made his choice. He thought of the terminal message that Mansur had delivered at their Geneva meeting. But he knew that Mansur would need his services for one last time. Of that he could be sure.

Then, he would be free to take care of what else needed to be done, but this time, on his terms.

Jackson was watching him. It had all happened so suddenly. The two sides of the equation had almost balanced. What he knew and what Crosfield's letter had revealed. But how the two were connected he could not be certain.

Crosfield broke the silence once again. "Hugo. I have no right to ask you but I need your help one final time. You'd have every reason to say no but I hope you won't. Someone's life will depend upon it."

Strangely, Jackson was not surprised at Crosfield's request. Jackson looked at Crosfield's impassive expression. Neither man could guess what the other knew but the implication was all too clear. Jackson's instinct had been right.

If he had not come to see Crosfield, he would not have known. Crosfield had no way out. He recognized that. What Crosfield was saying, however, was that Hedizah's life would be at risk if he did not agree to his request. Jackson knew that he had no choice. Inside the pit of his stomach he felt a sense of deep concern, a warning that he could not ignore.

He put out his hand. Crosfield shook it, almost warmly.

"Tell me what you want me to do."

There was a moment's silence. Then Crosfield spoke, slowly outlining his instructions. Jackson listened and confirmed that he would do what he had been asked.

"Thank you. And Hugo, there's another thing. If I don't get another chance to say so, I'm very sorry about your parents."

Jackson nodded his head and slowly walked to the door.

"I'll await your call."

Crosfield watched him leave.

Chapter Seven

Monte Carlo, Monaco

Hedizah Mansur looked through the tinted side window of the Rolls Royce Silver Cloud as the chauffeur gently eased the vehicle away from the kerb. The ornate gilded portico and the richly lit windows of the Grand Casino started to slip behind them. The tall illuminated palms of the square in front of Monte Carlo's central landmark penetrated the darkness of the late evening. Soft shadows fell as other guests started to leave. There was an air of secure and sustained opulence, reflected in the confident and deferential demeanour of the liveried attendants, as they escorted their charges to awaiting limousines.

"You looked gorgeous, Hedizah. Everyone said so. Hardly anyone could keep their eyes off you."

The mature sound of the well tuned engine almost masked his words.

Mansur touched a switch discreetly placed beside the ample leather rear seat and moved closer. The light dimmed. The vehicle started to make slow headway down towards the main yacht harbour.

Hedizah felt his hand slip down her dress, and gripped the seat. She felt cold in the palms of her hands and a dull pain in her fingers, as she pressed her nails into the soft upholstery. Her body stiffened as his hands moved to her thighs.

The evening momentarily flashed before her eyes. Since the television interview and Mansur's return from his latest trip abroad with Herlov, his attitude towards her had hardened. His demands had been greater. His obsession with what seemed to Hedizah to be a final or determining scheme had become more sinister.

She had arrived at the villa in Villefranche less than an hour before him after her journey from Paris. Sophie had met her and had done everything she could to conceal her departure.

Hedizah's thoughts had careered between the interlude of love and ecstasy that she had shared with Hugo, and the gnawing uncertainty at the identity of the caller who had left the telephone message at the hotel.

Whether this was behind Mansur's change of attitude, she had dared not speculate. But nothing had been said.

Then he had announced that they were to attend and host a gala charity reception in Monte Carlo. It would be an evening of long ball gowns, white tie, champagne, celebrities and the media, set within the sumptuous portals of the Grand Casino. Mansur would watch as others played for stakes that he could dwarf. His attentions would, however, be elsewhere.

The occasion, so soon after the event in London, would cement the name of Rahman Mansur in the minds of the other philanthropic entrepreneurs who would be attending. They too would similarly seek to validate their claims to posterity, amidst the green baize tabletops, the martinet croupiers and the smiling racketeers in their executive suits.

Hedizah knew that just as Hugo remained her hope, her yearning for the future, so she had to continue the pretence with Mansur for the present. Sophie knew as well as she did that Hedizah's life depended on it.

But Mansur had gone further this time. He had demanded that she wore a dress that, he knew, would humiliate her. He had purchased it for the occasion – a black gown, backless with tiny straps, low cut to the point where only a silver brooch drew together the two sides of her costume above the waist, and wide slits revealing her thighs.

It was everything that she hated. Whether it was modesty or religious reserve, Mansur had determined to destroy it. He had flaunted her beauty and her body to an extent that had made her physically sick. She could only keep her composure at the thought of the care and respect that she had found with Hugo.

Suddenly, as Mansur's attentions intensified, the car came to a halt. The lights on the yachts in the harbour were nearer now. The Royal Palace, illuminated in fairy tale splendour, lay immediately ahead.

Mansur pulled himself away. He spoke abruptly. "I have business to attend to here. The car will take you home."

Hedizah glanced out as the car door was opened. She recognized the exterior of the office. She had been there once. It belonged to one of the Globex International offshore corporations. The street light in front of the main entrance shone down, casting a shadow along the pavement.

"Good evening, Miss Hedizah. I hope that you enjoyed your evening. I'm sorry I missed it."

The guttural voice of Max Herlov was unmistakable. As he leant forward, to assist Mansur to step out, he looked at Hedizah with what seemed an air of concern.

"Permit me saying so. You look magnificent."

Hedizah had noticed the look before. She knew nothing about Herlov except that he had been Mansur's right hand man for a number of years. His face told all. He was clearly not a man to cross, and yet, on occasion his eyes said something else. Hedizah could only guess whether it was a sense of guilt, loneliness or even, deep down, a sense of compassion.

As Mansur moved away from the car, Herlov held her glance. "I wish you well. Take care."

Then he was gone. As the car drove off, Hedizah looked back. Herlov was watching the rear of the vehicle and speaking into his mobile phone. The car accelerated up the slope from the harbour through the quiet narrow streets of the principality. Within a short time, they had arrived at the access to the lower Corniche and the winding journey back to Villefranche.

The chauffeur drove swiftly. Hedizah reached for her wrap and settled back into the seat. She felt cold. Thoughts of Hugo dominated her mind but she could not rid herself of the last image of Max Herlov. He seemed to have deliberately shielded himself from Mansur's view.

Soon, she was asleep and awoke only when the car slowed again some forty minutes later. It was near to midnight as the car approached the outer security gate of Mansur's mansion. Ahead lay a tree-lined avenue leading down towards the main house, the office area and the staff quarters. Beyond lay the dark outline of the coast.

Hedizah sat up, expecting the car to enter the complex without stopping. The gates routinely opened electronically when approached by any car belonging to the Globex corporate fleet.

Instead, the car stopped. The chauffeur alighted and picked up the security phone on one of the gate pillars. The arc-light beyond shone down opaquely on the man's face. Hedizah realized, for the first time, that she had never seen him before. She recalled hearing Herlov calling up the car before leaving the casino but had paid no attention at the time. Now she immediately felt a sharp sense of anxiety. Instinctively, she reached for the internal rear door handle. It was locked. Her throat felt dry. She wanted to shout but no sound came.

Hedizah saw the chauffeur nod as he replaced the entry phone. The gates opened and the car drove through. She banged on the connecting glass behind the driver's seat but the man continued to look impassively forward.

The drive to the house took several minutes. The avenue eventually levelled out and the car turned slowly in a wide stone-flagged parking area. The oak-panelled front door of the house was set behind a flint archway covered in bougainvillea.

The car stopped. The chauffeur alighted and walked towards the rear door. Hedizah looked out. There was no other vehicle to be seen. This was unusual. Almost invariably, Mansur insisted that the offices were covered on a twenty-four hour basis by operational or management staff.

The door opened slowly. The man nodded his head.

"Sorry if I gave you a fright, Miss Hedizah. There was some problem with the security access. Mr Herlov warned me by phone before we left Monte Carlo. I should have told you."

Hedizah pulled her wrap more tightly around her. The chauffeur's words did little to allay her concerns. As she stepped from the car, she noticed that lights were shining from the first floor apartment suite that she and Sophie occupied. When she had been out with Mansur in the evening, Sophie always waited for her in the main hallway and they went up together.

Everything seemed too quiet. There were usually people about at most times of day or night but tonight there was no one.

The chauffeur ushered her towards the door. "Please go in. I'll take the car to the garage and come in through the side entrance."

Hedizah nodded and waited for the car to ease away before turning the door handle and entering the house. Sophie was nowhere to be seen. Hedizah looked around the hallway and through the doors into the main reception rooms. She was alone.

Immediately she began to feel a sense of panic gripping her body. She searched frantically and in vain for some familiar feature that might assuage her fear. She looked behind her, thinking for a moment to pull open the main door and run. Once in the garden, she could quickly climb down to the boat dock below, or find somewhere to hide behind the summer house on the terrace. No sooner had she started to turn than she heard the door locked from the outside.

Once again her throat tightened. She was unable to cry out. Then, throwing her wrap aside, Hedizah decided to go up to her apartment suite. Perhaps Sophie was there. Perhaps she had been unwell. Perhaps that was why the lights had been turned on.

She ran up the main winding staircase to a galleried first floor landing, threw open the glass door leading into the hallway and hurried towards her private suite.

There were three rooms before her private entrance. The first door in front of her accessed a kitchen and laundry room. The other two doors were on the right. The first was the entrance to Sophie's own room. It was open.

Hedizah rushed in. Sophie looked at her despairingly at the instant that

Hedizah emerged through the door. Her face was bruised, a thin trickle of blood seeped from the side of her mouth, her blouse was torn and she was gagged tightly by a ligature that bit into her cheeks.

Sophie was kneeling on the floor, forcibly held by two men dressed in black and wearing ski caps and goggles. One gripped her neck and held an automatic pistol to her head.

Hedizah threw her hands over her mouth. But still no cry would come. In an instant the man with the gun leapt forward, grabbed Hedizah by the shoulders, swung her round and pinned her arms behind her back.

As he did so, Hedizah's dress was torn open. The man's hands moved to her waist as he tried to wrestle her to the ground. At the same instant, Sophie, summoning all her strength, forced herself free from the man with the gun. With both arms in front of her, she threw herself protectively towards her mistress.

Hedizah stumbled forward, tripping over her torn dress, and fell to the floor. As she did so the man brought up his pistol and fired one shot at close range. Sophie's head erupted in a flash of blood and bone as her body crashed to the floor. Hedizah, by now lying half naked, finally found the strength to cry out.

The two men recovered their balance and stood over her as she pushed herself, terrified, backwards against the side of a chair.

Both men tore off their caps and goggles and looked down at the dishevelled blood-stained girl writhing at their feet. They then grinned at each other.

Suddenly the door was kicked open. Both men sprung back instinctively. Hedizah grabbed a cushion displaced in Sophie's fall, and struggled to cover her body.

Pytr Majec entered the room slowly. He was taller and heavier than the other two men, who appeared instantly to relax when they saw who it was.

Hedizah recoiled further as she looked up at his scarred and pock marked face.

"So Pytr, as always, you've arrived in time to join us in some fun. You never trusted us to enjoy ourselves on our own, did you? Still, there's time for the three of us before we have to get the young lady out of here. What do you say?"

Majec looked at the two men. They had worked for him in the bloody chaos of the Balkans when Serbian renegades had rewritten the rule book on the horrors and atrocities of war. Daily they had waged that war against women and children, over the bodies of the menfolk whom they had butchered.

Majec hesitated. Hedizah pulled herself frantically into the corner of the room. The two men moved towards her, turning their heads towards Majec.

"Come on. Nothing ever stopped you before."

But, somehow, Majec had grown tired of the vengeful misery that he had inflicted on the innocent. He had fled the region and taken employment with Mansur. He had done his master's bidding when required, but things had changed.

Now, he looked at the terrified form of the young girl less than a metre from his feet. Like so many others had been before, she was vulnerable and defenceless.

From behind his back he brought forward a snub-nosed Heckler and Koch machine pistol.

One of the two men was standing over Hedizah. Majec spoke quietly. "Leave her be." The two men smiled. The one standing over Hedizah knelt down as he started to tear at her dress. He sounded relieved, as he shouted back at Majec, "So that's how you want to play it."

He put his hands on Hedizah's breasts. As he did so, his body collapsed under a single shot from Majec's weapon. The other man wheeled around. Majec kicked him in the groin, stamped on his right instep and fired a second single shot from point blank range into his face.

Hedizah screamed. Majec left the room. He returned a few moments later with a bag and casually tossed it towards Hedizah.

"Please. Dress yourself. I'll be outside. When you're ready, I'm afraid you'll have to leave with us."

Hedizah sobbed uncontrollably. Her dark eyes streamed with tears.

"Don't worry." It was almost more than Majec could bring himself to say. "You'll be safe with me." He quietly closed the door.

* * * * * * * * *

The port of Bosasso, Somalia

Ronnie Simpson watched Douk El Sanah carefully peel back the tarpaulin, its oil skin cover cracked dry by years of exposure to the heat and dust. He looked across at Bertrand, who was seemingly trying to read his thoughts. Both men's faces showed the same sense of doubt.

The three men were standing on a craggy windswept bluff overlooking the broken harbour wall of the port of Bosasso. The Gulf of Aden opened up before them. The calm blue water shimmered in the intensity of the noonday sun, stretching away to the Red Sea in the west and, to the east, the Horn of Africa and the Indian Ocean beyond. Below lay a ramshackle series of wooden buildings that had once formed the headquarters of the port administration. Ahead, an untidy collection of Arab fishing and trading dhows swung gently in the harbour. Some displayed a furled sail at their masthead and others revealed stripped-down motors and open holds. Everywhere the heat hung heavily. A haze of dry dust enveloped several individuals as they made their way between piles of crates, ropes and seafaring equipment littering the wharves.

The tarpaulin slipped to the ground.

The young face of El Sanah broke into a wide smile. "There you are, my friends. What do you think?"

Simpson stood up and passed his hands along the burnished steel of the tripod. Already it was feeling hot to the touch. "I don't believe it."

The Australian's voice could scarcely conceal his incredulity.

El Sanah grinned broadly at the two strangers. His mouth revealed a fine set of gleaming white teeth.

"As you can see, it's a British Army Mark II Vickers General Purpose Machine Gun."

Bertrand looked quizzically at the water-cooling jacket and fingered the belt feed mechanism.

"Well oiled."

El Sanah's enthusiasm seemed undimmed. "Of course it is, Monsieur Bertrand. We have to look after what we have here."

Simpson looked at the younger man and spoke without malice. "Is this a serious weapon or a museum piece?"

Bertrand and Simpson almost anticipated El Sanah's reply.

"Nothing here should surprise you."

Simpson shook his head as El Sanah walked around the weapon and looked at the other two.

"It was captured by the Turks at the siege of Kut."

This time Simpson felt unable to restrain his words. "You have to be joking."

The response was emphatic. "Certainly not."

Simpson persisted. "You mean it really is a First World War weapon?"

El Sanah clapped Simpson on the shoulder "It's ninety years old and still working."

Suddenly his voice became more serious. "It's had many proud owners and been well maintained down the years, as you can see."

All three men laughed aloud.

El Sanah's tone was unchanged. "You've a lot to learn about what we do here, how we've survived and what we hope for."

There was an expectant pause. As suddenly as it had hardened, El Sanah's voice softened. "Let's just say, there's never been a shortage of armourers, from Kabul to Addis Ababa."

The atmosphere lightened again.

Bertrand had listened to the crisply spoken young man talking in faultless English. The day before, he and his men had, without doubt, been prepared to kill both himself and Simpson if anything had gone wrong with the cash delivery. But he could see now that it had been a necessary gesture of good faith that they were seeking, a commitment to a shared cause, almost a form of binding agreement, a bond that needed to be tied.

They had been told that the money had found its way to the Catholic Hospital. But Bertrand remained puzzled at the motives of El Sanah and his band of men. Within days he would be relying on them to carry out the operation that had brought him to the dusty remote terrain where he now found himself.

Two other men, dressed in rough vests and jeans, appeared quietly from behind where the group was standing. They looked impassively at Bertrand and Simpson and spoke hurriedly to El Sanah.

"It's time to move."

Simpson assisted one of the men in manhandling the weapon down a short stony incline towards a battered and paint-scarred Chrysler pick-up truck. Within minutes, the members of the little group were hanging on to the sides and roof of the vehicle as it lurched along a dry, rocky track, towards a low promontory some two kilometres distant.

As they rounded a rocky outcrop, two other bearded men, clad in dirty brown robes, appeared from nowhere and waved them down to the shore.

They had come to an inlet where the soft sound of gentle waves on the sandy beach gave an unreal quality to the scene that greeted them. Some 300 metres off shore lay the twisted and rusted form of the wreck of a coastal freighter. The shell plating, in way of the main deck, was open to the sea. The bridge and accommodation lay gutted and buckled, and the funnel and main mast leant outboard at a crazy angle.

The contrast between the tranquil idyll of the deserted bay and the distorted shipwreck was not lost on any of the men, as they stared out to sea.

It was El Sanah who broke the silence.

"It's how things are here. Beauty and ugliness sit side by side. We've grown up with it. It's been the same for decades."

Bertrand spoke slowly. "I'm not sure that I understand."

Bertrand looked at the younger man. He saw integrity, intelligence and a sense of mission. He had always been suspicious of the idealists whom he had met during his years with the Legion in Africa and elsewhere. Zealots and bigots, in his view, had agendas and motives more suited to their paymasters than the wretched people on the ground whose interests they professed to protect.

Perhaps he had judged them harshly. Perhaps if he looked closely in the mirror and asked himself what had persuaded him to accept his current mission, he would find that the answer did not come easily. Maybe it was a mixture of motive, opportunity and perhaps a desire to try to put things to rights, at least in a small way.

El Sanah pointed out into the bay. His voice now assumed a note of command.

"Watch this, gentlemen, if you please."

Within the few minutes that they had stepped down from the truck, an untidy squad of some further six or seven men had run up the short incline from the beach. They carried the Vickers down to the shore. As Bertrand and Simpson looked down, they could see it being mounted on the decked bow of a low cutter drawn up on the shingle. The boat's heavy-duty outboard motor idled in the shallow water. Two of the men returned to collect several ageing and rusty ammunition boxes.

Simpson looked at them suspiciously. "You're going to tell me that the rounds have been fashioned by your friends specifically for this old relic."

El Sanah's expression changed again. His reply came lightly. "Of course, old style .303 bullets manufactured in the proper style."

Simpson's voice sounded doubtful. "I believe you."

The Australian looked at Bertrand, who raised his eyebrows.

El Sanah's eyes for an instant seemed to show a sense of hurt but his reply was quietly defiant. "You still look doubtful. Trust us. We won't let you down. I swear."

"I know you won't." Bertrand's tone now sounded rueful, almost apologetic.

El Sanah sighed and raised his arms. "Follow me. I'll show you why you should believe me."

El Sanah's tone told Bertrand that a barrier had been reached. He knew that a fragile bond of trust could be shattered by an innocent wrong move, an unexpected tone of voice or a misconceived gesture. In the situation that they faced, the position could change in seconds. He had seen men die when, only moments before, their assailant had been a friend in a foreign land or even a fellow foot soldier. This was such a moment.

"We don't doubt you and your people. We know what you can do and why you're doing it with us. You must forgive a couple of weary old soldiers tramping over your land looking for a bit of adventure."

The younger man wheeled around. The smile had returned. Perhaps the moment had passed. Bertrand was not so sure.

They had reached the foot of the incline. A second boat, with a curved prow and low waterline, was being readied. An older, bearded man, with a red scarf and battered flak jacket revealing tough, muscular, tattooed forearms, seemed to be acting as quartermaster.

He waved cheerily and beckoned to Bertrand and Simpson to join him. The three men shook hands and peered over the boat's sleek wooden frame. On the narrow decking below, another man was carefully prising open several lightweight steel crates and extracting their contents.

Within minutes, the cases were unpacked. The man displayed a formidable armoury of automatic weapons, grenades and ordinance still bearing testimony to their provenance; armaments factories from China and North Korea to the Ukraine and Georgia.

"Are you satisfied?"

Bertrand looked around. El Sanah was now smiling gleefully and holding a whistle to his lips.

"It's time to start. I'm giving the order to embark in two minutes."

Bertrand glanced at Simpson. There was doubt in his eyes too. Perhaps the all important moment of danger may have passed and trust been restored but, when it came to the real thing, they would adhere to the old maxim of keeping their eyes forward and back.

El Sanah motioned Bertrand and Simpson back up the beach. He glanced at his watch, waited and then gave a shrill blast.

Six men appeared from nowhere and scrambled into the two boats. In each, a helmsman was already on station and the outboard engines on standby. The boats powered into life, leaving a surge of water in their wake as they raced outwards from the shore towards the narrow headland, to the right of where the three men were standing.

A swathe of rough water hit the beach. The bows of each of the boats curved upward, slicing through the calm sea. The crews ducked down as the spray raked the still air.

Suddenly, all was quiet. With the roaring sound of the engines gunned down, the sea once again was almost tranquil.

Bertrand could see the helmsmen in both boats raise their arms. He glanced at El Sanah whose head was lowered, still peering at his watch. Seconds later he gave two further long blasts on the whistle.

The response was instantaneous. The boats roared back into life and were shortly racing across the bay, describing a wide arc to the seaward side of the wreck. In what seemed only seconds, the first boat halted at the starboard stern of the old vessel and the other boat took up station on the port side, opposite the bridge wing.

Suddenly, in response to the crack of a yellow smoking flare, one of the crew of the first boat opened fire with the Vickers gun, sweeping the foredeck with a deadly clatter of machine gun rounds. On the other side, the crew fired several rocket-propelled grenades at the superstructure, followed by the dull crump of a shoulder-fired surface missile.

It took less than half a minute for the central topsides structure of the vessel to catch fire. Thick black smoke and flames rapidly enveloped the hulk. As the fire took hold, each boat drew close to the vessel. Scaling shackles and ropes were thrown up, and each boat disembarked a three-man boarding party.

A red flare signalled that the men were aboard. The exercise was over. The boats drew close. The men disembarked slowly. The wreck was left smouldering, her steelwork amidships already splitting and buckling under the intense heat.

El Sanah called his men back to shore. He motioned Bertrand and Simpson to sit down and await preparation of the midday meal on the open fire that was starting to kindle.

"Arab coffee or juice? Which would you prefer?"

The slow distinctive voice of an elderly man wearing crisp white robes and a red checked headdress contrasted strangely with the cacophony and chaos that had prevailed just moments before.

"May I ask you a question?" Bertrand spoke softly. It was as if El Sanah was expecting to be asked for an explanation.

"Please feel free."

His words came slowly. "How did you find yourself here, fighting a private war with men under your command? What do you expect to achieve? Why did you agree to assist us?"

His questions sounded more earnest than Bertrand had intended. He wiped his forehead and reached for the desert forage cap that Simpson passed him.

El Sanah looked into the distance. "This is a harsh place. It always has been. The earliest Christians lived only 300 kilometres from here. But from time immemorial, all this land has seen is death, starvation and tribal conflict that left poverty and destitution in its wake."

Bertrand was tempted to interpose that the young man's comments need not be confined to Somalia. It was a tale that all Africa knew too well. He decided to hold his tongue.

El Sanah continued in a matter-of-fact, almost resigned voice. "The last decades have been worse than ever. Foreign states have sponsored their own warlord to gain control of any area of strategic value to them. Sudan, Ethiopia and activists from across the Islamic world have all come and gone."

The young man paused. His tone hardened once more. "They leave nothing but smashed villages, burnt crops, no water and the detritus of modern war. Even the mighty United States came and left."

Simpson listened impassively. Bertrand sensed his mood. "What brought you back?"

El Sanah looked at the ground. Bertrand could not be sure and looked away. It was a private moment. He had seen many brave men cry one last time. He hoped that for this young man it might be different.

"My mother was from Kenya, my father from India. They met and fell in love when they were both studying at the University of Cairo."

"Go on." Bertrand's tone was gentle, encouraging.

"They went to America where I was born and grew up. Both had known poverty as children. They came here under a United Nations programme to run a school and clinic. I never saw them again. They loved the people. They felt a sense of destiny amidst all this."

It was Simpson who interposed. "What happened?"

The reply came in a measured, dignified tone. "Both killed – shot dead and their house burned down around them."

Bertrand and Simpson looked at each other. Before either could speak again, El Sanah continued, this time with hatred in his voice. "It seems that their local sponsor changed sides without telling them."

Simpson spoke first. "I'm very sorry, mate. Are you here for revenge or to put matters to rights, if you can?"

El Sanah stood up. He looked at the other men, who were seated beside him and had been listening to the conversation, without understanding.

His reply seemed to Bertrand almost to lack conviction. "Both, in a way, I suppose, but mainly to help those who, without our efforts, would die by the hundreds."

Bertrand felt that he had to ask the question. "Even if that involves piracy, ransom or murder?"

"Yes, if it's necessary. If it helps to save lives, restore a sense of tradition and give a meaning to this place for the future, the answer is yes. That's why I'm willing to help you."

The still of the midday was interrupted by the clatter of Bertrand's satellite phone. He listened and then snapped the unit closed. "We'll need that help sooner than we thought."

* * * * * * * * *

Keith Michel

The Mediterranean Sea

The dull throb of the *Aegean Dolphin*'s main engines gave little comfort to Georgios Milakis. As he peered over the starboard side bridge wing, he could see the vessel's wake describe a tender curve, her stern navigation lights showing sharply against the dark of the night.

"All secure." The voice of the First Officer came over the bridge tannoy.

It seemed only a short time ago that he had received orders about the rendezvous. The call had told him that this was to take place off the eastern coast of the island of Malta. Once the arrangements had been accomplished the vessel was to make full speed to Tripoli to load her cargo. No other details had been provided.

Several hours outbound, Milakis had received a radio telephone call telling him the course that he was to lay and the positional coordinates where the vessel was to stop. Milakis realized immediately that whatever purpose lay behind his orders, carrying them out would be dangerous in the extreme.

The satellite weather forecast showed strong squalls and heavy wave and sea conditions in the area where the vessel was to heave-to. There was no safe anchorage position, nor available shelter from the land. He only hoped that whoever was navigating the vessel with whom they were to rendezvous was prepared for what he was likely to find.

The weather had been worse than expected but the *Aegean Dolphin* had made good speed and passage. The vessel had borne the conditions well. Whatever else had happened at the shipyard, there had been no attempt to pare down the expense of the vessel's technical overhaul. The rendezvous time had twice been changed and the radio officer had been ordered to set up a secure communications link with the other vessel. Special call signs had been established. Milakis suspected, but could not be sure, that the other vessel would be an ocean-going motor cruiser. If so, she would be fast, highly powered, low in the water and bristling with the latest maritime technology. He could only guess at the purpose of what was intended.

It was pitch black when the lights of the other vessel were spotted by a bridge lookout through a torrential rain storm after the vessel had moved into radar range. The *Aegean Dolphin* was beginning to pitch and roll heavily. Slowly the other vessel began to close. She was an ocean-going motor yacht, as he had expected.

Despite the worsening conditions, Milakis managed to turn the *Aegean Dolphin* to provide a leeward side. The smaller vessel bucked and tossed in the waves as her navigators struggled to bring her alongside.

The deck lights of the *Aegean Dolphin* had been switched on and the beams of two spotlights cut through the swirling rain to reveal the sleek form of the suncruiser. The *Globex Seaquest* had been built to withstand most sea states, but neither vessel was equipped to easily deal with the transfer of the yacht's crew and their prisoner in the conditions encountered.

The commander of the *Globex Seaquest* did his best to bring his craft hard up against the *Aegean Dolphin*. The buffeting waves risked rending open the thinly structured sides of the yacht against the surging steel plates of the larger vessel.

Milakis had no choice. He took the Chief Officer, Bosun and several seamen forward on to the main deck. Wrapped in oilskins and capes, after several abortive attempts they managed to secure a line to the bow of the yacht.

A change in the wind direction swung the *Globex Seaquest* hard against the midships section of the *Aegean Dolphin*. A second line was secured and a steel roped ladder thrown over the side.

Majec was the first to board the *Aegean Dolphin*. As soon as he had done so, the wind direction changed again, causing the yacht to rise up and crash down in an eddy of seawater. Majec called to his men from the shelter of the covered companionway along the *Aegean Dolphin*'s main deck.

There was no time to be concerned about securing the lines. What they all now faced was a rapidly worsening situation where lives were at risk and the entire transfer operation was under threat.

Milakis pulled himself to the side of the vessel and looked down. Two men were holding onto a slim, lightly dressed figure. Milakis could see that it was a girl. She was desperately gripping the bottom rung of the ladder as it swung uncontrollably in the troughs of the waves that were hammering the sides of both vessels.

Then, for an instant, he saw her face. A man on the deck of the *Globex Seaquest* was fastening a rope around her waist as one of the deck hands on the *Aegean Dolphin* threw down another line with a securing clip.

He had just made the clip fast when a surge of water tore his hands away and flung him back on the deck. Milakis could see that the girl was frozen with fear. Her arms were locked tightly around the ladder. Her head was pushed forward in a vain attempt to protect her face from the swirling wind and sea. The smaller vessel bucked suddenly and the forward securing line snapped, causing the bow of the *Globex Seaquest* to sheer away.

The girl's terrified scream could be heard above the roar of the wind and waves. The rope ladder started to swing outboard. Another crew member from the yacht grasped his way forward to try to climb on to the ladder and pull the girl upwards. As he did so, the yacht swung back, threw him from the deck against the side of the *Aegean Dolphin* and then into the water between the vessels, which immediately closed over him.

Milakis caught Majec's eye as they both peered downwards into the swirling sea. A wave of water knocked Majec back on to the deck. At the same instant Milakis made his decision. He grabbed a life vest from the deck rail, hurled the securing line towards the Bosun and climbed up and over the ship's side.

Below, the ladder was swinging free. The girl was still gripping the bottom rung, her face set as if a death mask. Suddenly there was a further sharp crack and the second line to the yacht snapped. It swung upwards, narrowly missing Milakis, as he desperately fought to lower himself down. He could see several faces above him in the gleam of the spotlights.

Slowly he edged his way down. His freezing hands gripped the sides of the rope ladder. The girl's body looked limp. Milakis forced himself somehow to quicken his descent.

The *Globex Seaquest* was now well away from the side of the *Aegean Dolphin*. Milakis could hear the snatched sounds of the yacht's auxiliaries, as the crew battled to restart the main engine and drive the vessel into open water.

The girl's face looked up. She struggled to push her numbed hands towards the next rung. Milakis was almost above her now.

Suddenly he heard a deep throb as the engines of the *Aegean Dolphin* started to power up. He felt a surge as the turbines thrust the vessel forward. At the same time he could feel the vessel starting to turn. In an instant, he realized that the helmsman and engineers had seen that unless the vessel got underway, he would be lost and the girl with him.

In a matter of seconds only the rope ladder fell back against the vessel's side. It gave a moment of respite from the wind and sea

Milakis could see that the *Globex Seaquest* had manoeuvred around the bow of the *Aegean Dolphin* and into comparatively calmer water.

He was now next to the girl on the ladder. He pulled the rope around her waist towards him. Snatching at the line from above him and swinging free, he managed to secure the clip. He started to pull her upwards, slowly, painfully, rung by rung.

Within minutes, hands reached down and they were both pulled over the rail on to the main deck. The girl slumped forward.

Milakis caught a glimpse of her dark eyes, frozen with fear and cold, her face bruised from the wind and swell, her body limp with fatigue, and her clothes soaked through.

Majec had regained his balance. He bent over Hedizah and felt her pulse.

His words were lost in a squall of rain sweeping the deck. "She's alive."

Milakis struggled to his feet. He called the Bosun who was now hoisting up the ladder.

"I need to get to the bridge. Take her to her cabin."

The old Filipino seafarer called one of the deckhands to secure the ladder. Then he gently picked up the girl in both arms and made towards the main deck entrance to the accommodation.

Majec and Milakis eyed each other.

"Well done, Captain. That was a brave thing to do. I'll get the steward to look after her."

Strangely, Milakis felt that the words were well meant. He wondered why. It was as if the gaoler and his charge were now on the same side. But Milakis doubted that the moment would last.

The vessel was underway now and Milakis made his way to the bridge to resume command. Majec followed him.

The weather started to abate. Milakis expected that Majec would want him to radio the yacht, to steam for a few miles and then turn around to try to pick up the rest of the crew of the *Globex Seaquest*.

Milakis picked up the bridge binoculars. He could see the other vessel starting to turn and figures running out on to the deck. Majec looked out impassively and down at his watch.

The two men eyed each other. Then, as Milakis raised the binoculars a second time, the night sky was lit up by a blinding flash. The shock waves from the explosion less than 200 metres away reached the bridge of the *Aegean Dolphin*. Instruments shook. Two outer windows cracked and shattered. Burning debris crashed down into the water.

The *Aegean Dolphin* continued to pick up speed. Milakis looked to Majec for instructions.

What remained of the fractured hull of the *Globex Seaquest* continued to burn fiercely. Of her crew there was no sign.

Milakis suddenly felt Majec's face next to his own.

"I hope that I can still count on you, Captain." The voice was mocking now. Milakis shook himself back to the present. He tried to rub the tiredness from his eyes. He knew that Majec had detonated the charge that destroyed the motor yacht and what remained of the crew on board. Majec had said that he had enough men to control the *Aegean Dolphin*. The remainder were dispensable.

Milakis set a course for the port of Tripoli. The vessel had been ordered to arrive at the military port at dawn.

Port operations took less than six hours. Milakis and the crew were confined to their cabins, as military personnel from the terminal, under Majec's supervision, loaded the vessel's cargo.

Milakis had decided that those who had provided the satellite phone secreted in his cabin needed to know what had occurred. Confinement to his quarters during loading at Tripoli provided the opportunity.

Once Milakis had seen the name of the *Globex Seaquest* on the name of the motor yacht he had immediately realized what his voyage was all about. There had been rumours, nothing more, about the fate of the *Globex Mariner* and her cargo in the Red Sea some six months before. There had been talk in seamen's bars that somehow the real story had been covered up. No one knew. But there was talk.

Now it was clear to Milakis. He could only speculate about the components of the cargo being loaded on his vessel at Tripoli, but the surrounding evidence pointed to a clandestine military-type shipment. His orders were to make full speed for Alexandria, to transit the Suez Canal with the first available convoy, make fast passage down the Red Sea and await orders in the Gulf of Aden.

Then he had recognized Hedizah Mansur. The steward had told him that she had survived her ordeal and was asleep. Her cabin had been locked as instructed. One of Majec's men was patrolling outside.

He had thought little of the rescue. He had seen it as merely part of his job. The call on the satellite phone was brief. He had no inkling of the identity of the man to whom he spoke and he had no clear idea of what he intended to do. What he did know, however, was that his own salvation, that of his crew and the life of the young woman now similarly incarcerated onboard, almost certainly depended on whatever he decided.

The instructions that he received during the call surprised him. At a given position, Milakis must ensure that the Chief Engineer disabled the main and auxiliary engines for at least two hours. Nothing more had been said.

* * * * * * * * * *

The Duchy of Luxembourg

Emil Douchert stretched uncomfortably. He looked at his watch, picked up his briefcase and travel bag and headed for the line of taxis. There was no queue, and within minutes the cab was moving away from the imposing glass canopy in front of the main railway station in the Duchy of Luxembourg. The traffic slowed as it approached the business centre. Early morning mist hung over the imposing gothic castle and enveloped the parkland in the valley that ran through the city.

The pause gave him time to reflect on the last twelve hours. He knew the risks that he had run to let it be known that Bertrand was sending Simpson down into Somalia. But, like everything he had done since his enforced expatriate life had begun he had needed cash to feed an ever-worsening drink and drug addiction.

Douchert had somehow managed to maintain the outward pretence of running a legal practice in Djibouti. In reality, his very presence depended on his willingness to permit his office to be used to give a cloak of legality to transactions that elsewhere would not have proved possible.

That was how he had first come to know of Rahman Mansur. It had been a familiar story. There had been an unannounced visit, the threat of exposure, the non-negotiable fee and the complicit acceptance that non-compliance with instructions received would result in his certain death.

He had not been told any details. His task had been solely to provide a conduit for a series of payments to officials in Saudi Arabia to ensure that a coastguard investigation into the loss of a vessel in the Red Sea was suitably compromised.

Not for the first time in the deepening moods of depression that his drink and drug habit had forced upon him, he suspected that the illicit funds that he had been asked to legitimise comprised a bounty for murder.

Douchert had nowhere else to go. His office had become what passed for his home. It had been late in the evening. He was barely sober. The caller stated that Rahman Mansur wished to speak with him personally. He would receive the call in fifteen minutes. The caller's tone revealed that he had no choice.

Mansur stated that he was speaking on a secure line. Douchert should be aware that what was to follow was to remain secret and confidential. Mansur had sent one of his staff to Djibouti to shadow Douchert with orders to kill him if there was the slightest doubt in his mind that Mansur's instructions were not being carried out to the letter.

It appeared that Mansur's Globex organization was involved in the sale and transportation by sea of a sensitive cargo whose destination was undisclosed. An unexpected event had occurred that, if left unchecked, would imperil the operation. Whilst Mansur would take steps to neutralize the threat, the immediacy of the situation required that a cash deposit of twenty million United States dollars be established within forty-eight hours, in a manner that was untraceable through normal financial sources.

The arrangement should permit drawdown of the money at a nominated branch of a European bank, whose identity had yet to be revealed. Douchert was to use his resources to set up a secure financial instrument to achieve this. His fee, conditional on a successful and untraceable payment, would be 100,000 dollars. He was to have all the necessary arrangements in place and to attend a meeting with Mansur and one of his advisers within twenty-four hours.

"Number Four, Rue du Commerce."

Douchert alighted from the taxi, paid the fare and looked both ways down the narrow cobbled street. The door in front of him gave access to a mid-Nineteenth Century Belgian merchant's house. It was Douchert's first visit to Europe for years. He had almost forgotten how long its history was. In Djibouti no one was interested in the past. The present was too uncertain.

He punched in the security code that he had been given, and entered slowly. The vestibule contained an ornate gilded mirror and several antique Chinese vases on a highly polished walnut table. There was the sound of voices in a room to the right. He knocked and carefully pushed open the door.

A small, well fitted boardroom had been created at the rear of the house, which opened out on to a leafy garden, bound by high red-brick walls. The sun glinted through long French windows, which were slightly ajar.

He recognized Max Herlov. He was the man who had visited him before. Douchert recalled only too well that Herlov had made him coldly aware of what was expected of him in the wake of the loss of the *Globex Mariner*.

Douchert also recognized Mansur from his many media photographs. In person, he looked greyer, thinner in the face and hair and with narrower and meaner-looking eyes than he had imagined.

He did not know the third man who had been standing up, looking out of the window, but he too looked drawn and haggard. His cheeks were hollow and eyes sunken with dark smudges below them. The man spoke in clipped tones to introduce himself.

"Michael Crosfield."

Crosfield motioned him to sit down. Herlov nodded to Douchert. His tone was surprisingly formal.

"You've spoken to Rahman Mansur but you have not met, I believe?"

Douchert nodded nervously. Mansur looked up from the papers in front of him but said nothing. The four men sat down at the narrow table opposite each other.

Mansur spoke first. "What have you got for me, Maître Douchert?"

Douchert placed his briefcase in front of him and extracted a number of carefully ordered files and documents.

"May I see them, please?" Crosfield spoke quietly.

Douchert hesitated. Mansur's reply was swift and cutting. "Mr Crosfield is a lawyer too. I've been his major client for ten years or more but things have unfortunately changed, Michael, haven't they?"

The name had sounded familiar when he introduced himself. Then it came to him. He recalled immediately that Michael Crosfield was the Senior Partner of Layton and Springer, the international firm of lawyers based in the City of London. In days long forgotten he thought he could remember dealing with one of their young associates.

Douchert was cautious and hesitated again. Mansur looked at him coldly and spoke with a mild sneer in his voice.

"Monsieur Douchert. You can trust Mr Crosfield. After all, you're two of a kind. You're both lawyers on the run, fugitives from your home jurisdictions. Isn't that a fair description, Michael?"

Herlov looked blankly at Crosfield. He needed to know where he stood. Things had changed since the meeting in Leipzig but there was no going back now.

Hedizah Mansur was on the *Aegean Dolphin*. All depended on whether Pytr Majec could be trusted to keep what he knew from Rahman Mansur.

Herlov had made his choice. What troubled him was that Mansur was acting as if he suspected nothing. Herlov, not for the first time, began to question whether his decision to ally himself with Crosfield as a means of saving his own skin had been ill-conceived.

Mansur must have noticed the silence.

"As I said, Michael, our friend from Djibouti has nothing to fear from us, does he?"

Crosfield bit his lip. He felt his shirt tighten across his back, his palms dampen and a tingling pain in his stomach. He needed no reminding of his position.

Mansur continued mercilessly. "I suppose that you should confess to Maître Douchert that you are unlikely to be returning to your office, at least in the near future. It's an open secret I'm told. The Justice Ministry has issued an international warrant for your arrest on charges of fraud, and more particularly, my friend, because you failed to surrender your various passports in answer to a police warrant."

Crosfield leapt to his feet and threw himself at Mansur. "Fuck you, you bastard. Without me, without what I've done for you, you'd still be selling propane off the back of a shitting pick-up in Karachi."

Mansur thrust his hands up towards Crosfield's throat and forced him back towards his seat. Herlov made to intervene but sat back as he saw Crosfield slumped in his chair.

Crosfield lifted his head. He was tired and not a little frightened, but he remained determined to see through what he had gambled on, perhaps for the last time.

He needed no reminder of the dangerous predicament in which he found himself. It had perhaps been inevitable that, at some point, he would have to face a future, alone, a fugitive or worse.

But his luck had held. Following his meeting with Jackson, Crosfield had received an anonymous phone call. He immediately left the hotel.

With the aid of a cash bribe he had secured a seat on the last helicopter flight of the day to Penzance. He had then taken a taxi to the municipal airport and boarded the first available flight to the continent.

Having arrived in St Malo on the French coast, he had received a text message from Max Herlov, stating that the meeting with Mansur was to be in Luxembourg, the following day.

Using a driver's licence in an assumed name, together with a passport issued by the Republic of Panama, he paid for a hire car that would never be returned. He had arrived in Luxembourg earlier in the morning.

Mansur looked around him. Crosfield noted that his patience and temper were wearing thin. He spoke angrily.

"Can we get back to the purpose of this meeting? I don't want to have to waste my time with you any longer than I have to."

Crosfield looked down at the table. Herlov sat with his eyes staring out of the window.

Douchert cleared his throat.

Doubts about what he had been told were beginning to worry him. The years of double-dealing, deceit and self-abuse in a faraway land were suddenly starting to fall away. For reasons that he did not know, nor could understand, the integrity and independence that had been his inspiration, as a young lawyer in France long ago, were beginning to return.

"I know that it's not my business to enquire, Mr Mansur. I can, however, explain what I have achieved so far. I believe that it adequately protects your interests and complies with your instructions."

He hesitated as if thinking better of continuing.

Mansur looked at him. His eyes revealed his hidden anger but he knew that he needed Douchert to deliver. He breathed deeply and gave a thin smile, nodding to Douchert.

"Please continue."

Douchert cleared his throat and spoke slowly. Somehow he was surprised at his own self-confidence. "I don't mean to exceed my authority but, given the unusual nature of the transaction and its urgency, it would help me if you could tell me what has happened."

He stopped speaking and then, almost as an afterthought, continued. "It's so that I can be prepared for any questions that I might face when we complete the banking documents tomorrow."

He was expecting a serious rebuff, if not a violent one, but none came.

Mansur stared down at the table. He spread his hands in front of him and then stood up. Walking across to the windows, he looked up at the high brick walls and turned to the three men in front of him.

"The answer to your question, Mâitre Douchert, is that unless this payment is made, I have reason to believe that a project in which I have invested greatly and in which I believe passionately will be compromised. I cannot allow that to happen."

Crosfield and Herlov avoided each other's eyes. Neither could be certain whether Mansur's sharp glance was directed at either or both of them, or neither.

Douchert had little doubt that what Mansur wanted could be achieved. He had been a fool to risk all for a meagre cash commission for leaking details of Simpson's secret trip into Bosasso. He knew that Bertrand would realize who had broken trust. When he arrived back in Djibouti someone would be waiting. He had to have something to trade.

He persisted. "Forgive me, Sir, but if I am to complete this transaction successfully, I need to know what lies behind it. If I don't, others may have obtained information, maybe false information, which they will surely use to their advantage."

Mansur's expression was unchanged. He looked once more out into the tiny garden and pulled at the florid drapes that shaded the room from the bright sunlight. He turned round again.

"I accept what you say, Mâitre Douchert. You have a right to know in order to do what I'm asking of you."

Crosfield shifted uncomfortably in his chair. He was beginning to perspire. He felt cold sweat running down his neck and forehead. He dared not move to wipe it away.

"Gentlemen." Mansur folded his arms. He spoke with a combination of disdain and authority. "I hope that I can trust you all. I also hope that no one here has betrayed that trust."

The atmosphere tightened.

"Assuming that I am right, I can tell you that my wife, Hedizah, is missing; the French police have appointed a magistrate to investigate the murder of her maid in my house and the theft of a motor yacht moored at my private dock."

No one spoke.

"Additionally, the message that I have received states that harm will come to my wife if a ransom payment of twenty million dollars is not made within the due time."

There was another pause as Mansur walked back towards the table.

"I hope that satisfies you, Mâitre Douchert. Now, please tell me how you propose to deal with the payment."

Douchert nodded, inclined his head and reorganized the documents in front of him. He again spoke with confidence.

"I believe that we can deal with this by a specific form of letter of credit."

He looked apprehensively at Crosfield. Whatever his position now, Michael Crosfield had been the senior partner of a formidable firm of international lawyers. There was little that he did not know about the documentary formalities of global finance.

Douchert continued. "The credit has been opened through the State Bank of Djibouti, which is a client of mine."

Douchert felt Herlov giving him a searching glance. Herlov pulled out a pen and a piece of paper from his pocket. Mansur watched Douchert closely as he went on.

"They will issue the credit in favour of a private bank, owned by a member of one of the ruling clans in Saudi Arabia. The bank has an office in Kuwait. That bank will issue a second letter of credit to an offshore bank with a post box address here in Luxembourg. They in turn will confirm the credit to a local branch of the Tyroler Landesbank NV in Austria where the cash payment can be made against a coded security exchange."

Herlov appeared to be noting down the key points. Having done so, he replaced the pen in his pocket.

Douchert looked up at Mansur's urbane expression. The smile was unchanged. Mansur nodded to Herlov, who began to push back his chair.

"There are only two further things that I want to say."

The other three men at the table looked at each other. For the first time, a real sense of menace was present in the room

"The first is that all that matters to me is the mission, for which I have worked all these years. It has to succeed. Nothing else matters. That includes, in case you need to know, the fate of my wife. The second is that, if any one of you has had any part to play in this charade, I give you my word that you will die."

A deathly silence descended. Then, as quickly, it disappeared, as Mansur's mood suddenly lightened again. The smile returned.

"I assume then that the meeting is over. We have completed all our business, I believe."

Douchert was hesitant to speak again but there was a final detail that he needed to clear.

"I'm sorry, but there is one more thing. I need someone to deliver a power of attorney to the bank in Kuwait."

He paused before continuing. "I would go myself but I don't think that it would be wise."

There was no response. Douchert looked across the table.

"Mr Crosfield. I don't suppose you have anyone who could fly there tonight? The document is here already engrossed and executed."

Crosfield looked up. He saw Mansur's dark eyes peering into his own.

"I do, as a matter of fact. One of our young associates will be able to help you."

He continued quickly, as if trying to disguise what he was about to say. "His name is Hugo Jackson. He'll be here in an hour, Maître Douchert, if you could wait."

Mansur stiffened, looked at Crosfield and Herlov, and walked towards the door.

"Goodbye, Michael. I don't think that we shall be seeing each other again."

Crosfield looked up and said nothing. Inexplicably he felt an inner sense of relief. For a moment he almost felt in charge of his own destiny once more. His words came slowly this time. "I don't suppose we will."

Mansur and Herlov walked out. The door closed. Douchert noticed that Herlov had left the piece of paper on which he had been writing. He picked it up. The front page contained some indecipherable notes regarding the letter of credit. For no good reason, he turned the paper over. On the reverse side, Herlov had written two words, *Aegean Dolphin*.

Douchert reached into his pocket for his mobile phone. There was a text message asking him to call Karl Stedman at his office in Djibouti. He did so. When he had finished, he was alone. Crosfield had gone.

Chapter Eight

En route Dubai to Djibouti

Jackson looked down through the window as the aircraft began a slow turn to the east. Sunlight was already streaming into the cabin. Below, he could see the dark rocky outcrops of the desert terrain and the jagged lines of the low cliffs and shoreline of the Red Sea. The sharp rays of the early dawn reflected on the pale blue water, revealing strangely patterned sand spits and, beneath the surface, the exotic shapes and colours of pristine coral reefs.

Suddenly the plane began to bank and, as quickly again, to level out and start another turn.

"Ladies and gentlemen, the Captain has received a weather report from Djibouti. It appears that visibility at the airfield is presently too restricted for normal landing procedures, due to an unexpected sandstorm. We have been asked to enter a holding pattern until the storm clears. We hope that the delay will not be too long."

The announcement continued by instructing the passengers on the first flight of the day from Dubai to Djibouti to fasten their seat belts and sit back.

Jackson breathed deeply and closed his eyes. He had enjoyed little sleep over the previous forty-eight hours. That it had been the most turbulent period of his life now seemed immaterial.

Jackson had agreed to assist Crosfield for the one last assignment that he had requested. He did so because his instincts at the time had told him that, unless he accepted, Hedizah's position might worsen.

But there had been another reason as to why he had travelled to Luxembourg on Crosfield's instructions. Whilst there was no logical connection, the timing was too much of a coincidence.

Jackson had returned to his apartment in London immediately after the

Tresco meeting. He was becoming concerned. Two calls and several text messages to Hedizah's mobile phone had gone unanswered.

Anxiety for her safety had been replaced by cold fear. He had felt helpless. The longer the silence went on, the greater his concerns increased. He made one further desperate attempt to contact her. He called the villa in Villefranche. He hoped at least that he might be able to leave an oblique message with Sophie. But somehow he was doubtful.

His doubts proved well-founded, when an answering machine stated that, owing to technical problems in the area, all calls were being rerouted to Globex International's local office in Monte Carlo.

There was a list of mobile phone numbers to contact. Hedizah's was not among them. Jackson began to realize that Hedizah's disappearance must somehow, however remotely, be connected with the issues surrounding Crosfield's flight and the ramifications of the *Globex Mariner* trial. But there remained no hard evidence.

By chance, he had boarded an earlier train than he had intended from Brussels to Luxembourg. He had time to spare when he arrived and decided to walk the short distance to the house where he had been instructed to meet. As he turned out of a narrow alley in the old market district and into the Rue de Commerce, he had been forced abruptly to step back as a black limousine with tinted windows pulled out quickly from the kerbside.

He could not be certain. He had seen Rahman Mansur in person only twice before, at his father's funeral and at the charity reception in London.

Jackson's instinct, however, had told him that the passenger in the nearside rear seat was the man who, almost certainly, was behind the events in which he had become embroiled. He was also the husband of the young woman from whom, since their first lovemaking in the strangely quiet ambiance of an old medieval village in France, he knew that he could never be apart.

Whether Mansur had seen him or not he did not know. The car was gone in an instant. The door to the house where the meeting was to take place was unlocked. Jackson had quietly entered and noticed that the long windows to the garden were open.

He walked in and found a man in his late sixties standing alone. He wore a crumpled white suit and a cream open-necked shirt. When he heard Jackson approach he had turned and held out his hand. His face looked ashen, his thin grey hair receding and his face revealed unhealthy smudges beneath both eyes.

"You must be Hugo Jackson. Permit me to introduce myself."

The two men had shaken hands.

"Emil Douchert. I'm a lawyer of sorts from Djibouti."

Jackson had replied uncertainly, "I'm sorry but I must be in the wrong place. I was expecting to meet Michael Crosfield."

"Michael Crosfield left about an hour ago."

There had been a pause before the older man ushered Jackson to a seat. Douchert had pointed to a set of crisp-looking legal documents on the table. He went on to explain the nature of the letter of credit transaction that had been agreed. Crosfield had left instructions for Jackson to travel immediately to Kuwait and present a duly executed power of attorney to the local branch manager of the Saudi Arabian bank. Once the document had been authenticated, the bank would confirm the opening of the credit line, allowing the end user to draw down the secured payment in cash at an agreed location.

Jackson had sensed that Douchert wanted to tell him more but was unwilling to do so in the meeting room.

"I know that time is short. I have to travel to Dubai but maybe we've time for a quick lunch?"

Within minutes, Jackson and Douchert were seated at an outside table in a modest café close to Luxembourg's main railway station. The two men ordered a meal and ate slowly.

"May I call you Hugo?"

Jackson could not help but note a slightly winsome tone to Douchert's question, as if he was seeking to relive or recall something in the past. He had watched as Douchert's eyes drifted into the distance, beyond the bustle of passengers scurrying towards the terminus.

Douchert's words had come quietly. "It wasn't always like this, you know. I wasn't always a broken-down expatriate lawyer eking out an existence far from home. I didn't always take commissions from clients who were willing to pay simply because I was worth marginally more to them alive than dead."

Jackson spoke compassionately. "I'm sure that you don't mean that. But why are you telling me this?"

This time Douchert's voice was stronger. Jackson sensed that he had made up his mind.

"Because I now have a chance to see something through that's worthwhile. And I realize that if I don't, another life will be wrecked, just like mine has been."

Douchert had smiled at the younger man. "Believe me, I'm not telling you this out of self pity. It's too late for that. I can't decide what you should do but you've a right to know."

Jackson had put down his knife and fork. "Please tell me if it would help."

Douchert nodded. Jackson could not be sure but he thought that the older man's eyes were beginning to glaze over.

"After my national service in France I graduated in law from the University of Bordeaux and joined a small practice in Limoges. It wasn't up to much, mainly low-grade public and criminal work. But I believed in the law in a naïve kind of way."

Douchert seemed to hesitate. Jackson had urged him to continue. "Go on."

The Frenchman had looked at Jackson intently. "While I was there I fell in love with the daughter of the local Count. Claire Helene. We planned to marry." There was a further pause. Douchert had extracted a faded black and white photograph from his pocket, and passed it across the table.

"She's beautiful." Jackson had spoken admiringly. He realized that this had been the love of Douchert's life. In his mind's eye he could only see Hedizah.

"Thank you."

A waiter appeared and cleared their half-eaten plates. "Coffee, gentlemen?"

"No thanks."

Douchert had waited for the diners at the next table to leave before continuing. Jackson suddenly saw into the eyes of a man with a broken heart that he had carried for many years.

"One day a file arrived at my office from the Deputy Prosecutor's office. A railway worker had been found dead in suspicious circumstances." Douchert had looked away.

"My father was a doctor in a little village quite close by. When I showed him the file he was very agitated. It was the last time that I saw him alive."

Jackson had spoken softly. "What happened?"

Douchert had held his hands together on the table. "It took me months to find out, but it seems that, in the War, my father and the dead man were in the Resistance, operating in the Limoges area. There were betrayals. No one knew who. When I visited the railway worker's house, his widow gave me a sworn affidavit deposed by her late husband testifying that the Count whose daughter I was in love with was the collaborator."

Jackson had looked steadily at the older man. Douchert had continued more hurriedly.

"Someone in my office leaked the contents of the letter to the Count. Within a week my father was found poisoned in his surgery, Claire Helene had been sent away, my apartment was burnt out and a criminal malpractice charge against me had been filed in the local court."

Jackson could see that Douchert was near to breaking down. He had put his hand on the older man's shoulder. "I'm sorry."

Douchert swallowed hard. "Thank you. I never saw or heard of her again. The next day, I found an air ticket to French Central Africa and a small fortune in colonial francs."

Jackson felt that Douchert needed to complete his story. "So you never went back?"

"Not for years. By then it was too late and I was on a downhill slope."

Douchert had paused and looked at the crowds in the square. "You could say I still am."

Jackson had reached down for his briefcase. He wanted to check the file of documents that Douchert had instructed him to present to the bank in Kuwait.

"I should be going."

"Yes, we both should."

The two men had begun to walk towards the rail terminus.

"Hugo. You are a young man. Your life is ahead of you. I wouldn't want you to waste it like I've done."

Before Jackson could speak, Douchert had held up his hand. "Let me finish if you will. I didn't fight back when I should have. I took the easy way, degrading myself day by day under a foreign sun. Drink, drugs, corruption. I sold out."

Jackson stopped. The crowd around them had thinned. He looked at Douchert. It had come to him in an instant.

"This is about Hedizah Mansur, isn't it? She's missing. I know that now. All this, is it to set her free?"

Douchert had nodded. "Follow your instinct, Hugo. And my guess is that before too long you'll hear from someone who knows what's really going on."

Douchert smiled. "Take good care of those documents, my friend."

In a moment the jostling crowd had returned and Douchert had disappeared.

"Excuse me, Sir. Please put your seat upright. We'll shortly be landing in Djibouti."

The stewardess leaned across Jackson's seat as the aircraft's pilot announced that the sandstorm had cleared. Jackson rubbed his eyes and looked at his watch. It had been only fifteen minutes since the last announcement. He looked down to his right and noticed a folded piece of paper.

It was less than eight hours before, as he was leaving the offices of the bank in Kuwait, that he was called by the duty receptionist to a house phone in the office lobby. The recorded message was plain. The voice was clear. It was that of an articulate young woman with a faint Australian accent. Jackson was not to return to London. He was to make an immediate booking to fly to Djibouti via Dubai. Further instructions would follow.

Jackson unfolded the piece of paper.

"Cabin crew, we have two minutes to landing."

The message was typed. It told him to leave the terminal building at Djibouti and to look for a white Mercedes saloon. It would be parked immediately opposite the main exit.

Upon disembarking, and exiting the airport, Jackson shielded his eyes from the low afternoon sun and approached the car. The driver got out and opened the door.

"Welcome to Djibouti. My name is Karl Stedman. I'm a kind of general dogsbody here. But today it's more serious. We need to move quickly. My instructions are to deliver you to the security office in the main port area. There you'll meet another young man, with a mission to achieve. He's a naval officer and his ship is sailing on the evening tide in two hours."

* * * * * * * * * *

Ehrwald, Austria

Crosfield had made good time. He had changed vehicles at Frankfurt Airport and had reached the outskirts of the Bavarian town of Garmisch-Partenkirchen sooner than he had expected.

The lower pastures of the Austrian Alps ahead were still green and thick with grass. In the distance a few peaks remained clothed with a light covering of snow. He pulled the car into the forecourt of a small hotel, a timbered building with a sloping roof, galleried balcony and wall paintings depicting the celestial blessing of harvests long ago.

"Do you need a room, Sir?"

The softly spoken words of a middle-aged woman in traditional dress came as a surprise.

"Thank you. No, thank you, I'm just stopping for lunch." Crosfield found himself smiling at a pretty face with healthy cheeks and faded blue eyes. It had been a long time. Perhaps it had been the same for her too.

He looked around at the cosy dining room and warmed his hands before a slow burning log fire. Behind him stood several empty wooden tables draped with checked table cloths and beyond, shuttered windows with long drapes and traditional candle lights hanging low.

He smiled again. They were alone. They both knew that. Then the moment passed. The woman gave a gentle sigh and turned away.

"Thanks. Which way to the bathroom please?"

"It's that way. I'll put a menu out for you."

The passage was adorned with sepia photographs of past hunting scenes and winter sports from the hotel's early days. Crosfield closed the door to the bathroom and looked at himself in the mirror. He had not washed or shaved since the meeting in Luxembourg and had hardly slept since he had left London for Tresco. His face looked grey and ashen.

Pulling off his jacket, he loosened his collar and sluiced cold water over his face. He breathed heavily, grasping the washbasin in front of him. The call should come through at any time.

He had not planned to do it at the outset. Perhaps initially he had been motivated by a desire to do harm to Mansur. Strangely, Crosfield had felt a sense of betrayal, especially after the Geneva meeting.

But that had not precipitated his decision. That had been determined by his reckless failure to heed his instincts and cut his losses. The encounter with Ralph Lennard had proved that.

Majec, he knew, was nothing but a hired hand, with no loyalty to any cause except his own. He was also canny enough to keep moving.

Crosfield had no desire that harm should come to Hedizah Mansur. He had persuaded himself that her kidnapping and ransom was the only means whereby he could satisfy Lennard and his creditors.

But events had moved too quickly. Perhaps it had been inevitable. The authorities in the United Kingdom had reacted with the full force of the law. Within hours he had become a fugitive from justice. His agenda had changed, irrevocably.

When Max Herlov had shown up at the meeting in Leipzig, Crosfield had to assume that Majec had talked. Whether he had done so out of ignorance, cunning or self preservation did not matter.

That Herlov and Majec had kept their silence had caused Crosfield to conclude that both men had reason to believe that their allegiance to Mansur might be coming to an end.

How they would deal with the kidnap and ransom, Crosfield could only speculate. All he had needed was confirmation. The demand would be made and the arrangements for payment would then be put in place.

Crosfield had no doubt that Douchert's scheme to pay the ransom would work, but he could not be sure as to whom Mansur's parting words at the Luxembourg meeting were directed. He could only hope that there would be time enough.

If the next twenty-four hours went according to plan, he might survive. He might also come to terms with what little of his conscience remained.

Crosfield left the bathroom and made his way to the restaurant. The woman had slipped off her cardigan to reveal a shapely figure with a darkly patterned ankle-length dress in Tyrolean costume with a low cut neckline.

He felt himself fighting the desire to take the woman upstairs as she beckoned him to do, and in an intensity of brief physical release to ignore or postpone what needed to be done later in the day. But it was not to be.

"I'm sorry."

The woman looked away and took his order. The silence of the parlour was broken by the rattle of Crosfield's mobile phone.

"Crosfield? It's Lennard. I do hope that you're not going to let me down."

"Why should I?"

"Well. Talk about the mighty fallen. It's all over the papers now."

Crosfield looked out on to the little village square outside the hotel. The woman was still looking at him. He gave a half smile and turned away.

"I said, Crosfield, that it's all over the papers now. I enjoyed reading about it. The headlines said that a top City lawyer had been charged with corruption and perverting the course of justice. You should be proud of yourself."

His words sounded slurred.

"If you want your money, Lennard, you'd better listen to what I have to say."

"You're in no position to threaten me. There's an international warrant out for your arrest. Just make sure you deliver before they get you. If you don't, I'll find you wherever they take you. You know that."

Lennard coughed. "Do you hear me, Crosfield?"

"I hear you. Meet me where we agreed at four o'clock. And come alone."

"You'd better be there."

Crosfield ended the call, put down the cash to settle his account and left the room. The woman pulled aside the drapes in the hallway and watched him drive away.

Within an hour, Crosfield had negotiated the narrow, twisting road beneath the towering face of the Zugspitze and had crossed the Austrian border. A few minutes later he parked his vehicle opposite the civic centre in the village of Ehrwald and walked towards the side entrance of the local branch of the Tyroler Landesbank.

He rang the bell and was ushered into a bright, open office. Its long windows overlooked a green valley and winding stream that cascaded down from the lower mountain slopes behind.

"Mr Crosfield. This is a most unusual transaction. We are a small country office. We all live and work here. We're not used to handling huge sums of cash."

"I understand. But I assume your Head Office received my instructions yesterday morning?"

"Thank you. It was something of a relief."

The young bank official, no more than twenty-five years old and dressed casually in a checked open-necked shirt and jeans, smiled and removed his glasses.

"All I require from you, Mr Crosfield, is the secure access code which I need you to key into our system. That will allow me to release the safety default in our strong room downstairs. The first part of the cash payment under the letter of credit can then be released."

Crosfield nodded. "I understand."

There was a moment's hesitation before the younger man spoke again. "Mr Crosfield. You are only collecting the first part today, aren't you?"

"Sorry if I startled you. Yes. I'll be back as agreed at six o'clock this evening to give you instructions for payment of the balance."

The atmosphere lightened as Crosfield typed the code into the terminal on the young official's desk. He returned several minutes later as Crosfield stood up and stretched. He felt a sense of calm. There was more to be done but that would come later.

The two men descended to the tiny vault.

"It's been checked and counted. Two valises double-locked. Please sign here."

Crosfield picked up the cases and the two men walked up to the ground floor.

"Bring your car round to the secure parking behind the bank. I'll open the door as soon as I see you."

In less than two minutes Crosfield was driving away from the village. He stopped beside the tall spire of the Catholic Church, the low afternoon sun catching the ornate gilt roof and richly described stained glass windows.

He quickly sent a short text message confirming the pick up and felt strangely relieved that an acknowledgement was immediately received.

He then made a call to Ralph Lennard.

"I'm on my way. I'll meet you in the Gipfelhaus Bar in half an hour."

Crosfield did not wait for an answer. There would be time enough for him to park the car beside the ticket office. Although it was late summer, the gondolas were still running on the ascent to the upper station on the southern face of the Zugspitze. There, he would change to the elevator for the summit. He had no doubt that Lennard would be waiting.

Crosfield could not be sure but he felt a slight surge of confidence through his veins. Maybe, just maybe, he would pull it off.

He carried the two cases into the main hallway of the lift station, and purchased a return ticket for the summit. A few moments later he felt a surge of power as the long steel cables hauled the gondola towards the top.

Crosfield alighted from the gondola and crossed the narrow platform to the outer veranda. The cold wind struck his cheeks as he walked the short distance round to the elevator to the summit.

The ascent lasted several minutes before the elevator stopped at an open hallway leading out on to the winter ski plateau.

Crosfield walked towards a row of lockers, verified the number, and inserted the two cases. He withdrew the key, checked that the locker to the right was empty and unlocked it.

The entrance to the Gipfelhaus bar was adjacent to a souvenir and sports outlet, busy with late summer tourists. Crosfield looked around him. A party of hikers were noisily recounting their exploits of the day. Several mountain bikers approached the open gateway.

Crosfield entered the bar and saw Lennard immediately. He was sitting at a wooden booth decorated with traditional artefacts from the region, old ski equipment and a panoramic painting of snow-covered peaks to the south. He was also evidently drunk, as Crosfield had hoped he might be.

Lennard saw Crosfield but made no attempt to get up. "So, Mr Crosfield. Even the great and good have to pay their dues."

Crosfield said nothing.

"Sorry, that wasn't very kind, was it? I'd forgotten. You are in deep shit, but I can't say I'm sorry. Lawyers and their like always get up my nose."

"I assume that you don't want another drink?"

"Why not, if you're buying. But can you afford it?"

Crosfield approached the bar. There were few other customers. Those that were seated nearby seemed oblivious to Lennard's bragging tone.

"By the way, Crosfield, you should meet Lena. Here, why don't you sit down next to her. She'd like that."

Crosfield glanced at the young girl at Lennard's side – slim, shapely, highly made up with fine white teeth and short cropped red hair. Her face and eyes told their story. Her expensive clothes did nothing to hide a timidity verging on fear. Crosfield watched as she stroked Lennard's bull neck as though her life depended on it.

"She's from Bulgaria. You'd never think she was only sixteen, would you, Crosfield?"

Crosfield leant over the bar, reaching for the two beers that he had ordered. As he did so, he removed the locker key from his jacket pocket and slid it behind an ashtray.

"You make me sick, Lennard."

"You're in no position to judge me. You're stuffed and you know it."

Crosfield sipped his drink and watched as a stocky man with a sallow complexion approached the bar. He purchased a packet of cigarettes. Then, with his eyes on Crosfield, he carefully took the key as he swept his change into the palm of his hand.

"I hope that you've remembered what we agreed." Lennard pushed his pock marked face towards Crosfield. "I want half my money in cash today. The other half's to be transferred to my Bermuda account tomorrow. I'm watching you."

He pulled the girl towards him, forced his lips on to hers and pressed his hand into her loins. "It's good when you're on top. You should remember that."

Crosfield watched the other man cross the hallway and then walk into the elevator.

A few more minutes would be enough.

Lennard pushed the girl to one side and finished the beer that Crosfield had bought.

He stood up, thickset, menacing and without a hint of intoxication.

"Let's go get my cash now. I'll see you at the bank at ten tomorrow to do the rest."

Crosfield led Lennard and the girl towards the elevator. There was a delay. The unit remained at the lower station level.

Lennard appeared not to notice. He kept his eyes firmly on Crosfield and held the girl's hand with a force that was clearly hurting her. The elevator finally arrived. They entered and within a few minutes were walking towards the lockers.

"I'll lead on." Crosfield walked briskly ahead. He approached the locker where he had left the cases. Keeping his back to Lennard he quickly reached into the next door locker and retrieved the key before giving it to Lennard.

The two cases were withdrawn.

"I hope that you haven't made a mistake with this, Crosfield."

Crosfield threw him the keys to the two cases. "Check it now if you want to."

"I'll do it in my own time tonight. I know where to find you."

"As you wish."

Lennard picked up the cases. "You're coming down with me, Crosfield."

"Very well."

This time there was no delay. The gondola arrived and in less than ten minutes they alighted at the lower station.

Lennard nodded to Crosfield. "Until tomorrow then. Don't go away, will you?"

The girl looked at Crosfield, confused, frightened and humiliated. Crosfield could do nothing. He bit his tongue. He had no idea that Lennard would not be alone.

He watched as Lennard heaved the two cases into a black four wheel drive SUV parked on the far side of the approach to the ski station lift. He pushed the girl into the passenger seat. Crosfield saw her face turn towards him.

Lennard started the engine. Within seconds the vehicle was engulfed by a blinding flash and explosion, quickly followed by a roaring crescendo of flames.

Crosfield shuddered.

"Too bad about the girl." Standing beside him was Max Herlov. At his feet lay the two cases that Crosfield had deposited in the locker. The switch had worked.

"My fee, I think."

"You're a first class bastard, Herlov. You know that, don't you?"

Herlov smiled and held out his hand. "You're right, my friend. But it's what I'm good at."

* * * * * * * * * *

The Gulf of Aden

Hedizah Mansur felt the warm sea breeze on her face. She folded her arms and leant forwards over the ship's rail. The Saudi Arabian coast slowly slipped by.

She had been confined to her cabin for the two days after the nightmare of her transfer from the *Globex Seaquest* to the *Aegean Dolphin*. She had slept for most of that time, numb with exhaustion, fright and misery.

The ship's steward, an amiable Greek islander, with four decades of life at sea, had been instructed to look after her. Her cabin had been locked but she was now free to walk out on to the main deck.

Pytr Majec had told his men that they were to keep an eye on her but if any one of them were to touch her they would meet the same fate as the two who had attempted to do so in the villa at Villefranche.

Hedizah was trying to come to terms with what had occurred. Nothing made any sense, however much she tried to reason. The violent death of Sophie, her friend and confidante, had shocked and terrified her to such an extent that she could see no way of ridding her mind of the senseless brutality that she had witnessed.

Then, she began to feel a deepening sense of guilt and responsibility. She wondered whether or how it might all have resulted from her love for Hugo Jackson. She saw his face come and go. She felt the warmth of his body as she lay in her cabin. She shivered with fear at what might have become of him if what had befallen her and caused Sophie's death was a wild act of revenge orchestrated by Rahman.

She could not help but notice the constant armed security that had been imposed throughout the vessel. There were secrets on board to which she was not privy. Knowing looks from the seamen hinted as much as they went about their daily shipboard tasks.

She prayed not only for the soul of Sophie but that whatever events might unfold, she and Hugo would survive to find each other somewhere in the future.

"How are you feeling now, Miss Hedizah?"

She turned and found Milakis standing next to her, closely shadowed by one of Majec's armed guards.

Hedizah pulled the denim jacket round her shoulders. The steward had found her a rough set of clothes that he had been able to suborn from the ship's cook.

"Thank you again for what you did, Captain. I don't know why I'm here or what the future holds, but I know that you saved my life."

Milakis gave Hedizah a half smile. "It was risky but it was worth it. Let's say no more about it."

Hedizah saw that Milakis was looking into the distance. There was a crackle over his radio receiver. She watched him turn his head towards the bridge wing two decks above them. He spoke quickly in Greek and then closed the connection.

"That was the Navigating Officer. We've got to change course. There's some kind of naval exercise going on at the southern end of the Red Sea."

He could sense Hedizah's sudden anxiety. He knew that there was little he could say.

"Nothing to worry about, I'm sure."

The man shadowing Milakis watched him speak with Hedizah and thrust an automatic pistol into his jacket. For a moment he took in the view of the shimmering sea, the gently sloping coastline and the swift passing of several dhows, low in the water as the wind licked their slanting sails.

He had worked for Majec before in the badlands of the Balkans. His father had been killed in the Caucasus, fighting an independence battle against the might of Russia that was lost before it had even begun. He had needed to support his mother, sisters and brothers. Now he longed to be back with them on their tiny communal farm in the Ukraine.

He saw the face of his mother, looked at Hedizah, and wiped away a tear. He knew that he would never see her again. With all that he had done and witnessed, he was not sure that she would even recognize him.

The *Aegean Dolphin* began a slow turn to starboard and the wind suddenly caught Hedizah's dark hair.

Milakis knew that he had to ask her. In less than twelve hours it might all be over.

He had received a message on the satellite phone, which he had continued successfully to secrete in his cabin. The caller had told him that he must ensure that the vessel suffered a breakdown or technical failure at a position that he had been given.

Hedizah's mysterious arrival on board had changed everything. If, as he believed, Israeli intelligence wanted his assistance by reporting from the vessel, the reason had to be linked to her kidnapping.

He had decided to risk all and make an unprompted call to the unknown contact to which he had first spoken. There was no disguising the surprise in the voice that had responded when Milakis told him of what had transpired and how the vessel was now holding a prisoner on board.

Hedizah spoke quietly. "Captain, I should be going inside."

She looked towards the young guard who nodded. Milakis would have to make his decision within seconds.

It was obvious to Milakis that Majec and his men had been hired to protect whatever cargo his vessel was carrying. They were to repel any attack on the high seas or to thwart any unwanted interest at whatever destination port they might be bound.

There had been little risk thus far, which probably accounted for the tolerably relaxed security regime that Majec had imposed. But as the vessel steamed southwards, after leaving the secure waterways of the Suez Canal, their vigilance had increased. They knew that the real threat was yet to come.

Milakis and his crew had seen Majec's team weld the high calibre cannon on to the hatch cover of the number two hold. The weapon had a free arc of fire both port and starboard and, as the weapon's testing showed, it would have the capacity to reduce the vessel's bridge to a smouldering ruin in seconds.

Milakis had weighed up the options and had decided. He would make clear that he fully understood his new orders. He made sure that Majec had seen him lay out the charts and instruct the Navigating Officer to plot their new course as well as give the crew their lookout watches.

But his instinct told him that the only realistic option that he had was to adhere to the instructions of his unidentified contact on the satellite phone. It was Hedizah's capture and her presence on board that had made up his mind.

His only problem lay in communicating instructions to the Chief Engineer to fabricate, realistically, on time and at the stated position, a breakdown that would disable the ship for a sufficient period. What was to follow he could only guess at.

Hedizah moved towards the companionway door. Milakis looked at the young woman. That she was quite beautiful was beyond doubt. But there was something else. She had a rare sense of serenity and an evident courage beyond her years that had impressed both loyal seafarer and hardened guard alike.

Now Milakis had to ask her something. Everything might rest on her answer.

"Miss Hedizah. Forgive me. It's nothing really, probably only a silly question at a time like this. But you do speak Hindi, don't you?"

Hedizah gave Milakis a wide smile. Her eyes told him what he wanted to know. "Of course, Captain."

She gave him a long look and opened the door to the passageway to her cabin. The young guard continued to stare over the ship's rail.

Milakis had his answer. The only crew member on board from the Indian sub continent was the Chief Engineer. It would not be difficult to arrange. A message could be passed in Greek to the steward and relayed to Hedizah in her cabin. He would instruct the Chief Engineer to take a short break from his watch to pass Hedizah when she next came on deck.

One brief sentence in Hindi would be all that was required.

* * * * * * * * * *

Djibouti, Gulf of Aden

Bertrand had hoped that his previous visit to Djibouti would be his last. But he had no choice but to return. There was only one benefit that derived from the summons which he had received from Douchert. It would give him time to reflect on the final preparations that still had to be put in hand.

After the showcase assault on the derelict wreck, which El Sanah had organized for his benefit, there was still much to do and little time to accomplish it. It was no small relief, therefore, for Bertrand to learn by satellite phone from Wenger on the *Emden* that the *Aegean Dolphin*'s passage out of the Red Sea and into the Gulf of Aden would be delayed. Her change of course would give them another twenty-four hours.

Whatever the reason for Wenger's message, Bertrand would finalise his plans. They would deploy three high-speed craft and use the failing afternoon light as cover for the assault. He would lead the first boat, Simpson the second, and the other would be commanded by El Sanah himself. Each boat would contain a helmsman and three armed men.

Bertrand would have to leave the final weapons dispositions to Simpson. He would also have to ensure that the local seafarers whom El Sanah had recruited knew the backwaters of the craggy coastline east of Bosasso. They would lie up there during the day before H-hour arrived.

El Sanah's recruits were not, as Bertrand had learned, without experience of the tasks that would be required. Their hands had already been bloodied in earlier encounters. But they were still local fishermen and coastal seaborne traders. Cash and food for their families was their priority. Idealism for the greater cause of Somalian national recovery was the province of El Sanah, and his educated elite.

Bertrand knew that these men had worked the local waters all their lives, but they were nervous. They were not concerned with the forthcoming encounter. They knew the odds. But what concerned them were the unseasonable storms that had whipped up the coastal seas over the last few weeks.

They were ill at ease. The delay was auspicious. The dark fleeting clouds building up over the inland rocky terrain told them that the weather might prove to be their worst enemy.

But there was nothing more that Bertrand could do. In twelve hours he had to be back in Bosasso. The ageing single-engine aircraft, chartered for the return flight, was his only hope of returning in time.

Fog had delayed their arrival into Djibouti. He could not afford more than three hours on the ground if the aircraft was to get him back before nightfall.

Bertrand felt an unexpected twinge of nervousness in his stomach as he pushed open the door of the taxi at the end of the alleyway. He made his way quickly through the morning throng towards Douchert's office and rang the bell.

The building appeared closed up. The blinds were drawn in the ground floor windows. He looked up. The air conditioning unit, perched precariously on the wall above, was switched off.

Bertrand looked at his watch. He knew that he was late. He had intended to challenge Douchert over what must have been his involvement in El Sanah's people seizing Simpson, but somehow that no longer seemed important.

Douchert was what he was. Bertrand had had no choice but to engage him. Now it seemed that Douchert's involvement had changed. He had made clear to Bertrand that what he now knew might affect the very objectives that Bertrand had been given.

Somehow, Bertrand detected a change of tone in their conversation. It was almost as if Douchert felt an element of some indefinable concern. Over what, Bertrand could only speculate. He wondered whether Douchert's own fate was in point.

As he peered up again at the shuttered building, he felt a tug at his sleeve. It was Masoud.

"Come quickly, Monsieur. There is little time."

Bertrand followed the boy through a network of narrow winding alleys until they emerged into a small square, tucked behind several derelict houses adjacent to the old port trading sheds. Ahead, behind a rusted grille fence, lay the once symmetrical lines of a series of tombs and gravestones. Dust, dead wood and neglect over time had reduced the once immaculate foreign cemetery to just another forgotten corner of a former age.

Masoud pointed Bertrand towards the crumbling brick façade of what looked like a family mausoleum. A few flowers, recently picked, lay strewn at the entrance.

"I'm glad that you could come." Douchert spoke quietly, as he stepped out from the shadows.

Bertrand stopped.

Douchert was exhausted, grey and frail. He was a sick man. He looked at Bertrand and spoke slowly. "I'm sorry about Simpson."

Bertrand's reply came without rancour. "I assume that you leaked what I told you."

Douchert shrugged his shoulders. "I'm afraid you're right."

Bertrand could not bring himself to challenge what he had suspected.

"For a suitable fee, to keep you in what you needed?"

Douchert made no attempt to deny it. "Yes, a suitable fee to keep me alive."

Bertrand nodded and turned away. The square was quiet. Of Masoud, there was no sign.

Simpson's and his own life had been put at risk in a show of local bravado. It was, without doubt, the direct result of a sad and solitary man needing to feed his lifelong addictions.

Bertrand could feel no anger now for what had occurred. He knew only too well what drove Douchert and those like him. They were fugitives from their own land, driven solely by the need to survive. It was as simple as that. He had seen it many times before.

Time was running short. He turned back and faced the older man.

"You said that it was urgent, Douchert, that it might change everything. I hope that you're not lying to me now."

"No. There's no time for that."

"Go on."

Douchert paused for a moment before continuing in a voice that Bertrand could not fail to notice expressed concern.

"Do you know that someone has another agenda for your vessel?"

"Meaning?"

"I know what you're planning to do. I didn't know why when we first met but perhaps I now understand."

Bertrand was becoming impatient. "Tell me what I need to know."

Douchert looked hard at the younger man. "You have a conscience, I believe. That's a rare commodity in your world and mine."

Douchert walked slowly down the dusty gravel pathway towards the twisted metal gate that led out into the square. Masoud had returned. He was waiting, an envelope in his hand.

"I'm leaving here, Bertrand. I was in Europe only forty-eight hours ago. I'm going back to France. It's been too long. There's something that I have to do."

Bertrand allowed Douchert to finish.

"In case you didn't know, there's a hostage being held on the *Aegean Dolphin*. It's Mansur's wife, Hedizah. Don't ask me how I know, but it's the truth. I can't tell you who's behind it but I can tell you that I've just completed arrangements for a ransom of twenty million dollars to be paid for her release."

Bertrand stopped walking. He felt the heat of the late afternoon sun on the back of his neck as it shone down through a gap in the broken down building behind him. Douchert was telling the truth. Bertrand had no reason to disbelieve him.

They reached the gate. Douchert smiled at Masoud and turned back to Bertrand.

"Monsieur, if you and your friend survive what you are planning to do, please take care of Masoud. Perhaps he should go back to Dubai. I imagine that you could arrange that."

Bertrand held out his hand. "I imagine we could. Thanks for what you told me."

Douchert breathed heavily and coughed. His words were scarcely audible. "I don't know if I'm right, but for Rahman Mansur what your vessel is carrying may be more, much more, important than the fate of Hedizah. But then I expect you knew that anyway."

A party of worshippers passed by, answering the afternoon call for prayers. Douchert and Masoud were gone.

Bertrand stood for a moment and looked around him. There was something eerie, almost prophetic, in the atmosphere of the old graveyard.

He found an iron seat with flaked paintwork just inside the exit and sat down. He pulled out his mobile phone and keyed in the number that Ann Sutherland had instructed him to call, day or night, should an emergency arise. She answered quickly and Bertrand made his report. She told him to return to Bosasso as he had planned and that he would receive further instructions within six hours. Bertrand relayed the number of the satellite phone that he had left with Simpson.

It was that phone that Simpson was using when he called Bertrand minutes later.

"Listen, mate. I think we may have a problem. Despite all that bullshit the other day, I think our friend, Douk El Sanah, may be playing a double game. Word tells me that the cash you brought down has gone elsewhere than we thought. Watch your back. I'll be waiting for the plane."

Chapter Nine

Nicosia, Cyprus

Herlov knocked on the door. He looked sideways along the winding street. The brass nameplate was tarnished and the doorway dirty and uncared for. The ground floor windows were shuttered.

The office of Kalil Osman, Advocate and Notary Public, was housed in an old brick building in an outer suburb of Nicosia. The green line dividing the city was one street to the south, placing the office marginally within the Turkish area of occupation of northern Cyprus. A United Nations flag hung limply over an untidy police post manned by conscripts from South Korea.

The midday heat haze sat heavily and there was a dry dust in the air. A battered school bus rattled by, emitting thick black exhaust smoke.

There was a short delay before the door was opened. An elderly woman appeared, dressed in black with a faded grey headscarf.

"They're expecting you upstairs."

The woman offered a toothless smile and retreated inside.

Herlov stood aside as Mansur strode into the hallway and up the narrow winding staircase. It had been several years since he had visited the office.

Crosfield, over the years, had successfully shielded the activities of the Globex group of companies from scrutiny by international regulators. However, he never knew the truth of the manner in which Mansur had been able to protect his own clandestine personal fortune.

That had only been achieved through the complex unregulated environment available to those who could successfully manipulate the antiquated legal system of the Turkish state.

Kalil Osman had bent every rule to enable Mansur to conceal his personal wealth. A fabric of trusts and silent corporations had been established in jurisdictions where the western norms of international finance and commerce held no sway.

Mansur knew that Osman would not be there. He lay dying, old and alone, in a grim hospital less than a kilometre away. Mansur was impervious to his fate. Things had moved on. The care and scrutiny that the old Lebanese lawyer had brought to his client's affairs mattered little now.

All that was required was an undistinguished and covert venue for a meeting that Mansur had not himself demanded. Osman's office provided that.

Herlov and Mansur reached the first floor. They turned into an ill-lit area that passed for a reception and waiting room. Colonel Lev Barshok, dressed in brown lightweight slacks and open-necked white shirt, stood up as they entered. His manner was gruff, as was his mood.

"I suggest that we sit here, away from the window."

Barshok motioned Mansur and Herlov to two cane wicker chairs.

The elderly concierge set down a wooden tray with cups of thick Turkish coffee and glasses of orange juice. She left quietly and pulled an upholstered screen with Byzantine motifs across the top of the stairway.

The drinks were left untouched as Mansur and Barshok eyed each other intently, seeking to analyse the strategy and agenda that one or other would adopt. It was Barshok who spoke first.

"I think, Mr Mansur, that we need to be frank. There's much at stake, much to lose and less to play for than when we last met."

"I don't understand why you say that, Colonel. I agree that we needed to meet but, with respect, I disagree with your analysis of where we stand."

Mansur's tone was forceful but his manner was urbane and reasonable.

Herlov adjusted his chair. He would bide his time. As he well knew, both men could remove him at an instant. He had now safely banked the success fee that had unexpectedly come his way from Crosfield and he decided to allow matters to take their course.

Barshok looked down at the back of his hands and straightened his fingers.

"By the way, Major Rawazi sends his apologies."

Mansur continued to give Barshok a cool stare. He too would wait and see how much the other man knew or intimated that he knew or didn't know.

It was Barshok who again spoke first. "Well, let me tell you what I have learned and reasonably believe to be true. Please correct me if I'm wrong or you disagree."

Once more, Mansur's reply was non-committal. "Go on, Colonel. I'm listening."

"Very well."

The officer's tone was now crisp and matter of fact. "First, I understand that the investigating magistrate has completed his preliminary report into what occurred in Villefranche. He is, I believe, expected to make a public statement shortly. Then, he will almost certainly request the opening of a criminal enquiry into the disappearance of your wife, Hedizah, and the murder of her maid."

Mansur responded as if expecting a question. "That has nothing whatsoever to do with me, Colonel, as you know."

This time Barshok permitted himself a wry smile. "I believe you, Mr Mansur. I am sure that neither event involved you personally. However, once the magistrate's report is published the press will be free to do their worst, doubtless with a little monetary persuasion from those who would like the story to run."

Mansur replied almost before Barshok had finished. "I've lived with the media and press for a decade. Nothing has changed. Since you have opened the debate, please tell me something that I don't know."

Barshok's smile had gone. His expression seemed to suggest that time was on his side.

The two men sat motionless. Their eyes met again, seeking out what hand the other might be concealing or intending to play.

Barshok drank slowly from one of the cups and carefully replaced it on the table.

"I'll continue if I may."

Herlov sat impassively as if watching a fencing contest or a display of Chinese shadow boxing.

"Secondly, Major Rawazi's sources, which are said to be reliable, have passed me intelligence which goes to the root of our mutual understanding."

The hint of irony was not lost on either Mansur or Herlov. Mansur, this time, wanted to make his point before Barshok had a chance to continue.

"Our understanding, Colonel, was simple. I made a payment which underwrote the consent of your two governments to allow me to proceed with the transaction which we agreed at our last meeting."

Barshok's reply came quickly. "Just so, Mr Mansur, but as we both know, the basis for the transaction has changed. We were proceeding on the basis that the delivery of battlefield nuclear weaponry into the Kurdish region of northern Iraq was a strategy which we were willing to support. This was particularly so, as you had made it plain that the Kurdish Revolutionary Council supported both your plan and your avowed political ambition."

Mansur's face imperceptibly tightened.

"We believe that recent events have altered the picture. The Council's membership has changed. Their aims are different now. Their long term strategy is under review. They are not sure that they need an expatriate sponsor any more, or if they do, there may be others on their shortlist. Am I right?"

Mansur needed no reminding of what had occurred only days before. Several of the Council's members, men with whom he had fought, and grown up with, had been assassinated. A suicide bomber had exploded a petrol tanker next to the building in Mosul which had been the intended secret location for their recent meeting.

Barshok continued slowly and deliberately, as if in a court room encounter with a witness who might be unable to tell the truth because he did not wish to admit it to himself.

"It's fair to say, Mr Mansur, is it not, that the central theme of your strategy for taking power for yourself is no longer viable?"

Mansur was not going to allow the cross examination to continue its course unchecked.

"As I made clear to the Council at our last meeting, irrespective of recent events, it was their decision at the end of the day and theirs alone. My own ambitions and aims have not changed."

Barshok said nothing. Herlov caught Barshok's eye as Mansur's tone, for the first time, displayed a hint of anger.

"You of all people, Colonel, know that my business is no different to your own line of work. Priorities change. They often change unexpectedly and at short notice. The key to success is being adaptable. There's often no time to reflect on a previous plan. What's needed is to make sure that the next one succeeds in its place."

Barshok sat back and took a sip of coffee. He sensed that he was getting the upper hand.

"I am sure, Mr Mansur, that your ambitions are unchanged but, as I've said, the position on the ground is different. We were willing to countenance what you proposed. We saw it as an opportunity, even a diversion from the world's attention. It might even have been a short respite from the daily round of hostility to our very existence."

Herlov looked at Mansur. He could not be sure but something in his body language had altered. The room began to feel cool despite the fierce heat outside.

"Colonel, my Kurdish comrades may have no use for what I have offered them now. But, as you say, events change. They will need me, and what I can offer, before long. I can wait. Time is not of the essence. The middle east is long on history, as is the story of Israel."

Barshok knew now that he had been right to call the meeting.

"I take it that you have found other buyers?"

Mansur realized too that they had reached a turning point.

"You must have assumed that in the circumstances I had no other course open to me."

Barshok stood up and put his hands on the table. He looked at Mansur but said nothing. Mansur, too, remained silent.

Herlov felt the moisture starting to form in the palms of his hands. Barshok straightened and walked across the room.

"Mr Mansur. That is your decision. We have to respect that. But it is not a decision that we can support. My instructions are to counsel you against any course other than to abort the voyage of the *Aegean Dolphin*."

It was Mansur who now gave a wry smile, as if he had expected to hear what he had just been told.

Barshok continued. "I assume, therefore, that your decision is made."

"It is, Colonel. I respect your advice, of course, but I have no choice."

Barshok stood beside the window. It seemed strangely quiet outside. He reflected for a moment and decided to try once more.

"Mr Mansur, if you did what we suggest and abort the voyage, we would be prepared to assist you. We could look after the operational side and the logistics. The vessel could proceed to a port where the cargo can be discharged and stored. We would secure the shipment and keep it secure until we had each resolved how to proceed."

Mansur pushed back his chair and made to stand up. He nodded to Herlov. The meeting was over.

"Thank you, Colonel. That, if I may say so, sounds similar to most of the proposals that your countrymen have made to me over the years; a non-negotiable, one-way option to suit the State of Sion. No, thank you. I appreciate, but reject, what your superiors propose."

"Very well, Mr Mansur. The position is clear."

The soldier reached down to pick up a small leather case from beside his chair. He extracted a bank cheque drawn on a leading Italian bank, payable to the bearer.

"Here is your fee. We are returning it in full. You paid us for the price of silence, and whatever covert support that you might require if your operation succeeded. You obviously don't need us any more, or what we have to offer."

Barshok handed the cheque to Herlov. He then moved to the top of the staircase.

"Mr Mansur. One final word, if I may. Be sure, before you proceed, that you are still master of your own ship."

Mansur watched Barshok's face. As Mansur had expected, he had known all along. He looked hard at Herlov and started to walk slowly down the stairs. As they reached the narrow open doorway, Mansur turned and spoke in Herlov's native tongue. He had never done so before.

"My friend, we have been through interesting times together. Until recently, it never occurred to me not to trust you. But I did warn you, several times. I hoped that you would stay loyal to me."

Mansur looked into Herlov's face with an expression of regret and resignation. "I'm disappointed, Max, I can't deny it."

He stepped quickly through the door and ducked to his right.

Herlov watched him go. In the same instant he looked across the street. A man was standing immediately opposite. Herlov stared at him, unable to move.

Two muffled shots followed in rapid succession. They struck Herlov in the chest and head. He fell dead on to the pavement in an instant.

Mansur beckoned to the man opposite and walked quickly towards a car parked some twenty metres away. The narrow street opposite led to a checkpoint across the green line and the road to Limassol in the Greek-controlled south of the island.

He snapped open his satellite phone. It was answered in seconds.

"Majec, this is Mansur. Herlov is dead. Listen to me. Your orders are confirmed. On no account is the vessel to be delayed on her passage to Karachi. If you face any opposition you are to proceed as I instructed you last night. You are to execute a crew member unless the vessel is given clearance and free passage. If that fails, you know what to do next."

Majec looked out from the deck of the *Aegean Dolphin*, across the still evening sea. Mansur knew that Hedizah was on board. Herlov was dead. Majec had little time to decide how to proceed, if he was given an option.

* * * * * * * * * *

The north Somalian coast

Bertrand lowered his binoculars and motioned with his right hand towards the storm clouds settling over the sea to the east. The wind was freshening and waves began to rock the three boats as they lay anchored inshore of a rocky bluff some twenty miles east of the port of Bosasso.

He looked across to the other two boats. Simpson was standing at the bow of the next craft, beside the Vickers machine gun. El Sanah was in the last boat. The crews sat awkwardly. Each man wore a chest flak jacket and life vest. They were starting to break out their weapons, a combination of locally modified Kalashnikov rifles and several Heckler and Koch light machine guns. Simpson would man the Vickers when the attack began.

Bertrand called to Simpson and El Sanah to check that the boxes of grenades and phosphorous smoke canisters were securely stowed. When the men's weapons had been checked they would begin the final distribution of ammunition. Then waterproof covers would be fitted to withstand the expected heavy spray once they made open water.

Bertrand and Simpson reckoned that, assuming the *Aegean Dolphin* had been disabled at the position they had been given, there would be at least an hour's passage from where they were presently concealed.

They had trained as best they could on the basis that the vessel would be stationary. They had repeated the exercise against the target wreck. If the *Aegean Dolphin* was underway, however, and those on board had been unable to disable the main engine, the attack would be against a moving target.

Either way, neither Bertrand nor Simpson was certain that the men under their command would be reliable faced with a real contact. They were also increasingly uncertain whether they and El Sanah could be trusted to see through what had been planned.

Bertrand feared that Simpson's warning about El Sanah's doubtful loyalty and ambivalent ideals might prove to be uncannily correct.

He checked his watch. Time was moving on. They had less than four hours until the start of sunset. He knew that darkness came quickly in the region.

Then he settled his back and kit against the wooden bench. Every soldier hated the waiting before an action and the call to fix bayonets. Suddenly those days seemed far away, as if what he was now doing was the beginning of something new, rather than a continuation of an earlier life.

Bertrand thought about Ronnie Simpson and Runah. She would be waiting in the tiny home that they shared together in Dubai. He thought about Alix Wenger and his wife and young family in Hamburg. Perhaps it was the old sergeant in him. He hated to see loss of life amongst comrades. But he needed Simpson's experience and he knew that, without Wenger's helicopter and his commandos from the *Emden*, they would be struggling.

The boat began to sway more heavily. He saw the wind whipping round the men and their equipment. It was what he was trained for. That's why they had hired him, but it would be the last time.

Milakis, on board the *Aegean Dolphin*, had also seen the weather ahead. If he complied with his instructions and the vessel was stopped at the given position, they would be exposed to serious danger from wind and sea. Without power, there was a real risk of being swept on to an offshore reef or one of the craggy promontories that distinguished the coastline.

Milakis felt sure that whoever was behind the clandestine instructions that he had elected to follow now knew that Hedizah was a prisoner on board.

He had made every attempt to ensure compliance with Majec's orders to make full speed for Karachi but the atmosphere on board had changed. Majec and his men had altered their routines. They were becoming edgy.

Milakis looked down from the open bridge wing. He could count no fewer than six men on the foredeck alone. Each was taking cover with his weapon at the ready. Majec himself was standing on the number two hatch cover beside the curved steel stock of the heavy cannon. Its tarpaulin had been removed and a full belt of ammunition hung down from the breech.

All depended on whether Hedizah had played her role. It was a situation that was as bizarre as it was dangerous. Milakis knew that. He also knew that, unless the message had reached the Chief Engineer, the lives of Hedizah, himself and his crew would be at even greater risk than they were now.

Suddenly, the ship vibrated heavily. The vibration was followed by a loud grinding sound that echoed up from the bowels of the vessel. Within seconds the main engine had stopped. The rhythmic throb of the propeller driving the vessel forward had gone. The vessel's bow lifted and then slipped away to starboard as the wind and sea from the north east caught the vessel's topsides.

Milakis, the Navigating Officer and the helmsman were momentarily thrown off their feet. Milakis struggled to regain his balance. Through the bridge windows he could see that Majec was pulling himself up and was starting to run towards the stairway to the bridge.

Sound and light alarms rang and flashed in front of him. Milakis realized immediately that whether Hedizah had managed to convey the message to the Chief Engineer or not was immaterial now. The vessel had suffered a major disabling breakdown of a type that could imperil them all.

Milakis looked ahead over the vessel's port bow at the darkening sky. Already the boat was heaving uncomfortably in the growing swell.

Majec reached the bridge at the same time as the telephone rang on the steering console.

The loudspeaker cut in. The Chief Engineer spoke calmly and professionally.

"Captain, I'm afraid it's bad news. We've lost a main bearing and I think that we may have a fission fracture in the crankshaft. We need to get to sheltered waters."

There was a pause before he continued. "The auxiliaries are also out. There's been some kind of electrical fault. It happened last night on the midnight watch. We've had no time to sort it out."

Milakis knew that the message had been received. Hedizah had done as he asked, but events had moved on, dangerously.

He spoke calmly into the telephone. "Do we need assistance, Chief?"

The Chief Engineer replied in a matter-of-fact tone. "Captain, you have no choice. You have to put out an emergency call. It's a job for a salvage tug. That's if you can find one in this region."

Milakis put down the receiver and looked up to find Majec pointing an automatic pistol into his face.

"Captain, I sincerely hope, for the sake of you and your crew and that pretty lady below, that this is not some kind of foolish stunt. You know what my orders are."

Milakis smiled. "You heard the Chief Engineer. What do you think?"

There was a silence as both men eyed each other.

Milakis' words came quietly. He sensed that the others on the bridge were also looking to him for reassurance. The vessel rolled heavily as the force of the sea started to bear down on the bow.

"Mr Majec, it's quite simple. Unless we can find a tug to tow us to sheltered waters, the vessel is in danger of being swept ashore. You can see the storm ahead. We may be able to get our anchors down but, as you heard, there are problems with the auxiliary engines."

Majec stood looking at Milakis. The Navigating Officer and helmsman said nothing. They kept their eyes firmly on their Captain's face.

There was almost a sense of panic in Majec's response. "No one's going to call until I have permission. Until then this ship is going to be locked down. I want everyone at their posts. No exceptions."

Majec pulled out his short wave radio and relayed his orders. Milakis could see movement on the foredeck.

"Captain, you and the other two stay here. I want the girl up here. Get the steward to fetch her."

Milakis kept his eyes and head upright, scanning the surrounding waters, watching the vessel's head falling away against the heightened swell.

As he did so, he slowly allowed his right hand to slide down under the bridge communications console. His fingers edged carefully along the underside until he found it.

Majec had turned away and was opening his satellite phone. Milakis pushed the switch and as slowly withdrew his hand.

Stelios Kyriakos had done his job. Whatever instructions he had received from the vessel's new owners, he had made sure that an AVPS unit had been fitted. The Automatic Vessel Position System was the latest regulatory requirement imposed by the International Maritime Authority to combat terrorist or pirate attacks on merchant ships. When secretly engaged, within minutes the position of the vessel under attack would be known to all naval vessels operating under NATO or UN directions in the immediate area.

* * * * * * * * * *

A village in the Austrian Tyrol

The tall imposing house with its long sloping roof and neatly shuttered windows was almost out of view. The wide sweep of the gravel drive and the slender pine trees alongside gave the sanatorium a sense of tranquillity and seclusion. Behind the house, several snow-tipped peaks remained in view.

Crosfield stopped the car beside the timbered gatehouse. He noticed the bright flowers hanging in well tended baskets beside the ground floor porch.

He looked back. They would now be inside the house and Anna would be in her bedroom. Crosfield pictured the room that he had left only minutes before. It was bright, airy and with a sunny southern view. It was Anna's world, the only one that she would ever know.

It had of course been wrong to sanction the kidnap and ransom of Hedizah Mansur. He knew it at the time but, as with everything else, that was the past. He could only hope that, whatever the outcome, more lives would not be lost.

After the Luxembourg meeting, Crosfield had posted a notarised declaration to the Justice Department in London. He had testified by sworn statement that Hugo Jackson had played no part in the *Globex Mariner* affair. Whether officials and investigators believed him or the rest of his attempt to exclude the partners and staff at Layton and Springer from like responsibility, he would never know.

But, having made up his mind, he had tried to use what remained of his legal acumen to put other matters to right.

The young manager of the bank in Ehrwald had accommodated his instructions with almost a sense of approval and relief. After the deduction of Herlov's fee, fifteen million dollars of the ransom payment remained available. Half was to be paid to the sanatorium for Anna's lifetime care and the other half to his late sister's cancer charity in London.

He had left a modest balance in an offshore account for himself. It would be sufficient to cover the cost of what he needed to do.

Crosfield started the engine. He held the steering wheel tightly in his hands. Anna's face came and went. Mentally and physically disabled, and condemned to a life of lonely solitude, she would forever be helpless and dependent on the care of others.

He turned round and tried to capture the scene again, the final moments on the terrace as he said goodbye to her for the last time. He could visualise her wide and distant eyes that would never see and never recognize. Crosfield would try, like nothing else he had ever done, to retain that image.

Within hours he would be gone. He picked up the passport. It was one that he had kept for last. They had done a good job with the name, photograph and identity details. It would pass muster, at least where he was going.

He checked the tickets in the same false name. They were all there – a train from Innsbruck to Vienna, a flight to Cairo, a connection in Abidjan and the final sector to Freetown in Sierra Leone.

He had been told that the upcountry refuge for the scarred survivors of the civil war asked no questions. They were short of everything; money, volunteers and equipment. Perhaps there he might do some good. Crosfield removed the handbrake and started the slow descent into the valley below.

* * * * * * * * *

On board the Emden

There was a sharp knock on the wardroom door.

"We've received an automatic alarm signal from the *Aegean Dolphin*." Wenger let himself in quickly. "She's just over an hour's steaming distance from our current position."

Jackson stood up. He had been on the *Emden* for nearly two days and had been mainly confined to his cabin. His voice reflected a sense of uncertainty.

"You weren't expecting that, were you?"

Wenger's response was confident and to the point. "No. We can only assume that there's been an incident involving Majec and his men on board, or that there's a genuine emergency. With the ship's communications not available, this was the only way that the master could alert us."

Jackson felt the nerves in his stomach tighten. This was the moment that he had been waiting for. Now it had arrived, he knew that he had to put his trust, if not his life, in the hands of the young lieutenant who was to lead the operation.

Wenger was dressed in iron grey combat fatigues and was carrying a lightweight pack.

"The Captain has cleared the helicopter to take off in twenty-five minutes at 1535 local time."

He looked at Jackson and gave a boyish grin. "Against his better judgement, and mine, he's agreed to let you come along for the ride. It won't be a picnic, believe me. The wind's getting up and a rapid descent to a moving deck under fire is always a bit of an eye opener. But, if you want to win your girl, my friend, here's your chance."

Jackson was not deceived by the deliberately self-deprecating tone. He knew that the risks involved were reckless and dangerous; risks that, as a young climber, he had been trained to avoid.

He had been surprised to learn that his request to join the mission had been granted. But, as the last weeks had demonstrated only too clearly, his life was no longer determined by events of his own making. This time, however, he had a chance to challenge the pattern. The initiative for once had been with him and he had seized it.

Wenger opened the pack. "You'll need these."

He routinely removed a life jacket, upper body armour and an automatic pistol.

Jackson had had less than half an hour's training on the weapon in the *Emden*'s lower deck armoury.

"Are you confident with this?"

Wenger was still smiling but his voice had changed. There was now a sense of grim reality in what he was asking the other man to do.

Jackson nodded his agreement. "As ready as I can be."

He noticed that Wenger's face had hardened.

"Good. Get kitted up and report to me in the hanger in fifteen minutes. Stay close and good luck."

Jackson began to pull on the equipment. He thought of his late father, the funeral in the mountains of Switzerland, and the first time that he had seen Hedizah. She had shown him not only her passion and her care but her courage. There was nothing less that he could do than to ensure that they both survived the next few hours.

The *Emden* was beginning to turn to line up for the helicopter's take off. It was time to go.

* * * * * * * * *

On board the Aegean Dolphin

Pytr Majec looked around the bridge of the *Aegean Dolphin*. There was a smell of fear. The small group was looking at him. No one spoke.

Milakis knew only too well what the gradual rolling motion of the vessel would mean if steps were not taken immediately to call for assistance. The

Aegean Dolphin would be in mortal danger.

The storm was approaching from the north west and, without motive power, the heavily laden vessel was being slowly turned abeam the waves. White flecks began to show on the wave tops and the troughs between waves were gradually deepening. The jagged coastline for the moment remained two nautical miles off the starboard quarter. If the vessel turned, soon she would begin an unstoppable drift towards the shore.

Hedizah Mansur stood beside him. Dressed in rough seaman's garb, and with her hair tied loosely at the neck, she stared at Majec and the other guard who had brought her up to the bridge.

Her dark eyes revealed nothing. Her fine face, scarcely lined with fatigue, demonstrated tight lips and a strong jaw. It was evident that this young and beautiful woman would not show her feelings. What was more, Majec saw in her an inner courage that chilled him.

Not once had he been faced with the dangers that Hedizah had experienced over the last few days.

He knew inwardly that it had taken no such courage on his part to become the man he was, an assassin and street executioner who had inflicted countless atrocities against the weak and vulnerable.

He was also beginning to panic. He knew it and could not be sure that the others had not sensed it. Majec snatched up his mobile phone and called again. There was no answer from Herlov. He was feeling increasingly alone, desperate to have someone tell him what to do. This was a real crisis. His life depended on a decision being made.

Suddenly, it was no longer easy to hide from the past. Before his eyes he could see the constant image of a young Kosovan boy shot in the neck for living in the wrong street. He could see himself laughing as the boy's mother and sister were dragged upstairs.

The vessel lurched heavily again. Majec was no seaman but it was obvious to everyone that the vessel would shortly be in real peril if assistance was not called for.

Majec dialled again frantically.

There was still no answer from Herlov's mobile, not a flicker of recognition. He tried for the third time the scrambled emergency number that he had been told to call, if all else failed. His hands began to perspire. He wiped them on his tunic and tried again. The same message was repeated.

He could not tell whether it was the voice of Rahman Mansur or not. All it said was that Mr Mansur was presently unavailable. He had boarded a Globex Corporation aircraft at Limassol in Cyprus and was expected to land in Beirut in approximately one hour.

****

The north Somalian coast

Simpson raised his right hand in the leading boat. The *Aegean Dolphin* was nearer to shore than they had expected.

Bertrand had received a report over his satellite phone. The *Emden* had monitored the emergency communication from the *Aegean Dolphin* and had relayed the vessel's position to Bertrand, as the three boats had started their passage out from the shore.

Bertrand acknowledged Simpson's signal. They were now less than 800 metres from the port side of the *Aegean Dolphin* as she continued to swing towards the coastline without power, increasingly at risk from the freshening wind and sea.

Bertrand could immediately see that the conditions were already far worse than they had expected. They had planned for an assault in conditions that would permit a rapid direct approach. But the height of the waves was already slowing them down. Bertrand could see that the vessel's hull was beginning to pitch and roll. Simpson, with the boat mounted with the Vickers, could still make a frontal attack on the port side. But their ability to mount a fast scaling operation over the vessel's stern in the seas prevailing and under likely fire looked dangerous in the extreme. They had, however, no choice.

Timing was tight as Bertrand knew it would be. The diplomatic negotiation and business exigencies that had allowed the whole operation against the *Aegean Dolphin* and her cargo to go ahead had been tortuous.

To enable those involved in government and elsewhere to adopt a policy of denial, the *Emden* could only be seen to be assisting in response to an onboard emergency. Whilst Bertrand knew that Wenger and his commandos could sweep in and save the day, they had orders to do so only once Bertrand and his men had boarded the vessel.

Simpson's boat moved ahead and increased speed. At less than 200 metres from the vessel, one of Simpson's team struggled to stand upright. He raised a shoulder-held RPG launcher. The sharp form of the rocket-propelled grenade struck the steelwork of the bridge deck of the *Aegean Dolphin* and exploded, causing little damage but emitting a dark trail of smoke.

Majec had seen the approach of the first boat. Ordering the other man on the bridge to keep Hedizah, Milakis and the other two seafarers in the

Captain's office, he ran down the two flights of stairs to the weather deck.

As he did so, he felt the first burst from Simpson's Vickers machine gun clatter and ricochet off the bulwarks and deck gear. Majec saw one of his men stationed on the poop fall with a gaping head wound.

Others were attempting to bring their weapons to bear. But the range and height of fire meant that they could not engage Simpson's boat. Majec looked over the side and saw the other two boats diverge, one on either side of the vessel, heading for the stern. The ship's bosun ran out from a position behind one of the anchor winches. Seconds later he was thrown backwards by a burst of short range fire, his body sprawled across a steel hawser, his chest bloodily ripped apart.

Simpson's boat had turned and was making a direct frontal approach. The bow of the light craft was bucking in the heavy sea. Majec slipped as he ran along the deck towards the raised framework of the number two cargo hold and the heavy calibre cannon. The barrel was swinging free as the *Aegean Dolphin* continued to roll helplessly.

Majec could sense that the sea was taking its toll. It was starting to rain. The shore seemed darker. It was also considerably nearer than minutes before. He scrambled up on to the hatch cover and swung round the twin handles of the weapon, struggling over an open sight to target the approaching boat. He could see Simpson crouching over the Vickers less than a hundred metres away.

Bertrand called for full power as his boat raced along the ship's side. As they turned to take up a boarding position at the port stern he saw El Sanah's boat round the *Aegean Dolphin* from the starboard side. Fire from the vessel was already crashing into the waves around them.

Bertrand motioned to El Sanah. Within seconds two smoke and phosphorous grenades were launched from each boat. They exploded on the deck of the vessel, aft of the superstructure. A thin column of grey smoke flecked with yellow and red flames started to spiral upwards as a coil of deck ropes began to catch fire.

The first grappling hook and line was projected upwards from almost under the vessel's stern. Bertrand could clearly read the name of the vessel and her port of registry immediately above him. A second grappling hook and line was fired. Each slammed down on to the deck. The rocking motion of the *Aegean Dolphin* allowed the hooks to slide free and anchor their stanchions on the bulwarks and railings.

Bertrand grabbed the first of the lines, his pack and weapon slung behind his back. Two other members of the boat crew braced themselves and dragged down on the line.

Bertrand's feet were against the steelwork of the vessel and he began to climb. A reserve line hanging from his pack was thrown up. The clasp hook snapped shut around a steel bracing wire on deck.

As he climbed, Bertrand felt himself being pulled outwards from the vessel's side as the hull continued to lurch. All depended on whether Simpson could occupy Majec's men on the forward part of the vessel.

He heard the clatter of further rounds from the Vickers hammer against the ship's sides and an agonised scream from somewhere above him. He could see the flames beginning to take hold on the aft deck. Another man was on the line below him and he caught a fleeting glimpse of the first of El Sanah's team preparing to scale the opposite stern section.

Simpson's boat was now less than fifty metres off the *Aegean Dolphin*. He had fired almost a full belt of ammunition before Majec could bring the cannon to bear. A thunderous report followed his first shot. Simpson felt the high velocity round tear past him and explode in the aft part of the boat.

The body of the crewman who took the full force of the shot was sliced in two. Another was thrown overboard into the wake of the boat. Simpson looked down and saw flames start to break out beside a box of flares and grenades.

The helmsman struggled to keep hold of the tiller. Simpson could see an ugly shrapnel tear on his forearm. Blood was starting to pour from the severed vein. He shouted to turn the bow towards the stern of the *Aegean Dolphin*. Already sea water was starting to flood over the boat's open sides.

The helmsman wrenched the rudder as far as he could. He then clamped his body forward over the tiller to stop it swinging back. The motor coughed but they were making way.

Majec took aim again but the boat was moving out of his line of fire. Simpson looked up and saw one of the ship's crew wrestling with Majec's men. Others ran along the deck, firing down at Simpson's stricken craft.

The guard on the bridge pushed Hedizah and Milakis towards the cramped office aft of where they had been standing. The helmsman and Navigating Officer were already inside.

As they reached the door, Milakis stopped for an instant. The guard was behind him with a machine pistol in the small of his back.

In an instant Milakis lifted his right heel and stamped down violently on the toes and instep of the guard's right foot. He screamed in pain. Milakis swung round and elbowed him in the jaw.

As he did so, a single shot was discharged, striking Milakis in the left shoulder, passing through the flesh and cracking into the wooden panelling behind.

Hedizah grabbed Milakis as he fell. The guard tried to fire again but before he could do so the Navigating Officer was on top of him and, with one blow to the guard's forehead, knocked him unconscious.

Milakis slumped to the floor. Hedizah ripped off her seaman's jacket and pressed it against the wound. As she did so Milakis called hoarsely to the helmsman.

"Get down to the engine room. Tell the Chief that unless he can get some power from the auxiliaries, he's to get his men up."

As he slumped forward, Hedizah cradled Milakis' head in her lap. His words to the helmsman were scarcely audible.

"Try to find the Chief or Second Mate. Tell them to check with the engine room as well. If there's no change, ring the alarm and give the order to abandon ship."

Other crew members were moving from their stations. The Second Mate lay dead on the deck and the Chief Officer was trapped in the officers' day room, along with several others.

At the stern of the vessel, Bertrand and two men were now on deck, taking cover behind the raised steelwork of the aft hold.

Majec had abandoned the cannon on the number two forward hold when Simpson's boat had moved out of his line of fire. He and his men were now taking up positions on the upper deck, pouring down light machine gun rounds on to Bertrand and his two men below.

The fire was beginning to catch. Deck equipment and several drums of oil and paint were burning fiercely. Bertrand rushed through the smoke and looked down over the stern.

The waves were lashing the boats below. The remaining men of his party were pulling themselves up towards the weather deck on the scrambling net that Bertrand had thrown down. He expected to see El Sanah and his team scaling the starboard stern to support their position. They remained dangerously exposed on the port corner of the deck where they were pinned down by fire from above them.

Instead, he saw El Sanah's boat drawing away. Bertrand heard the clatter of bullets striking the winches beside him. He stood up, motioning El Sanah to head back towards the *Aegean Dolphin*.

As he did so, El Sanah turned towards him. The boat steadied in the trough of a wave. Bertrand saw him raise his fist in a clenched salute and swing his weapon round into the firing position.

Simpson had seen it too. His boat had struggled against the waves to round the stern. The helmsman lay dead over the tiller, the deck of the boat was smouldering and the engine had failed.

One of El Sanah's men stood up and opened fire. Simpson ducked and leaped forward on to the steel platform supporting the Vickers. A wave broke over him but Simpson gripped the handles of the weapon and opened the belt release.

A wave washed his boat to within metres of El Sanah. Bertrand saw Simpson hold his position and open fire. As he did so his face and body were torn apart by rapid fire from the other craft. But his fingers never wavered from the trigger.

El Sanah's boat and its occupants were decimated by the point blank fire from the Vickers. Bertrand thought that he saw Simpson trying to raise his head. He imagined for an instant the Australian giving a grin and a thumbs-up sign. But then he was gone. His boat, burning and weighted down with the Vickers, turned over and sank below the stern of the *Aegean Dolphin*.

Majec and his men were gaining the upper hand. Only two of Bertrand's team had reached the deck. He heard shouts from below but could not see his boat. He ducked down as another incoming fusillade cracked into the steel deck equipment around him. The other two were looking to him for orders.

Suddenly, Majec showed himself on the deck above and ran to the other side of the vessel. Bertrand could see him raise his weapon and dispatch an RPG down towards the water abeam the stern.

Seconds later there was a blinding flash and explosion, followed by an agonised scream. Bertrand knew that his boat and its remaining occupants were gone. A third man, who had succeeded in reaching the deck, was cut down by another of Majec's men, hidden behind a life raft two decks above.

Bertrand knew he had to regain the initiative. Checking his weapon, he reached into his pack. Motioning to the other two men to follow, he hurled a phosphorous grenade at the bulkhead shielding the doorway access to the accommodation block.

As the projectile exploded a searing flash obscured the area immediately in front of him. Bertrand ran forward, firing upwards and to his left. He heard the slump of a body fall beside him. To his right the other two men charged forward. In the seconds of confusion that followed, Bertrand reached the access door and saw one of the men trip and fall. His head struck the deck and he lay still. The other man was behind Bertrand.

The fire on the deck was now taking hold. The grenade had ignited other flammable materials and a sheet of flame shot across the stern area. Bertrand needed to reach the bridge. But they were only two now.

He could hear Majec shouting to regroup his men. Bertrand needed to get inside, to find and arm several of the crew members who he guessed would have been locked in their cabins or a mess room.

He pulled at the door. He could hear Majec still shouting orders as he ran down the stairway from the deck above. Unless he could get inside they would be trapped. The door stuck fast.

Bertrand turned with the other man, backs to the accommodation, and raised their weapons. They had no time. Either they took their chance to rush out and try to secure access to a higher deck or they would die where they stood. The smoke continued to hang thickly and Bertrand could see the fire spreading along the port side of the vessel.

Then he heard it. From over the forward part of the vessel came the roaring sounds of a helicopter.

It drew rapidly closer. Bertrand knew that the helicopter would have to make its approach over the starboard bow. Unless he could give covering fire there would be a massacre as Wenger's men attempted a fast rope descent to the deck.

He ran forward. In seconds the two men were on the first rungs of the outside stairway. The smoke had lifted a little. Two of Majec's guards were at the top. They opened fire. Bertrand threw himself down. The bullets passed over him but struck his only surviving team member in the head and neck.

Bertrand was on his feet in an instant. He dispatched the first of Majec's men with a single shot. As he did so, his dying colleague threw himself at the other man, knocking him backwards. Bertrand clubbed him unconscious with the butt of his weapon. Smoke from the fire on the opposite side was billowing upwards. Bertrand looked down. The man had probably saved his life. He bent over him, closed his eyelids and ran on.

The Chief Engineer knew that their only chance of saving the vessel would be to restart the auxiliary motors. But he and the Third Engineer had done too good a job in disabling the equipment on the previous evening, in response to the message that Hedizah had delivered.

It was no use. The helmsman's orders from Milakis were that if they could not restart the motors, the order to abandon ship was to be rung. Already, fire alarms had started to sound automatically.

The Chief Engineer ordered his staff out of the engine room. Some crew members who had broken out of their cabins were running to their muster stations.

The officers in the mess room had made their escape though a connecting hatchway to the galley. The Chief Officer ran up towards the bridge.

Majec had also heard the sound of the helicopter. With the battle for the vessel's stern over, he ordered his men forward.

Bertrand ran along the lifeboat deck and saw the pilot turn the helicopter to make his approach. The aircraft released a smoke canister as its two doors opened and the first ropes were launched.

He threw a grenade on to the deck below. Majec was grouping his men on the bridge deck. They raced to gain height and a full field of fire as the helicopter descended.

The cannon on the number two hold was now unmanned. Bertrand saw the last of Majec's men on the bow run back and try to engage the weapon. He fired a short burst and the man's body slumped to the deck.

Alix Wenger was the first man down. He took cover beside the forward deck bulwarks and started to engage Majec and the remaining group of his men.

Bertrand ran down from the first deck, firing upwards as he did so. He saw the second and third members of Wenger's team fall as they took fire from the port bridge wing. Wenger had seen him and raised his hand, pointing towards each side of the vessel. They would storm the upper deck in tandem.

Bertrand took cover again. He was alone on the port side. Suddenly, beside him he felt another man pushing forward, his head down. Bertrand held him back. So this was the stranger Wenger had said would be coming along.

Wenger had told Bertrand that he had no choice. Those running the operation had given him clear orders that Hugo Jackson was to be given the chance to rescue Hedizah. The young man was only too aware of what little chance he had of succeeding or staying alive.

The rain was falling harder. The *Aegean Dolphin* was catching the stiffening wind broadsides. Already her bow was beginning to dip dangerously and the ship was struggling to right herself as the troughs between the waves lengthened.

Fire alarms were now sounding continuously. Away from the foredeck, crew members were preparing to swing out the lifeboats.

Hedizah Mansur had managed to drag Milakis to a sitting position against the dividing bulkhead between the bridge and the master's office. His shoulder wound was still bleeding but Hedizah had almost stemmed the flow of blood. She crouched over him as he lapsed into unconsciousness.

The bridge windows on either side of her smashed, and glass crashed to the floor. Bullets ricocheted against the steelwork above her head and tore into the wooden panelling of the door behind. She threw herself to the floor, shielding Milakis' head as she did so.

On the starboard side, Wenger and two of his team had forced their way up to the bridge deck. Three of Majec's men lay dead in front of them. Majec, firing as he raced upwards, grabbed the open access door into the bridge area and slammed it locked behind.

A single shot rang out from above and the second of Wenger's men fell, grasping his neck as blood began to pump from a severed artery. Whilst his colleague rushed out to pull the wounded man back under cover of the covered companionway, Wenger ran into the exposed deck area and hurled a grenade upwards.

As he raced back to try to force the door, he felt the ship heave and list heavily to starboard. He grabbed a railing to steady himself.

Bertrand had also reached the bridge deck. The last of Majec's men showed himself from behind a ventilator shaft. Bertrand motioned Jackson to follow him. The third of Wenger's commandos accounted for the man with a short burst from his machine pistol.

Bertrand was looking for the port side access. There was none. He called for Jackson and Wenger's man to follow towards a door leading to the passageway to the bridge. They staggered as the ship lurched heavily. Dark, acrid smoke suddenly blinded them. They shielded their faces.

Bertrand guessed that Majec and any survivors would try to hold the bridge. What he feared most was that with the ship in real danger of grounding or capsizing, and with nothing to lose, Majec might take hostages. Any hostages would almost certainly include the Captain and Hedizah Mansur, if they were still alive.

There was only one door to the bridge. If Majec reached it first and held hostages, there was likely to be only one outcome.

Bertrand felt the heat of the flames sweeping up from the stern. He could hear shouts from a megaphone on the deck above, calling all hands to the lifeboats. The ship's emergency sirens were blaring out. A distress flare exploded into a red ball of smoke above the foredeck.

They reached the door. Bertrand turned to caution Jackson to wait until he and Wenger's man had cleared the passageway.

The smoke curled around them again. As it cleared momentarily, Bertrand could see the figure of Hugo Jackson hanging precariously on to the exposed rungs of an escape ladder leading up to the side of the bridge wing.

Bertrand watched as spray from the waves crashing into the vessel's side swept over him.

As he wrenched open the aft door to the bridge deck accommodation, Bertrand looked up. The *Emden*'s helicopter was making a return sweep over the vessel. The clatter of its rotor blades drowned Wenger's shouted command to fix a charge to the locked access door on the opposite side. Another distress flare lit up the stern, as the fire began to gut the aft deck.

Bertrand was through the door and running down the passageway. A sharp report echoed as Wenger's men on the starboard side detonated the charge. The door flew open. A rattle of machine gun fire echoed along the corridor.

Less than thirty seconds later, Bertrand and Wenger were through the entrance and on to the bridge. In front of them, Majec stood with a machine pistol in one hand pointing at the head of Georgios Milakis as he lay bleeding on the floor. In his other hand he held a switchblade to the throat of Hedizah Mansur.

Bertrand and Wenger took up position, their weapons levelled at Majec.

His shouted words were scarcely audible. "We either leave together or these two both die before you kill me."

Milakis turned and groaned with pain. Hedizah suddenly grabbed Majec's hand holding his pistol. He wrenched it free, lifted the knife and raised his weapon.

Suddenly the vessel rolled steeply. A heavy explosion rocked the stern. Bertrand and Wenger were momentarily unbalanced. Each struggled to retain a grip on their weapons. Majec staggered against the steering column. As he did so, he lifted the knife to strike down on Hedizah's neck and levelled his pistol to fire.

At the same instant, two shots hit Majec in the upper back and head. His body jerked forward and fell to the floor. Jackson scrambled through the shattered port door, threw down his pistol and bent over Hedizah. It was over.

Within minutes, a general alarm had been sounded. The helicopter hovered lower over the foredeck as the ship lurched uncontrollably in the heavy seas.

Waves lashed the sides of the vessel as the helicopter winchman struggled to hoist the limp bodies of Milakis and the wounded men to safety.

The Chief Officer took command of the vessel's evacuation. Sea, wind and towering waves threatened the lifeboats as they gradually pulled away. The helmsman on each headed their craft to the shore.

Bertrand watched the trail of the helicopter as it set course to return to the *Emden*. Wenger had been the last to be winched off the deck. Bertrand hoped that they would meet again. He liked the young man. He had also survived.

As his lifeboat pulled away towards the shore, Bertrand could see the *Aegean Dolphin* swing round, her bow clear of the water and her hull crashing down before coming to a halt, grounding the vessel on a sand bar.

In the eddy of water, Bertrand thought that he could see a fleeting image of Ronnie Simpson's last moments. Simpson had without doubt saved his life. At that moment he knew with certainty what he had to do.

The lifeboats were moving to safety as the inshore waters slackened. He watched Hedizah and Hugo Jackson, crouched opposite him in the boat, wet, cold and bloodied, huddled in their life vests. As they sat with their hands gripped tightly together, Bertrand saw both the love in their eyes and the strength and courage that had brought them together.

These two young people had shown him what he should do. Perhaps then he might find contentment of a kind that he had never known and perhaps also his mother might rest in peace.

The shore line was approaching. Bertrand smiled as Hedizah squeezed Hugo's hand. Whilst safety was in sight, each of them knew that it was only the start of a new beginning.

* * * * * * * * *

Mumbai, India

The afternoon sun cast long shadows through the open veranda windows of the first floor lounge of the Rajasthan Hotel in the old business district of Mumbai on India's west coast.

The room was quiet except for the distant sound of rush hour traffic headed for the port, and the shouts of stall proprietors and traders in the street market below. The scent of oriental spices hung lightly in the air. Fans set high in the ornately painted ceiling hummed in unison.

Jackson stood up and walked over to the slim television, discreetly situated in a corner beside a softly cushioned sofa, resplendent in brightly coloured imprints of tigers, elephants and oriental birds with exotic plumage.

He returned to his seat. Hedizah placed her hand on his shoulder. She then tucked up her legs and leaned against him.

The caller had suggested that they might wish to watch the hourly news bulletin on the Call Asia Skyway channel. Camera images flashed the viewer into the news room of the Skyway studio in Singapore. An impassive news reader announced the main headline.

"Wreckage of the private jet of the international business magnate, Rahman Mansur, has been located in the Eastern Mediterranean about twenty nautical miles off the coast of Lebanon. Sources close to the search and recovery operation said that the aircraft was on a routine flight from Limassol in Cyprus, when it disappeared from radar screens at Beirut International airport. It is thought that there are no survivors. Several bodies have apparently been discovered at the crash site. Our freelance reporter, Ann Sutherland, has this report from Beirut."

The screen immediately switched to a wide boulevard with palm trees swaying alongside a sun swept beach and a shimmering blue sea with several tall hotel buildings behind.

A tall, fair-haired woman in her mid-thirties appeared with a microphone.

"Only days ago I was interviewing Rahman Mansur, the founder and owner of the Globex group of companies. Today Mr Mansur is reported dead and his business empire is collapsing."

She glanced down at her notes and continued slowly.

"Investigators are starting to trail through an intricate web of the group's transactions. Internal sources indicate that these investigations may uncover a catalogue of criminal activity, ranging from fraud, money laundering and tax evasion to environmental damage, conspiracy and even murder. Within days it is predicted that what has become known as the Globex phenomenon will be over."

There was a further short pause.

"As I speak to you, enquiries are focusing on the disappearance of Mansur's private yacht, the *Globex Seaquest*, and its possible connection with the wreckage of a vessel called the *Aegean Dolphin* off the coast of Somalia. There is suspicion that this vessel may be connected to the mysterious loss earlier this year of another vessel in the Globex group."

The image switched quickly to the open sea and then as quickly returned to the shore, as the report concluded.

"Lastly, we have just heard that the Israeli Defence Ministry has denied that Rahman Mansur's aircraft may have been hit accidentally by a missile during a naval exercise off southern Lebanon."

Jackson watched without emotion. It was clear that, regardless of who Ann Sutherland was, who she worked for, and whatever her role, the destruction of the Globex empire and, most likely, the death of its founder, had been their aim. The reasons why they had involved him no longer seemed to matter. Events had moved on in a way that they could scarcely have imagined.

Jackson's eyes had not left the screen. He could not know how Hedizah would react, if at all. He felt her head on his shoulder. Fate had cast them together and he would pray that fate would never keep them apart from then on.

Epilogue

A MONTH LATER, HEDIZAH MANSUR AND HUGO JACKSON were married at a private ceremony in the chapel of St John's College, Oxford. The ceremony was conducted by the pastor of the church of St Martin and St Paul in the Swiss village of Les Deux Croix where, fewer than four months previously, he had officiated at the funeral of Hugo's father, Richard. The bride was given away by Dr Alan Jenkins.

Whilst the firm of Layton and Springer survived a judicial and regulatory investigation, Jackson resigned his position to take up a research post in the Department of Anthropology at the University of Georgetown in Washington DC. He elected to write a PhD thesis on the interaction of global industrialization and the survival of ethnic tribal systems in the Twenty-first Century. The couple moved to an apartment in Alexandria, Virginia, where Hedizah began a teacher's training programme.

On completion of their studies they plan to move to northern India to raise a family. Hugo hopes to find a university lecturing post. If the opportunity arises, Hedizah wishes to teach and bring to her young charges some of the happiness that she enjoyed there in her childhood.

Jean-Yves Bertrand returned to Dubai. He had, as he had done so many times before, to break the news to a loved one. He told Runah that Ronnie Simpson was dead and that his body had not been recovered.

He also told her that Ronnie had saved his own life and the lives of others. Runah received the news with stoical calm, the sad legacy of her former life in Somalia.

After Bertrand had made his report, he turned down the offer of another assignment. He travelled back to Dubai and began to rebuild Ronnie Simpson's adventure and safari enterprise on the edge of the desert.

He saw Runah more frequently, as the days passed. They both knew that a time would come when they could be together. When that happened, they would bring Masoud back from Djibouti.

Georgios Milakis recovered from his wound. In recognition of his meritorious conduct on board the *Aegean Dolphin*, the maritime authorities in Cyprus reinstated his master's licence.

He declined the offer of a command with a prestigious Greek tanker company and opted to stay ashore. He became reunited with his wife and family, who moved to Piraeus where he took over a redundant marine survey firm. Shortly afterwards he changed its name to Kyriakos, Milakis and Partners.

Emil Douchert returned to the town in France where he had met and fallen in love with Claire Helene. He found her living alone with her maid, unwell and unmarried in a closed wing of the Count's chateau. Her father had died in mysterious circumstances soon after he had forced Douchert out of his homeland to conceal his wartime treachery. Claire Helene had tried, without success, to find Douchert and had become a recluse. After his return, they married quietly in the village and then, in failing health, moved to a villa in Arcachon on the Atlantic coast.

Alix Wenger lost five of his men in the attack on the *Aegean Dolphin*. He was decorated for his part in the action. On his return to Bremen, after a short period of leave with his young wife and family, he was promoted and seconded to the German foreign intelligence service.

He never returned home. Six weeks later, Captain Wenger was reported missing, presumed killed, in a secret NATO operation to track down and suppress terrorist activity in an undisclosed North African state.

Nothing more was heard of Michael Crosfield. The documents that he sent to the authorities exonerated most of those with whom he had worked over the years.

The findings and conclusions of an international board of inquiry into events leading up to the voyage of the *Aegean Dolphin* were never made public.

Colonel Lev Barshok officially retired from the Israeli army and went to live with his family in a seaside apartment in Tel Aviv. Unofficially, he continued to work for the Israeli Secret Service and maintained a deniable joint mission with Major Assad Rawazi.

The high commands of Israel and Syria temporarily discontinued their strategic aims in northern Iraq.

Ann Sutherland remained a freelance journalist and broadcaster with the *International Economic Monitor*. This continued to provide an effective cover for her role as Director of Operations at the World Commercial Bureau.

With its secret headquarters located in the offices of the International Atomic Energy Authority in Vienna, the Bureau continues to be funded privately by corporations and member governments.

The Bureau's constitution permits it to target and outlaw individuals and organizations deemed to pose a threat to the established business order. Adversaries from opposing political and economic interests can thus act in a way that would not be possible through normally recognized international channels.

Ann Sutherland wondered whether she had been right to involve Hugo Jackson, as she had done, but the case against Rahman Mansur and the Globex group was now closed. Its incidental and unexpected result was the happiness of two young people.

The relationship that had developed between Hedizah and Hugo had proved a challenge and a risk. But it had been a risk worth taking, and one of which her late co-director, Hugo's father, would have approved.

THE END

MELROSE BOOKS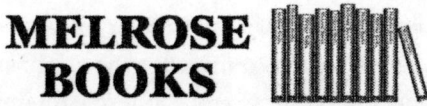

If you enjoyed this book you may also like:

Legacy of the Ancients
Kenneth Joul

Legacy of the Ancients has the inventive scope of high-concept science fiction combined with the breathless pace of a conspiracy action thriller

Matt Weston, a former Marine who lost a leg in a suicide bombing and now works for a government exploration agency as a special troubleshooter, travelling to the ends of the earth investigating missing expeditions, resolving crises, unraveling conspiracies and exposing cover-ups.

Size: 198 mm x 129 mm	Pages: 320	
Binding: B Format Paperback	ISBN: 978-1-906561-72-7	£10.99

Breaking the Surface
B.P Thompson

Breaking the Surface is an absorbing and deeply engaging novel which is set at the turn of the millennium, extending into 2071. An alternative vision of the world and its future, it is set in a parallel universe which is in most ways identical to our own.

The story centres on two key characters: Kim Barnes, a gifted blues singer wrestling with an intense conflict between musical purity and her envy of a former friend; and Frank McCombie, an intelligent and educated man who shuns the world and lives rough. Gradually revealed are hidden connections between these and other characters through their strivings for success and meaning.

Size: 198 mm x 129 mm	Pages: 368	
Binding: B Format Paperback	ISBN: 978-1-906561-73-4	£9.99

St Thomas' Place, Ely, Cambridgeshire CB7 4GG, UK
www.melrosebooks.com   sales@melrosebooks.com